THE FIFTH BOOK OF THE SMALL GODS

THE TWILIGHT FADES

BRUCE BLAKE

The Twilight Fades

The Fifth Book of the Small Gods

Bruce Blake

Comments?

Contact Bruce at: bruce@bruceblake.net

ISBN 978-1-927687-24-6

Prologue

THE PAIN AGAIN. RUTHLESS, inescapable, indescribable. It started inside her, radiating out; it pressed on her from outside her body. Everywhere and nowhere at once. Everywhere. Clenching, twisting.

N'th Ailyssa Ra gritted her teeth, raised her arm and set her palm against the wall for balance. She held her breath, shut her eyes tight, and leaned forward as much as her swollen belly and the thing inside causing her agony allowed her to.

"Breathe," Adesi said from where she stood behind her.

Ailyssa knew the woman's hand rested on her bare back, probably massaging rose oil into her taut muscles, but the pain swallowed it up in the swirl in her head. A strained noise squeaked out of her throat and she tried to locate the texture of rough stone against her fingertips, orient herself on the wall to her left. She wondered for an instant if she'd fallen, but the contraction devoured the thought as quickly as it did any other.

When the pain eased sufficiently for her to recognize a world around her, she let out her air in a long stream, cheeks ballooning with the force of it. Cool sweat clung to her brow, refusing to break free and roll away in droplets down her face, her neck. She drew another breath into her chest, and opened her eyes, the torment of her uterus subsiding enough to bear seeing again.

She stared at the floor, unable to see her bare feet past her belly. The tread of thousands of women over the turns of so many seasons had left the stone near the wall discolored and worn. It appeared black instead of the light gray of the rest of the chamber. She blinked, swallowed, and straightened, the muscles in her lower back spasming. Adesi noticed and redirected her ministrations to the spot. Ailyssa canted her head toward her.

"Thank...you," she said, each word riding on an exhausted breath.

Her friend leaned closer, whispered in her ear in a gentle tone: "Is it time for the pool?"

Ailyssa's gaze strayed to the circle of water at the center of the room, tendrils of steam rising from its surface where belladonna, chamomilla, and other leaves she'd recognize at other times floated. She gave a quick nod and Adesi's hands moved to her hips, guiding her away from the wall toward the bath. They progressed slowly for fear another contraction might grip her.

When they reached the pool's edge, a pair of the other Matrons—women who had given Goddess two daughters and earned the title Re, as Ailyssa hoped for this child to do for her—took her hands, supporting as she stepped from the floor onto the first stair. The warm water—heated by Goddess herself—washed over her foot, soothing. She descended to the next step, and the next, the tepid and healing liquid climbing to her ankles, her calves. When she got to the bottom, she lowered herself to her knees, fingers slipping from the grip of those aiding her as the warmth of Goddess' love enveloped her belly. She closed her eyes, inhaled the myriad smells, the black pepper oil warming on the infusers the most pungent of them. When she opened her lids again, N'th Adesi Re knelt at the lip of the bath in front of her; she placed a pillow there for her.

"Come, Ailyssa. Rest yourself here."

Ailyssa forced a smile and wondered if her current condition might twist it into a less recognizable expression. She shuffled across the bottom of the pool, the stone surface smooth and comfortable against her knees, and leaned on the cushion.

"I'm getting it wet," she exclaimed.

Adesi chuckled. "Don't worry about the pillow. Your only concern is providing Goddess a healthy daughter.

Daughter. Claris.

"What about Claris?" she asked, propping herself up on her elbows. The movement flared pain along her back, and she tensed in case another contraction came on, but it settled again.

The pool stirred, gentle waves lapping against her as the birth Matron descended the steps into the water with her. She thought to turn toward her and thank her for what she was about to do, but didn't.

"Claris is fine," Adesi said, brushing strands of hair from her friend's forehead and tucking it behind her ear. "She is with some of the other Mothers. Do not worry about your daughter. Concentrate on bringing a second into the world for Goddess."

Ailyssa nodded and lowered herself onto the pillow, the Matron's words rolling around in her brain like a marble in a bowl.

What if I birth a male?

Another contraction struck as the thought completed itself, punishing her for the simple act of considering the possibility. She grunted, squeezed Adesi's hand. Her entire body tensed; her spine arched, pulling her head up off the pillow again.

"It is not time to push yet," the birth Matron said. She knew the woman's name but couldn't think of it then. N'th something Re—another Matron younger than herself, the same as Adesi.

The pain engulfed her, stealing the world away. Adesi spoke in her ear—sounds without shape or meaning, possibly a reminder to breathe again. She huffed fast breaths in and out between her tight-pulled lips, panting like a dog after a long run. The action itself did nothing to relieve her extreme discomfort, but it at least distracted her mind from it, if minutely.

It passed, and she lowered herself onto the pillow, turning her head and pressing her cheek against its cool fabric, the tide of agony ebbing for the moment. She inhaled a deep breath through her nose, let it out forcefully between her lips, then repeated the action twice more. In this position, she saw another Matron sitting on a stool inside the worn ring at the edge of the room, one of three besides Adesi and the birther. She, like the other two, waited in case they required aid—to massage, or retrieve unexpected items needed; to bring water for drinking, or honor Goddess if a daughter came into the world; to clean a new babe, or dispose of a male child.

Male child.

Her mind flashed to the birth of her first baby. She remembered so little about it with her inexperience, the passage of time, and the herbs they'd given her to help the memories fade. The few details she'd ever been able to recall were the Matrons' disappointed expressions, and the wine-colored birthmark glimpsed on the baby's shoulder. They had shuffled the babe away as soon as they cut the cord connecting their lives, ending their shared experience. She'd seen a flash of its back before the Matron took it, holding the male child out from her as though disposing of something rotten.

What if I birth a boy again?

The thought left her mouth dry. She licked her lips with a sticky tongue, raised her eyes toward Adesi. Her friend understood and immediately gestured. The woman on the stool rose, retrieved a cup with a bamboo straw poking up out of it, handed it to Adesi. She lowered the mug until its bottom touched the pool water and the tip of the straw hovered near Ailyssa's mouth; she accepted it between her lips and sucked as best her body allowed. The cool liquid flowed across her tongue, bringing with it the vague earthy taste of Olvana's well. She took one mouthful, swirled it around inside her cheeks, then swallowed and sipped again, smaller this time. Finished, Ailyssa nodded her thanks, and Adesi returned it to the Matron, who returned to her seat until they required her assistance again.

The refreshment cleared her mind for an instant and she remembered that, should she birth another son, they'd take it away again. But what would happen to her? During her pregnancy, she'd worried over this, though she hadn't asked and couldn't remember hearing tales of any Mother birthing two males and heaping such dishonor on Goddess. She had vague recollection of a time in her youth, before her first bleed and when she was beginning to understand the role of Ra. A pregnant Sister who had previously birthed a male became so distraught over the possibility of it happening again, she'd taken the forbidden herbs and caused her baby's premature arrival. The child—a girl, it turned out—died, and they banished the poor young woman. Ailyssa didn't know where they'd sent her, nor did she ever inquire. She'd never seen her again, and the mothers told the tale to their daughters since in warning.

Another contraction gripped her, tightening her muscles until the cords in her neck stood out. She closed her eyes so tight, a flash of light jumping across the darkness behind them. She forgot everything else for the space of two heartbeats, but then Adesi squeezed her hand again, reminded her to draw air. This time, it passed with merciful quickness, and Ailyssa found the water she'd imbibed not sitting well within her. It roiled in her belly, threatening to find its way out, and she wondered if pain made it so, or the thought of bringing a boy into the world. Her belly answered with a lurch.

If it's a male, I hope they kill it and tell me it was stillborn.

Worry brought sour saliva to her mouth, but at least her gut settled somewhat.

If she gave birth to a child possessed of a cock, they'd take it away as they did before. This time, she hoped she didn't have to glimpse its pale, wrinkled flesh. Such a sight might leave her retching the meager contents of her stomach onto the birthing chamber's floor. Which of the Matrons' jobs was it to clean vomit up?

Please, Goddess.

A quick pain made her tense, but it waned.

Please let me honor you with a second daughter.

She exhaled a hard breath, drew another in between clenched teeth.

Please let me be Re.

Her belly seized again without warning and she cried out. Instead of intensifying and relaxing, the agony came and stayed, taking up residence in her soul, refused to diminish.

"It is time," the birth Matron said.

Ailyssa became vaguely aware of water lapping around her as the birther repositioned herself. N'th Adesi Re leaned close, lips nearly touching Ailyssa's ear.

"Push."

Any thoughts of male and female, consequences or happiness fled her mind, chased off by the repeated spasming of her insides. It went on and on. Whenever she stopped pushing and attempted to catch her breath, the pain tightened its grip, or Adesi told her to push again, commonly both at once. Light flashed before her eyes sometimes, alternating with darkness encroaching the edges of her vision. Ailyssa gasped and moaned, screamed and cried. Time meant nothing; her understanding of it left her, slipping away as her perception of life passing disappeared. The Matron with the cup of water came to her more than once during labor putting the tip of the straw to her mouth. Most of the fluid she struggled up its length spilled over her chin and dripped into the pool, but a few drops made it between her lips, giving her small measure of refreshment. Any more and she'd have spit it out for risk of gagging.

After a while, she collapsed on the pillow, both of her hands under her face and her elbows and forearms lying flat on the floor to either side. She panted and gasped as N'th Adesi Re dabbed her forehead and cheeks with a cloth, wiping away sweat and tears and spittle. She used her thumb to put a drop of rose oil under her nose.

"You are doing so well," she said. "Almost there."

Anger flared in Ailyssa's chest and she directed her eyes at the Matron, fixed her with a glare boring into her as she bit down on her back teeth, choking the inappropriate response threatening on her tongue. Adesi had nothing to do with her state; she was but a tool of Goddess who required her followers to go through this. If she didn't ask for daughters as tribute, Ailyssa thought she wouldn't have ever done what it demanded to find herself in this place. She'd have happily lived her life without being seeded and experiencing what became before and after it.

A more intense shock of pain gripped her, melting her anger. She turned her face toward Adesi, tears running from her eyes.

"Get it out of me," she pleaded. "Please get it out of me."

"Almost there," N'th Adesi Re repeated, dabbed her forehead again.

Ailyssa closed her lids. She suddenly became sure the life within her—now either fighting to come out while her body refused to let it, or struggling to stay in as she attempted to expel it—wasn't male nor female, but some hideous monster. It would emerge from her womb with two heads, or a tail, or perhaps claws and teeth, a horn on its head—an excellent explanation for her discomfort.

Her experience had gone beyond mere words—pain, agony, torment. All were such puny things conceitedly trying to impart the depths of her torture. Searing heat now, convulsions, a feeling like being split from crotch to neck. She held her breath, pushed. Veins popped in her neck, on her forehead and temples, and she wished for whatever hid inside her to either come out or kill her and relieve her misery.

Words swirled around her, noticed but unheard. Orders to push, encouragement, support. Everything said may have been in another language, or the sounds made by animals, until one phrase found her ears, spoken by the birth Matron in the pool behind her.

"Here comes the baby."

The reassurance she needed. She pushed, concentrating her effort more than she had been able to for far too long. Eyes closed, a protracted groan escaped her, and a small life shifted inside her. Instantly, she knew she'd love it—daughter, son, or monster. It grew in her, she'd fed it from her body. A part of her.

The pain increased as the baby's head stretched her, then its shoulders. She gritted her teeth against the sensation of being ripped apart, kept exerting force until the pressure of the child eased and it slid out of her; she exhaled a lengthy breath.

Ailyssa blinked sweat away and pushed herself up on her elbows, the pain excruciating, but so much more manageable compared to before. She pivoted, peering over her shoulder, glimpsed the baby as the Matron raised it out of the pool. One of the other women had entered the water without Ailyssa's notice; she clamped and cut the cord. Ailyssa smiled, a pained expression more worthy of being called a grimace, then laughed despite the tears sliding from her eyes. The babe wriggled in the birth Matron's grasp, but she didn't cradle it. She dangled it out in front of her, holding the child in both hands under its arms. She scowled, a detail escaping Ailyssa as the infant made its first sound—a tiny cry, a mewling tone like the bleating of a newborn goat. Her heart swelled with love.

She twisted around, water sloshing against her as she ignored the protests of her exhausted muscles. Ragged breath found its way in and out of her chest with the effort as she raised her arms, fingers splayed, awaiting the birth Matron to pass her the child.

Nobody in the room moved; the entire chamber held its breath, waiting. The two Matrons in the water stared at the baby dangling at arm's length in front of the birther. Her gaze flickered from the babe to Ailyssa, a frown pulling the corners of her mouth enough to crease lines down either side of her chin. She stood, the force sending a wave across the pool to wash against the new mother's chest, splash up into her face.

"My baby," N'th Ailyssa Ra said, voice faltering. The energy within her withered, replaced by a desperation to hold her child.

"It is male," Adesi said, leaning close. She did nothing to hide the note of derision in her tone. "N'th Nissa Re will take it away so you and Goddess do not have to witness it."

One of the still-seated Matrons rose and came to the edge of the birthing waters. She held out her hands, much the same way Ailyssa did, and the birth Matron handed her the child.

Ailyssa glimpsed the baby's face.

Its mouth opened, a tongue looking very pink against purplish lips poked out between them. As she looked at him, the hue of its skin faded. The babe's lids parted, and its dark eyes met his mother's.

Love and anguish exploded through her in equal measure. She leaned forward, reaching out farther and ignoring the cord hanging from her, awaiting her body's expulsion of the afterbirth.

"Give me my baby," she cried, her voice high pitched, shaking.

The Matron paid her no attention. She headed for the door where another woman grasped the handle and pulled it open.

Ailyssa leaned forward more, now on her hands and knees, began crawling across the pool toward the steps leading out of the water. The birth Matron grabbed her shoulders, stopped her from reaching her goal. She struggled against the woman's grip, but it held firm against her own flagging strength.

"Please," she said. "Please let me hold my baby. Please. Please let me hold my son. Please. Please."

N'th Nissa Re passed through the doorway and turned left. The way she carried the newborn out in front of her gave Ailyssa one more flash of his pinched face. She inhaled a sharp breath, stunned by his beauty, then he and the Matron disappeared. The door swung shut behind them.

"Give   me   my   son," she   shrieked. "Givememysongivememysongivememyson."

The number of hands on her shoulders doubled, pulled her backward until her shoulder blades pressed against the edge of the pool farthest from the exit, then kept her there. The birth Matron settled between her thighs, attending to the afterbirth, but Ailyssa ignored her. She could insert her arms to the elbows and extract her insides and she wouldn't care; she went on screaming—for her son, cursing the Matron and Goddess herself—until her throat went raw and she tasted blood. When she lost the ability to scream, she cried. Tears streamed from her eyes along the side of her face, down her neck, the salty liquid mixing with the water in Goddess' pool. They held her until her body discharged the birth sac, her last remaining connection to a child she'd never see again.

She banged her head against the pillow on the lip behind her, unable to fight in any other way. She shook her head side to side, sending tears flying. Still the grip on her held. Dimly, she heard the scrape of the door opening through her anguish, then the shuffle of bare feet on stone floor. The pressure holding her eased, and she opened her eyes.

All but N'th Adesi Re and the birth Matron had left the birthing chamber. Adesi took a robe from a nearby stool and held it open for the

Mother as she climbed out of the pool. They turned toward the door and Ailyssa caught her friend's eye.

"My son," she whimpered.

Adesi looked down at her, lip curled and brows lowered. She stared at her friend for a heartbeat, then shook her head and crossed the room, pulling the door closed after her and leaving Ailyssa alone.

The new mother who would never know her child leaned back until the water came right to her chin. She put an arm over her face to block light from her vision, and cursed her Goddess for doing this to her, cursed them all for taking away her baby.

I - Trenan - Departure

THE PRINCESS' BLOOD MIXED with the dirt outside the Green, turned it to pink mud which became hardened clay—a tiny sculpture representing nothing but death.

Trenan found it hard to divert his gaze. Fellick and Ive moved around him—the stocky fighter never far away—as they prepared themselves to depart. Did they mean to kill him, Teryk, and the girl? Leave them here to die? Make them a sacrifice to the black priests? After everything he'd been through in his life, it was all going to end like this: in failure and disgrace.

The master swordsman hung his head, tearing his eyes away from the grisly sight of the dead princess he thought of as his own, killed by the young man who actually was. How did this happen? How did he let it?

The muscles in his jaw knotted, and he swallowed hard. Many seasons had passed since the last times he wept, and most of them as he lay alone at night after losing his arm. And again when he realized he'd never truly love. Now they threatened, their presence clenching his throat, shortening his breath. But weeping wouldn't bring the princess to life; tears lacked the power to rescue Teryk from what he'd done or what the weapons merchants might do. Danya was gone, a fact impossible to change, but the opportunity to save the prince—his son—still existed.

He bit down harder, raised his head until he found the tall, spindly Ive. Seasons upon seasons of training and experience screamed at him to ignore this fellow and direct his rage toward the more dangerous Fellick, but sometimes one can overlook instinct when driven by vengeance.

Trenan set his palm flat on the ground, noticed but ignored sharp pebbles pressing into the heel of his hand. The muscles in his shoulder and arm tensed, readying to help propel him to his feet and at the gangly merchant who'd busied himself cleaning the dagger he'd provided Teryk with which to kill his sister. To his right, the prince sat with Danya's head in his lap, shirt and pants soaked with her blood. The sight of it ballooned in his chest; he coiled, ready to spring.

The instant he launched himself to his feet, a boot struck his, sent him lurching forward. Trenan flailed to catch himself, but his body twisted, making it impossible to use his one arm for such a purpose. His chin hit first, scraping across the ground, jarring his jaw and clacking his teeth together hard. Dirt found its way between his lips, grass poked at his eyes. The impact flashed sparkling lights in his vision, dazing him. By the time he recovered, Fellick's knee already pressed against his back.

"And where do you think you're going?" the stocky merchant growled.

Trenan struggled in vain under the man's bulk. Nothing besides the blunt knee touched him; no point of discomfort suggested a blade of any sort. If they meant to kill them, why not get around to it?

"You killed the princess," Trenan said, the breath attached to his words stirring the grass in front of his face.

"Strictly speaking," Ive said, "we didn't kill her. I may have supplied the dagger to your prince, but he put it to use. If you held us responsible for every death brought by a weapon provided by Fellick and Ive, then we bear the blame for a great number of deaths. Murderers of the highest order."

"The boy is not of his right mind," Trenan grunted, the knee on his back making speech difficult. "He knew not what he did."

"I believe my constant companion told you what came to pass was necessary. Did you tell him, Mr. Fellick?"

"I did."

Footsteps rattled stalks of dry grass as Ive made his way closer. Trenan lifted his head and watched the tall man's boots settle less than an arm's length from his nose. The merchant squatted so the master swordsman saw him, his long, thin limbs bent and intertwined, giving him the appearance of a spider missing half its legs.

"Mr. Fellick and I need to take our leave. Do you think if my friend removes himself from your spine you might dispense with any attempt to separate us from our lives?"

"Try it and see."

Ive leaned onto his haunches and Trenan squinted up at him. The surface of the veil glinted behind his head, lending it an otherworldly aura.

Given the opportunity, he'd gladly remove it for him by taking his noggin from his neck. He jerked his shoulder, intending to reach for the merchant, but Fellick predicted his attempt. The stocky man's boot stomped down on his forearm, pinning it to the ground and grinding the bones together, making him wince.

"Tut, tut. None of us will ever leave this accursed place if you can't agree to play nice."

The pressure on Trenan's back increased as Fellick's weight shifted. He leaned forward until his lips brushed his captive's ear.

"It's a hard and bitter thing losing someone you love, swordmaster. This we all know. I cannot imagine what it must be like to see it happen, but this had to be and the undoing of it is not possible. What you have left isn't vengeance; what you have is the opportunity to save your son."

Fellick lifted his boot and shifted his bulk again. The knee remained, but the effort in breathing eased. Trenan's mind reeled. Did he mean to threaten Teryk? With one of the royal children dead, his own life likely hung by a thread with a sharp edge pressed against it. If he lost the prince, too, the final cut became inevitable.

Ive stood. "Mr. Fellick and I have a wagonload of weapons to retrieve, along with several other things on our agenda. We are expected."

"Indeed we are."

"Can we come to an accord? We won't kill you or either of these children and you will give us the same consideration?"

The girl sat in such complete silence Trenan had forgotten her presence. Evalal, Danya called her. She bore at least some responsibility for Danya being here. He'd seen her in her green smock and mask, spiriting the princess away; of that he harbored no doubt. He raised his head, glared at her.

She sat unmoving, eyes darting from one man to another. Tears glistened on her cheeks, her skin flushed and puffy from her despair. Her gaze never fell on Danya's corpse. Trenan looked from her to the prince stroking his sister's hair.

"We have an accord."

The weight lifted from him. He took only the time to fill his lungs before jumping to his feet. It did not surprise him to find Fellick already with sword drawn, its point directed at him. In his other hand he grasped the crownsword in its scabbard, the belt wound around it. The weapons merchant first held it up toward him, then tossed it to the side. It bowled through a patch of tall grass and landed on the ground with a dull thump.

"You'll want that," the stocky man said, "but not until we leave."

Trenan pursed his lips, the tip of his tongue pressing against the inside of his teeth. After a moment, and against his better judgment, he nodded. Fellick returned the gesture but did not lower his blade—the master swordsman hadn't expected him to.

The two fighting men stared at each other across the patch of beaten grass between them. Somewhere in the distance birds sang. A fly or bee buzzed past Trenan's face, its sound dissipating as quickly as it had appeared. If he'd been counting the number of times his heart beat as they surveyed each other, he didn't think he'd have reached twenty before the whisper of Ive's boots broke the stillness.

The lanky merchant joined his companion, faced Trenan and bowed at the waist before straightening again.

"I believe I can speak for Mr. Fellick when I say the honor of meeting you belonged to us, master swordsman. I wish the circumstances had been different, less desperate; I'd like to think we might have gotten on quite well."

He turned and strode toward the hill where Trenan had left his warriors. He saw no sign of them at the top of the ridge and his already pained heart squeezed a little tighter. Perhaps they'd seen what happened and retreated—a disappointing decision, but better than the alternative.

Fellick paced away, walking backward with his sword pointed at Trenan.

"You won't want to hear this, but leave the princess here. Do not bury her. It is how it must be."

Trenan glanced at Teryk. He hadn't moved, but Evalal stood from her spot on the log, hands bound behind her as she stared after the merchants.

"And what of the girl?" he called after them.

"She will know what she is to do," Fellick replied. "Goddess guides her."

The stocky man spun and jogged after his friend. The instant he turned, Trenan bolted for the crownsword, tore it from its scabbard. He took one step after them, the rage of Danya's death filling him again faster than a blink.

"Don't!"

He glanced around to find the girl had stood and taken a few hurried steps toward him. She peered at him with her red-rimmed eyes and shook her head. The burst of anger disappeared as though her gaze acted as a salve to heal it. Trenan's shoulders sagged, he lowered Godsbane, and the tears he'd been suppressing flowed free.

The loss of blood had turned her face porcelain.

Trenan stared down at the princess, his chest tight and his throat clogged with sorrow. Her hair, caked with drying clots, lay spread across her brother's lap. Her murderer's lap.

How did this all come to be?

Trenan touched the hilt of the crownsword before raising his hand to his face—an old habit. Before today, knowing a weapon hung at his waist brought him the comfort only a soldier felt from a piece of cold steel, a confidence in realizing all the world remained in its place and everything would end the way it should. Brushing his fingers over it did no such thing now.

The master swordsman wiped his hand across his cheeks, scouring the dried tears from his skin. Teryk didn't look from his sister. The young girl perched on the log where she'd returned to after the departure of the merchants, also staring at the dead princess. Trenan wanted to comfort his son, or scoop Danya up and will her to life, but he did neither, instead crossing the space to Evalal. Her eyes flickered to his at his approach; he glanced away, circled to stand behind her, then knelt.

A square knot in the cord bound her hands, a tight and efficient choice for holding a prisoner. He'd used similar knots for the same purpose on many an occasion so understood how to release it. As his fingers worked, he spoke for the first time since Fellick and Ive disappeared over the rise, leaving the four of them—three, he corrected himself—on their own.

"I am Trenan." His voice cracked, and he cleared his throat but did not repeat himself.

She nodded. "I am Evalal."

He finished untying her and stood. The girl brought her hands in front of her, rubbed her wrists, but neither turned nor thanked him as he remained behind her, staring a hole in the back of her head.

"You are of the Goddess' order."

"Yes," she replied, though he'd meant his words as statement rather than question.

"You were the one with her in the square."

She nodded again.

"You took Danya from the Horseshoe. Brought her here."

The girl's shoulders rose and fell and he heard her breath sigh from her lungs. It wasn't agreement, but it served as confirmation.

Trenan's hand went to Godsbane's grip once again. He cinched his fingers around it, squeezed hard against its leather-wrapped surface until he felt his knuckles strain. His gaze moved to Teryk, watched the young man stroke his sister's hair with a palm now dyed red with her blood. He returned his glare to Evalal.

"It is your fault she is dead."

The girl stiffened. Others might not have noticed the change in her, but the practiced eye of a seasoned warrior scrutinized for such minute differences and tells. She expected him to grab her, to strike her, to run her through. A spear of guilt jolted him.

How many turns of the seasons has she seen? Twelve?

His mind drifted to memories of Danya at the same age; she'd been defiant and adventurous, full of life and laughter, sweetness and light. So many times he'd searched Draekfarren, looking for her and her brother during an impromptu game of hide-seek. How many times had he reprimanded her while struggling to keep a smile from his lips? More than he'd possibly remember and attempt to count.

The flash of reflection forced him to draw a deep inhalation, the summery scents of the meadow marred by the coppery battlefield stink of death. But this wasn't a battlefield, and the stink belonged to the spilled blood of a young woman as much a daughter to him as Teryk, the lone child of his loins.

His gaze returned to the back of Evalal's head draped by her straight, brown hair. her body remained tensed, awaiting his reaction, his punishment. In his time, he'd slain others her age—a truth in which he held no pride nor liked to admit aloud. Sometimes the work of a soldier, whose job was doing a superior's bidding, included unenviable tasks a man might not forgive himself for. Things capable of haunting one's memories for the rest of a lifetime.

Trenan released his hold on the sword's grip, the tension in his own muscles easing. He stepped to his right, moving from behind her, and the girl flinched. His guilt flashed again and, when no blow landed, Evalal cocked her head to peer at him over her shoulder, eyes wet and frightened. He looked away—the girl's gaze reminded him of Danya's after being caught doing something she should not have been up to. He came out in front of the log, stood between where she sat and where Teryk mourned his sister, his back to the siblings.

"I won't hurt you," he said. Saying so aloud helped dissipate the guilt in his chest, but the remaining sliver of anger and ache of loss clenched his gut.

She inhaled a deep breath, let it out through her nose, then nodded once. The tension in her face and shoulders did not disappear.

"I'm sorry."

The two words she spoke surprised him. Did they represent an admission of guilt? An expression of grief? He regarded her features, looking for a clue to clarify her meaning, but fear remained, disguising her intent. Trenan nodded, stood, closed his eyes.

Danya's face swam into the darkness behind his shuttered lids—not the blanched cheeks and chalky forehead of the lifeless version of her prone on the ground, but the pink and rosy, full of vigor princess he so loved. Then Ishla's image came to his mind. Her beauty and the hurt in her expression pained his heart as if someone prodded it with the tip of a dagger.

What will I say to the queen?

The complex web of emotions brewing inside him congealed into a knot in his gut. In his lifetime, he'd faced down foes twice his size, commanded armies, defeated fearsome warriors, but how would he face the woman he loved in secret? Tell her of her daughter's death and how the fault lay with him?

He raised his hand, pinched the bridge of his nose, hoping for it to aid him in controlling the tears threatening to spill forth again.

What's wrong with me?

He pulled a shuddering breath into his lungs, pressed his lips tight together. Neither action provided answers. For the first time in his memory, his mind failed to see its way through. He'd always believed in his ability to find a solution to any challenge, but no other problem had ever involved devastating the woman he loved.

He shifted his hand, covered his eyes with his palm. He needed to do something but found himself unable to gaze upon the grieving prince and his dead sister. If he did, he'd surely see Ishla's face where Danya's should be, her flesh painted alabaster by the artist known as death.

A touch at his elbow startled him. He jerked away, lowered his hand, afraid to find the queen standing before him, or the princess' ghost.

"You must go," Evalal said. A gentle shimmer of sympathy and understanding beyond her age replaced the fear in her eyes. "This is not a safe place for you and the prince."

Trenan blinked, sniffed, nodded. He half-turned, partially facing the girl, but able to look toward the royal siblings. He saw Danya's face drained of blood, not Ishla's—no sort of comfort or relief in reality.

"We can't leave her like this." To him, his voice came out small and weak. He cleared his throat, swallowed. "We must take her with us."

Evalal squeezed his arm to regain his attention. When he looked to her, he found her shaking her head.

"It's important she stays here."

His brows lowered toward the bridge of his nose and he considered questioning her, thought better of it. If he spoke the truth, he didn't relish returning to Draekfarren with her corpse either slung over his shoulder or draped over the haunches of a horse. Treating her thus not only struck him as disrespectful, he also knew he couldn't stand having to gaze upon her dead face. But if he returned without her instead of bringing her body, would the queen ever forgive him?

She will never absolve you.

His chest tightened around his heart, strangling it. He paused, waited for the sensation to pass; it eased but did not dissipate. He hauled a deep sigh in through his mouth to quell the last of it and nodded.

"Then we bury her."

Evalal shook her head again. "Remember what Mr. Fellick said? He said not to put her in the ground."

He glared down at the girl, lips pursed. Had she forgotten who he was? Master swordsman. Right hand of the king. Keeper of the royal children.

A swordsman bested by a weapons merchant. A glorified nanny who let a child in his care die.

The voice in his head spoke in the king's tone. He and Erral had been friends for much of his lifetime, but the cords of their friendship began fraying the night he lay with the queen. Though his regent didn't know, Trenan never found a way to act the same around him after. His actions and failures to protect his charges would undoubtedly sever those ties.

"But if we leave her, animals will pick her bones. I can't let that happen." He closed his eyes for a second, opened them again. "It's the least I can do for her."

"I'll stay with her."

Her gaze strayed from his, past him to the prince and princess. Fear and grief disappeared from her voice, replaced by what he interpreted as determination.

"It wouldn't be safe."

"The Mother of Death told me not to leave Princess Danya, no matter what."

"Mother of Death?"

Evalal nodded.

A shiver ran along Trenan's spine despite his best effort to suppress it. He'd heard the name before but never believed the myth to be a real person. He imagined her a hulking woman in a cloak, with scraggly hair, wild eyes, and the hands of a skeleton.

"She couldn't have meant for you to be with her even in death."

"No matter what."

Trenan sighed, his nose filled with the encroaching stink of rot. Not enough time had passed for Danya to be emitting the odor, so it must have been from the other fellow whose corpse lay on the ground near them. He did not recognize the man, nor did he understand what had brought him to this place; doubtful anyone left behind might tell him. He knew the death scent would attract predators as soon as the sun touched the horizon. How might a girl like Evalal keep herself safe, let alone the body of the princess?

"I don't think—"

She rose from her seat on the log, interrupting Trenan's protest. Her forehead came to the bottom of his chin, forcing her to incline her head to peer into his eyes. Despite her diminutive stature, her stance and demeanor spoke of conviction, courage, and single-mindedness. The master swordsman's desire to fight her wishes diminished.

"Goddess is on my side. She speaks through the Mother of Death, and I will do her bidding. I am not to leave the princess and the seed, no matter what."

The seed?

He opened his mouth to question her but closed it again, the words unspoken. The weight of fatigue threatened to overcome him, his limbs filling with wet sand, his mind fogging. Would returning Danya's body ease Ishla's sorrow over the loss of her child? No. Prevent the king from punishing him for failing to protect her? Doubtful.

Then what reasons did he have to return her to Draekfarren other than to cause himself pain every time he gazed upon her corpse?

None.

His shoulders sagged, his chin drooped to his chest, breaking the girl's gaze from his. He nodded, realizing the futility of trying to convince Evalal of anything but what her Mother of Death had told her. Trenan stepped away from her, turned toward Teryk, steeling himself as he did to once again view Danya's lifeless body.

Fresh tears glistened on the prince's cheeks. As Trenan inhaled another deep breath, he watched a droplet of Teryk's despair coalesce on the end of his nose, lengthen, plummet to spatter on her chin. The prince didn't notice it; the princess couldn't.

"You'll want to do something about the other one," he said, nodding in the direction of the unknown man's corpse. "Before the beasts come for it."

She looked across the grass toward the body, regarded it for a moment, then returned her gaze to Trenan, eyebrows raised.

"Burn it," he said.

The master swordsman crossed the few paces between them, set his hand on his son's shoulder. All his insides twisted upon themselves, clogging his chest, his gut, his throat. In his time as a soldier, he'd seen so much death, so much pain and suffering, things capable of driving a regular person mad; never had the sight of a corpse and the grief it brought affected him thus. For the first time, he understood each life ended by his own sword left someone somewhere experiencing exactly what now gripped him.

He struggled to keep from retching, swallowed the bile which rose into his throat.

"Teryk, my prince. My son. We must go."

His voice came out a rasp filled with regret and loss, barely more than a pained whisper, yet the prince raised his head. Anguish pulled his features taut. His eyes met Trenan's, but he seemed to be looking past him, through him. The sight of his son's distress tightened the knot filling his body, entangling his soul.

What will the king do when he finds out Teryk murdered the princess?

Worried about himself, he hadn't considered what consequences might await the prince when they returned to Draekfarren. Surely Ishla would prevent her husband from overreacting, at least for her son's sake if not himself.

He squeezed Teryk's shoulder, encouraged him to stand; he didn't move other than to continue stroking his sister's hair, as though doing so might cast some spell to raise her from the dead. Trenan looked at the princess' slack, red-streaked face. All her life he'd wished he'd sired her as he'd sired the prince. Countless nights he'd imagined a different life, where he and Ishla and their children lived together in peace and love.

What will happen if Erral realizes Teryk isn't his son?

Trenan's flesh turned cold at the thought. If it came out the lad was the master swordsman's offspring, none of them would be safe; not the prince, not himself, not the queen. But only one person knew their secret, and Trenan had left him at Ikkundana, a place he'd never be allowed to leave.

He couldn't take that chance.

"Get up," he said, his voice firmer and more his own as he spoke between clenched teeth.

Teryk didn't move, and unreasonable anger rose within the master swordsman. He shifted to put his hand under the prince's arm, to draw him up and away from his dead sister, but Evalal appeared at his side first. She shook her head at him, then crouched beside Danya's body, opposite her brother.

The prince turned his gaze toward the girl. She didn't speak, instead moving his touch from his sister's hair, replacing it with her own as she lifted Danya's head from his lap, placed it on hers. Evalal stroked her cheek, spoke words to the fallen princess too quiet for Trenan's ears, but her tone betrayed them as expressions of comfort and love. She nodded at Teryk, then gave her full attention to the corpse.

As if released from a spell, the prince stood. His knees faltered, and he grabbed Trenan's sleeve to steady himself, grief and the time spent kneeling leaving him weak. The master swordsman put his arm around his waist, led him from the girl and his sister toward the hill, to warriors and horses and the Windward Kingdom beyond.

Trenan glanced back once, intending to call out to Evalal, tell her to take care and be wary of hungry beasts, but the sight of the princess covered in her own blood once more stole his voice. Worries about the consequences to himself, but more so to Teryk and Ishla, rushed into his mind. He wouldn't allow anything to happen to his son or the woman he loved.

And Trenan knew he'd not return to Draekfarren. Perhaps never again.

II - Horace - Escapin'

*E*ACH BREATH HORACE DREW scraped his throat, rattled in his chest.

Some time ago, the onus on propellin' himself and the woman forward shifted from him to her, his job now bein' to steer them along safe bits o' ground like she were the ship and he the rudder. It'd taken all his concentration not to peek some more to see how the fight progressed but, after a while, the sound o' the fray ceased. Whether because it ended, or they got too far from it to hear, he couldn't say. He hoped for the second but, either way, not hearin' it anymore did little to ease his fear.

The familiarity o' the features hidden underneath the white skin stuck with him.

He were positive that, if not covered with blood, he'd have known the man. Part o' him held a desire to go back—certain the whole lot o' the creatures'd be dead—and examine the almost-recognizable face. He didn't. He never once glanced o'er his shoulder again.

They stumbled and fumbled through the brush, keepin' where he thought the shimmery green wall'd be to their port side. Ivy'd ran off this way, and he hoped if they continued in the same direction, they'd find the small, gray person. They traveled in silence, the lack o' sound weighin' on him until he couldn't take it no more.

"I'm..." He half-choked on the word, coughed. It hurt his throat to speak, but he pressed on with it anyway. "I'm Horace. Horace Seaman. What do they call you?"

She didn't answer immediately, as though unsure o' her own name. Then it occurred to him maybe she weren't only blind; might be she lacked the ability to hear and to talk, too. The urge to apologize made him open his mouth again, but he caught himself, chastised his silliness in his head.

"I am N'th—" She stopped, sighed. "I am Ailyssa."

"Ailyssa," he repeated, tryin' out the name. Not one he'd ever come across before, but the first thing she said rang a tiny bell in his noggin, though he couldn't recall why it should.

Silence fell again as they picked their way through an overgrown bramble. He touched her shoulder to guide her, and she stepped with care. It struck him she didn't move with the kind o' confidence someone who'd been blind a long time might, but she weren't blunderin' neither. Once they cleared the tangle, he glanced o'er at her, decided the time'd come to find out more.

"How is it you be findin' yourself here?" He lowered his voice, close to a whisper. "Behind the Green."

She sighed again, her unseein' gaze cast down toward her feet as if tryin' to fool him into thinkin' she possessed her sight after all. But that weren't why she did it, he figured. Even not bein' able to see, somethin' about her answer made her not want to meet his eyes. Knowin' his own tale, he expected it'd have to be a near unbelievable thing what'd happened to her so she ended up in this wonderful, deadly, mythical place.

"It's a very long story."

"Couldn't be anythin' but." He let a few strides pass by, noticed his legs wasn't as tired as they'd been before. "Far as I can see, time is a commodity we have lots of."

She nodded, eyes still directed downward, but didn't speak for a while. The ol' sailor considered promptin' her, but decided to wait. If she wanted to tell him how she arrived in the Green, she'd do so, but it really weren't none o' his business; they was merely two strangers what met in the woods and nearly got ate by creatures with no right to exist. Didn't owe each other nothin'.

When Ailyssa started speakin', the words spilled out in the manner o' water rushin' through a hole in a ship's side. Horace listened as she related her story, from the time her friend expelled her from what he'd have called a nunnery for not producin' a second daughter, all the way up to the moment the pale abominations attacked the animal guidin' her and keepin' her safe in this foreign place. At times durin' her tale, his throat threatened to close up as he fought to withhold tears, other aspects left him angered, but mostly he found himself appalled by the things what'd happened to her. Hearin' it made his own experience seem a quiet day upon a calm sea.

After she finished, they fell into silence. He desired to say somethin', find some words to make her magically better. But what should a man tell a woman who'd experienced expulsion from her religion, rape, loss, death, and blindness? The fact she were alive and sane told him all he needed about her strength, courage, and resilience. If he'd been through half o' what'd happened to her, he'd likely have given up on the idea o' livin' a long time ago.

She lifted her chin and directed her unseein' gaze toward him, lookin' at his face though she lacked the sight o' it. He peered at her, self-consciousness makin' him queasy despite knowin' she weren't peerin' at him. He looked anyway, and noticed the paleness in her eyes, like sheets o' translucent cloth covered them, both hidin' them and keepin' them from seein'.

"The way you speak makes me believe you are a man of the sea."

"I am," he said, clearin' his throat.

"You've listened to my sad story. How does a sailor end up here to listen to such a pathetic tale?"

"I...uh...fell off my boat and washed ashore."

Heat rose into his cheeks—weren't no good sailors what fell off their boats. He considered tellin' her about seein' the man floatin', about the idiot Dunal knockin' him o'er the side, about the God o' the Deep destroyin' the Devil and endin' the lives o' all the souls aboard her except for himself and the deckhand, but he didn't bother. She'd been through enough; no reason for him to heap his tales upon her. Besides, his story held a bunch more what happened he'd prefer not to tell, particularly what ended up happenin' to Dunal. He were startin' to suspect he'd never find peace with it.

"A while later, a little gray feller called Thorn fell on me."

Her forehead wrinkled, and she tipped her head to the side. It seemed plain to him she didn't understand what he were sayin'—why should she?—but she didn't ask him to repeat himself or explain. Didn't need to.

He stopped walkin', pulled on her arm to stop her, too, then leaned in close. What he meant to say weren't no secret, but it didn't feel right sayin' it out loud.

"The Thorn feller, he were—" He hesitated, swallowed, glanced around at the trees and brush on all sides, half-expectin' to find the white ghouls comin' for them, all covered in blood, or a troop o' short, gray creatures bent on keepin' the truth o' them secret. He didn't see neither. "Thorn were a Small God. He lived here behind the veil."

"You've seen a Small God?"

"Yeah. A few, actually."

The confusion didn't disappear from Ailyssa's expression, but this time she put words to her befuddlement.

"So you were already here when he...fell on you?"

"No, I weren't. And it were truly more like he were dropped than fell. Maybe even jumped on me."

The statement did nothin' to rid her face o' the crinkly forehead and raised brow.

"He'd escaped. Rode a bird he called Father Raven o'er the veil and outta the Green."

Now her eyes widened, her mouth opened and closed, then opened again. Reminded him a little bit o' a fish caught and thrown on the deck, gulpin' for water and worryin' about dyin'.

"Did he bring you here?"

"No. He's still out there."

She shook her head, the creases findin' their way onto to her forehead again. "Then how...?"

"Don't matter. He were taken from me by a man made o' clay. I'm not sure what might've happened to him, but I bumped into Thorn's sister, Ivy. I was tryin' my best to find her again when I came across them pasty-faced ghouls attackin' you."

Ailyssa inhaled a breath so big, it surprised him it fit in her chest, then she let it out all at once between her lips. Her eyes slipped away from his face, flickered about the area surroundin' them as though she might actually be seein' it. He considered askin', but guessed she'd've mentioned somethin' was it the case.

"Do you know where she is? Ivy?"

He shrugged, then remembered she couldn't see him do so.

"Can't be too far off," he said, unsure it were the truth but hopin' so. "She came this way."

Don't really know for sure though, do you?

"Let's not tarry, then. We have to find her."

She grabbed his hand and started walkin', leavin' him no choice but to go, too. Without him, how'd she find her way?

25

She took Horace by the hand, hoping the skin-on-skin contact might yield the same result as the nameless man's touch, giving her back her sight, but it didn't. Despite this, hope fluttered in her chest with gentle butterfly wings. It wasn't the first time she'd experienced it since her expulsion from Olvana; she'd also noticed it when Creidra found her, when Juddah rescued her, and when the nameless man's touch first returned her vision. Each time left her disappointed, but failure didn't stop the flit and quiver next to her heart.

A Small God.

Though she'd never seen such a thing—no one had—she knew they were real. Goddess saved them before she banished the other Small Gods to the night sky. She also knew Goddess had imbued them with some of her power—the reason they stayed behind the veil, away from the rest of the world. The thought of their magic had corrupted before.

A Small God might heal my sight.

She realized thoughts like these had led to depravity in the past—people wanting to use power not belonging to them for their own gain. But Goddess must have a plan for her. Why would she put her through so much if it wasn't to test her, to strengthen her for whatever was to come?

She allowed the sailor named Horace to guide her, suppressing the excitement brewing inside her. How long since she last thought about Goddess? For so long, she'd felt abandoned by the very thing she'd lived her life for. Now, somehow, lost behind the veil with a man she didn't know and her sight gone, no genuine hope other than the rumor of a Small God who may or may not exist, faith crept in. Faith she'd thought dead, something she'd never again have.

Goddess, I'm coming.

III - Trenan – The Cursed

*T*HEY CRESTED THE HILL with the sun sitting balanced on the treetops, its warm rays tinted the color of bile by the green curtain they shone through.

Trenan's thighs burned with the effort of dragging the prince along with him on their trek from the site of the princess' death to the top of the rise. The distance seemed farther than when he'd slid from his saddle and run down the grade to engage the weapons merchant Fellick with his sword. The expanse had appeared less then, but it also felt as though much more time had passed. How had the sun not set yet?

He hadn't looked back during their ascent, realizing the pain it would have brought to his already agonized heart. Each step away from the fallen princess and toward his uncertain future invited visions of the queen's face to his mind; each thought of her became another dagger to his soul, for he assumed he'd never see the woman he loved again.

But when they reached the top of the slope, all thoughts left him.

The brown grass on the hilltop lay beaten to the ground in a perfect circle. Trenan pulled his arm from around the prince's waist, lowered him gently when his legs wouldn't hold him, and moved toward the anomaly.

Every blade lay flat, pressed to the dirt like the bottom of a woven basket. Nothing marred the surface: no piece out of place, no scuff, no drop of blood, no footprints of human or animal. Trenan stepped up to the edge, hesitant to cross the threshold, and stared, his eyes tracing the outside. It wasn't until they reached the far side when he noticed the horse picketed beside the track at the distant end of the clearing.

His horse.

"What happened here?" he murmured.

Surely his warriors wouldn't have fled. He saw no indications to suggest so, but neither did he see anything insinuating a fight, as though women, horses, and black-robed men had disappeared, every one of them. No sign of retreat or departure. How?

He thought of the robed figures—priests of the mysterious brotherhood. Their existence a topic of discussion many times, he'd warned Erral they might pose a danger, but the king insisted they were peaceful and had as much right to their religion as did the followers of the Goddess. The crown, he said, possessed no power to dictate the whimsy of others.

Standing at the edge of a grassy circle yielded no clues to what happened. He knelt, reached a wary hand across the imagined border separating the ring from the world, pressed the tips of his fingers against the grass. It acted no differently than one might expect. He plucked some broken blades, held them up, let them drop. They fluttered in the air like any grass so released.

Trenan shook his head and stood, drew Godsbane from its scabbard at his waist. He put the sword's tip to the ground, knelt again, bowed forward until his forehead touched the crownsword's pommel.

"This day we have suffered so much," he said, voice quavering. "The world is lesser if we've lost these soldiers, a worse place without the princess."

He closed his eyes, inhaled deeply through his nose. The scent of dried grass floated on the air, a hint of the perfume of flowers growing nearby, and the vague bitterness of burnt orange peel—an odor with no right to be in this time and place. Could it have something to do with the priests?

"Keep their souls well," he said. "Protect them from further harm. Return them to the bosom of life."

As always, he knew not to whom he prayed, or if it made any difference, but if their Goddess might chance upon his plea, then these women deserved to have prayer and mercy more than any man he'd killed in battle. Gods—small or any other sort—or Goddess, they deserved honor and care.

Trenan closed his eyes and let his words float on the placid, warm air. Birds twittered in the trees and insects buzzed in the waning sun. At the far end of the clearing, his horse nickered. Inside him, in his chest, the day's losses gnawed at him, each one of the women's lost lives nibbling away bits of his flesh and parts of his being. Never had he endured loss in such a manner. He opened his lids, forehead still resting on the sword, and stared at the yellowed grass.

"What is happening to me?"

Was whatever befell his warriors leeching into him? Did the odor of burnt orange mean death looked to claim him, as well?

And the prince?

Trenan jumped up, sheathed his weapon and rushed to Teryk. He sat cross-legged where Trenan had let go of him, head drooping forward as though he didn't possess enough energy to hold it up. The master swordsman grabbed one of his arms, threw it around his neck as he encircled the prince's waist with his own. He gritted his teeth at the effort of lifting the young man's weight with no assistance but got him up, pulled him across the ground, feet dragging, and avoiding the circle of beaten grass. Teryk offered an insignificant amount of aid. When they reached the animal, he leaned his son against its flank. The horse raised its snout, directed a brown eye toward them, but did not move. Trenan's pulse hammered at his temples.

It concerned him whether the prince possessed the strength to sit a steed on his own, but after traveling so far with Dansil tied behind him before, he didn't think he'd be able to do it again.

"We have to get you on the horse," he said.

The effort he'd put into bringing Teryk here had left him wheezing, heavy breaths rattling in and out of his chest. This realization sped his heart faster. No reason such small exertion should leave him thus drained. He'd fought on battlefields for the best part of a day, marched without sleep through sunrise, sunset, and sunrise again, thrown fallen soldiers over his shoulder and carried them to aid. Why did this have such effect on him?

The smell.

It wasn't the odor of burnt orange, but the stink of magic. His throat tightened. He wielded a sword to fight evil men, not an unseen killer.

"Teryk," he snapped. "Get on the horse now."

The prince turned his head. Recognition flashed in his eyes, quickly doused by pain and grief settling back in. Trenan couldn't imagine his torment after killing his own sister, but they didn't have the time to mourn her in that instant. If they didn't get moving, they'd be lamenting at her side in the afterlife.

Trenan grabbed his son's chin, held his drooping head until their eyes met. He felt his breath rasping in his throat, his arm growing heavier. How long before he couldn't hold it up? How much time before his chest stopped drawing air?

"Get on the horse or we both will die."

Teryk blinked, a tear spilling over the edge of his bottom lid and tracing a shining trail down his cheek to be lost amongst his stubble. His head tipped forward almost imperceptibly. A nod? Trenan had to assume so. The prince raised his foot toward the stirrup, missed it on the first try. The swordsman cursed, reached down and guided his boot so it found its goal on the second. Pain shot along his spine as he straightened, and he grimaced, biting down on his teeth to keep from crying out.

What deviltry did the men in black leave behind?

He ignored the discomfort and crouched again, put his shoulder into the back of Teryk's thigh and pushed upward. The muscles in his legs burned as though someone had lit them on fire and the flames licked at his flesh, eating their way out. He let out a hard breath as the prince struggled his leg over the horse and settled into the saddle. When he held the reins in his hands and appeared stable, Trenan turned away, leaned against the horse's side as he struggled to catch his air.

To his surprise, a flicker of movement caught his attention partway along the clearing toward the top of the hill. Instinct brought his hand to the hilt of his sword, but he didn't draw it when he realized what drew his eye.

The roan stood perhaps twenty paces away, watching them and flicking its tail. He recognized it immediately: Yoli's mount. The recognition made his already short breath catch in his throat, but necessity forced him to push emotion aside. The distance to the horse seemed impossibly far to the master swordsman. He paused, hand resting on the flank of Teryk's steed, and attempted to collect his energy, but it proved elusive. If he didn't get them out of the place soon, he might not have to worry about breathing at all.

"Wait here, boy."

The words came out with more vehemence than he intended, but the pain in his back, the searing in his thighs, a throb in his head pressed him to hurry.

Trenan pushed off and started toward the horse, boot heels dragging in the grass. He breathed in through his nose, as deep as his aching chest allowed, and released his breath between his lips. Each step shot agony through his feet, his legs, along his spine.

More than halfway to his goal, the animal turned from him, moved away in search of more tender shoots on which to munch. Trenan's gut sank, crowding his knotted bowls. Of all the ways to die, this wasn't one he'd ever considered: death by breathing.

If he'd been alone, he might have surrendered to his body's desire to give in, fold up on itself and tumble to the ground. But he'd already lost a child he loved this day; he'd be damned if he let the other perish. He stared straight ahead, keeping the horse in the center of his decreasing eyesight.

"Stop, damn you." His voice rasped, each syllable tearing the raw flesh lining his throat. He tasted blood on his tongue but pushed on, increasing his stumbling pace until he lurched at the threshold of over-balancing. Miraculously, the steed found a green patch of grass and stopped to satisfy its hunger.

He reached the animal and grasped the side of the saddle in time to keep himself from collapsing. The horse nickered and flapped its tail at him but didn't raise its head.

Where are you, Yoli?

His body screamed at him to rest, to take a rest and find his breath to supply his muscles and brain with much-needed oxygen, but his speeding heartbeat and waning eyesight pushed him to continue. If he stopped, a moment might turn into eternity.

He shoved his fingers under the saddle, gripping its edge to steady himself as he lifted his leg to insert his boot tip into the stirrup. The first attempt proved unsuccessful, and he'd have pitched forward onto his face had he not been holding on. He reset himself, concentrated on raising his foot as high as fatigue allowed.

This time, his toe found its goal. He leaned in, putting his weight on the one foot, pulling with his hand, and leveraged himself onto the horse, belly pressed against the saddle's hard leather. The mount raised its head, flicked its ears. Whatever evil threatened to steal his life, it didn't seem to affect the horses. He'd have taken the chance to give thanks had his own existence not balanced at the precipice of ending.

He struggled his leg over, pulled his hand from under the saddle, and grasped the reins. His legs possessed barely enough energy to press his heels into the horse's side, his shoulders hardly the strength to pull on the bit and direct it toward where he hoped Teryk awaited his return. It felt as though much time had passed since he'd deserted the prince, yet the sun setting did not cause the encroaching dark, but a haze collecting at the edge of his vision.

The effort of reaching and mounting the animal left the master swordsman out of breath and nauseated. His heart thumped against his ribs as though it wanted to make its escape, leave him behind to fend for himself. He swallowed hard, forced a long inhalation through his nostrils. The fog around the outside of his vision expanded, narrowing his field of view. With his teeth clenched tight enough to hurt his jaw, he pushed his heels into the animal's side. Trenan's racing heart swelled, perhaps with hope of survival, perhaps threatening to burst, as the mount took its first step.

The white crowding his perception darkened, turning the gray of storm clouds, fading to black at the outside. He leaned forward, chest resting against the horse's long, muscular neck. The roan made its way toward the far end of the clearing where Teryk waited by the track. Even in his condition, he noticed it avoided crossing the threshold into the circle of compressed grass.

As they approached the other horse, Teryk sagging down against the animal, Trenan reached out to grasp the lead. His ass slipped against the smooth saddle and his heart jumped as he slid sideways. In that instant, knowing the impossibility of finding his way back on if he fell, a lifetime of regret flashed through the master swordsman's mind. Missed opportunities and taken lives, broken friendships and shattered hearts. If someone offered the chance to relive it all, he wouldn't sacrifice his arm to save the king. How different would his life be then?

At the last moment before he slid from his seat, Teryk grabbed his sleeve, gave him enough support to right himself. He breathed three sharp breaths to calm a heart he knew he couldn't slow, adjusted his position to keep from falling, and took the reins of the prince's horse between his fingers. He nodded his thanks to his son, but he'd already returned to leaning against the horse's neck, eyes directed away from Trenan.

The master swordsman pressed his heels to his mount's sides and the well-trained animal responded, heading down the dirt track, out of the clearing.

He rested his cheek against its mane, inhaling the familiar odor of horse sweat and leather. The animal's gait bounced him on the saddle and he worried the movement of the prince's steed might unseat him, but there was nothing to be done about it. Keeping his own seat had to be his priority. He gripped as tightly as his exhausted legs allowed his knees; his eyes slid closed and opened again. As the riders passed from the clearing onto the dirt track, the master swordsman thought he spied two figures at the fringe of the forest—one tall and lean, clad in a dark robe with a cowl covering his face, the other short, stocky, limbless but for a single arm. The fog in his vision obscured them, leaving him confused, and his mind no longer functioned well enough to process what he observed.

The master swordsman who believed in no gods or goddesses closed his eyes and prayed for the second time that day.

IV - Evalal – Shooting Star

THE ONE-ARMED MAN AND the prince disappeared before the sun completed its descent from the sky.

Evalal sat with her legs folded beneath her, Princess Danya's head resting in her lap. With the sun out, she hadn't minded the coolness of her companion's flesh as she stroked her forehead or cheek, brushed matted hair away from her face. But as twilight fell and night crept in, stealing the day's heat, death took on a different hue.

The evening wasn't cold, but the air felt cooler than before sunset, more so here than during their travels. Maybe because she'd curled up beside her companion and they'd shared their warmth. Now hers was the lone source, and the coolness threatened to steal it from her. Despite the sickening odor produced by the crackling flames, she wished she'd waited until nightfall to take Trenan's advice to burn the dead man. A few tendrils of smoke still rose lazily toward the sky from the charred grass, but any heat it might have provided was long since gone.

The veil separating the Green from the rest of the Windward Kingdom cast a dim glow—not bright enough to form shadows, but it transformed the princess' bleached skin to a sickly shade. Its diseased pallor agitated the young woman. She noticed the pins and needles creeping into her legs and feet, the nighttime sounds of the land. Gone were the birds and insects of the day, their songs and droning buzz replaced by eerier, more suspect noises.

Wind stirred the leaves, setting them rustling. Or was it a creature stalking toward them, drawn by the odor of dead flesh? The call of an owl brought gooseflesh along her arms. A growl startled her, made her cower until she realized it came from her own belly complaining about not being fed. She chastised herself for her silliness.

"Goddess takes care of us," she said to unhearing ears. "The Mother of Death says so."

She shifted her position, moving her legs to the side to give them much-needed relief. The prickling sensation in her muscles intensified, and she groaned aloud, covered her mouth at having made the sound. She held her breath, listening. If any beasts lurked close enough to notice, they gave no sign. After the space of ten heartbeats, she drew air into her lungs again, but the odor clinging to her hand forced her to pull it away from her face.

While sitting so near the dead princess, she hadn't noticed the gradual change in the way she smelled. The coppery scent of dried blood; the sweet, sharp odor of decaying flesh. The grisly bouquet turned her stomach, brought tears to her eyes. Sometimes she wished she understood why Goddess allowed things to happen the manner they did, but she was a novice, not yet N'th. She'd see the seasons turn many more times before being given the opportunity to become a mother. Though bearing a child wouldn't help her understand.

A tear spilled down her cheek and she reached up to wipe it away but stopped herself. She didn't think she could stand smelling the princess' death so clearly again.

Evalal lifted Danya's head from her lap, slid her legs out from beneath, then set it on the ground again and shuffled aside. The Mother of Death told her to stay with Danya, but said nothing about touching her at all times. She stood, knees shaky under her, and backed up two steps.

The air freshened, allowing her to fill her lungs and rejuvenate her aching muscles. She stretched. The leading tip of the rising moon showed over trees at the top of the hill over which the one-armed man had taken the prince. Its white light shone into the clearing, throwing shadows and forcing the veil's glow back toward the Green. It blanched the olive hue from Danya's face, turned her from sickly to bloodless. Not any better.

She raised her eyes skyward. Since her youth, she'd loved the nighttime. Though the stars shining after dark were the Small Gods who'd nearly brought the world's destruction, Goddess hung them in the sky with the moon sitting watch, making them precious. Anything so obviously created by Goddess swelled the girl's heart with love even as losing the princess bathed her with grief.

As she stood staring up and drawing fresh air into her lungs, a streak of light cut a path across the night, its life so brief, she suspected it might have been a trick of her eyes at first, played upon her by exhaustion and loss. But the remnants of it had barely faded from her vision before another one flashed, then another. Such a sight should have been beautiful and, for an instant, excitement rose in her at the spectacle.

Until she remembered what this rain of stars meant.

Evalal wrapped her arms around herself, feeling chillier than the night should make her. Before she left, the Mother of Death had warned her to be careful of the sky; she knew the prophecy as well as any other novice, perhaps better, but a sliver of her had always wanted to deny the likelihood of such horror happening in her lifetime. Part of her wished for the stars to be nothing more than pretty lights in the darkness.

Two more silvery lines knifed through the dark, these lasting longer, appearing larger. They crossed in front of her from her right to her left, disappearing beyond the tree line as though sucked up by the pull of the moon. She held her breath, waiting for more stars to fall. For a while, none came. The shimmering lights turned into non-threatening decorations on the black background, tiny diamonds bejeweling the night.

Evalal relaxed her grip on herself, releasing her hold on her elbows. She inhaled through her mouth, released it in a long huff, surprised to find the air wasn't cold enough to turn it to mist despite what her shivering body and goose-bumped flesh told her. The tension in her neck and shoulders loosened, and she raised her arm, wiped away the drying tears on her sleeve.

As she lowered it, she heard the rumbling growl.

She froze. The tautness which had disappeared a moment before sprang into her again, through all of her. Her throat closed up behind a lump preventing her from swallowing the fearful, bitter saliva filling her mouth.

It's just your stomach again, silly. Don't worry.

The excuse rang false. She waited, unmoving but for her eyes searching the surrounding area. In the moon's shine, she spied the ends of long grass moving. The wind? A predator? The growl again, closer. She couldn't tell from which direction it came.

She bent her knees, ready to spring away. Surely it was more likely for a hungry animal to leave her alone in favor of scavenging the already dead princess. Danya's death might save her.

You promised.

The voice in her head may have been her own, or maybe it belonged to the Mother of Death, perhaps Goddess herself. It held no chastisement, only expectation. She'd given her word, and more than her own life depended on keeping it.

Evalal's hands curled into fists. She took a step toward the princess, unsure how she might defend the corpse from hungry teeth but knowing she must.

The growl came again and this time she determined its direction, pivoted. The long grass bent before the animal she couldn't see. It mustn't be too large. The thought did nothing to ease her mind; she doubted a more diminutive predator would prove any less difficult to banish without a weapon.

Thinking about her lack of protection reminded her of Danya's death. The slender blade the prince used to slay her...what had happened to it? Everything had occurred so quickly. She remembered him pulling it out of her neck because the fountain of blood following it had squeezed her heart to the size of a grape dried by the sun. What transpired after remained fuzzy. She didn't think Teryk had kept it, but the one-armed man or one of the weapons merchants might have collected it. Considering the pride they—especially Fellick—took in their wares, the last option seemed most likely.

Still...

Evalal side-stepped toward the fallen princess, gaze fixed on the fluttering grass betraying a hunter's presence. The growling ceased, the terrifying sound replaced by another: a vague whistle. It confused her; she'd never heard an animal make such a noise. No matter. She couldn't let it distract her from finding the knife responsible for ending Danya's life—her one chance for survival.

She stopped when the side of her foot encountered the princess' body, knelt without taking her eyes from the beast stalking her. Reaching down, her fingers searched the ground beside her dead companion. She cringed as they found grass caked with dried blood, the once life-giving fluid crunching and flaking under her touch. Her gorge rose, and she swallowed hard around the lump in her throat, the effort hurting.

The threat of being mauled gave her greater focus. She pushed past the emotion of touching her friend's lifeblood, maintained eye contact with the spot where the growl had come from. Light glinted amongst the grass, two eyes glaring at her as she stared back. Her fingers searched the ground, the tip of one finding the edge of the blade, nicking her and drawing blood. She breathed a sharp, surprised breath through her teeth but grasped the leather-bound grip.

She rose, arm extended, the knife pointed toward the rustling grass.

The whistling sound grew, expanded. It became obvious the noise came from somewhere other than the creature, but she dared not take her gaze from it to find out where. Without a doubt, the instant she allowed distraction to creep in would be when the animal pounced. Whatever Goddess planned for her, she must protect the princess.

You might have thought of that before the prince killed her.

The voice in her head undoubtedly belonged to her this time. She pushed it aside; guilt needed to wait.

The animal's snout protruded from the grass, its dark nose shuddering as it tested the air, sharp teeth glistening between lips pulled into a snarl. Its fur shone a shade of coppery red, similar to the color of Danya's dried blood. The long, broad tail drooped behind it as it crouched, shifting from paw to paw, readying itself. Evalal pursed her lips, bent her knees, waiting to accept the predator's attack.

The whistle turned to a dull roar, grew to a rumble. The animal's demeanor changed. Its bared teeth disappeared; its flattened ears perked. The spring-like tension in its body shifted and its gaze slipped from the girl, moved upward to a place over her shoulder.

It wasn't until the beast bolted that she realized the clearing was lit as if by the rising sun. Evalal watched the small creature bound away through the grass before lowering the knife and turning slowly.

The falling star rushed across the sky, coming directly for her.

V - Horace - Searchin'

*E*XHAUSTED, *HORACE SLUMPED* ONTO the log, his fingers slidin' outta the woman's grasp as he did. Her expression switched to one o' concern.

"Is everything all right?"

"Tired." He heaved a chest full o' breath in with the word, released it again with a whoosh. "Need to rest a bit."

She nodded and began feelin' the air with her hand, realizin' her companion had put his ass down and tryin' to find an appropriate place for her to do the same. He waited a heartbeat or two to give her a chance, then guided her fingers to the damp surface o' the fallen cedar he'd rested himself upon. She smoothed her grubby robe and set beside him.

They sat in silence for a while, nothing but the sounds o' insects and birds, the rustle o' leaves and the creakin' o' ancient tree trunks; noises what, on other days, a person might've found soothin' and restful. For his own part, Horace fought unsuccessfully to stop glancin' back from where they'd come, watchin' in case pale figures flitted from one shrub to another. He figured enough time'd passed he shouldn't need to worry, but it were hard not to, knowin' how ferocious and nasty they was. Of all the ways he'd prefer not to die, he decided gettin' ate by a thing without a mouth might rate somewhere near the top o' the list.

"We won't find her, will we?"

Horace jumped a little, not expectin' her to speak. He turned his head and gazed at her starin' straight ahead, eyes not seein' anythin', and wondered what it must be like for her. Despite its threats and dangers, the forest were a beautiful place—beat bein' confined to a ship's deck for all one's livin' days. Flowers and trees and leaves, the small furry creatures what didn't want to eat you, and the birds hangin' out way up in the trees—better'n gawkin' out at the stinkin', roilin' sea. But she noticed none of it. Probably she'd be happy for the boredom o' countin' the waves when there weren't nothin' else to do.

"I don't know. It be a big chunk o' forest we're in here behind the green wall."

Horace'd put the futility o' their search outta his mind, but it came rushin' in again with her askin' the question. The ache in his legs grew, and he became aware o' the growl rumblin' in his belly. He leaned forward, placed his elbows on his knees and buried his face in his palms. It'd been some while since he felt like cryin', but it worried him this might be the time for it to happen.

"Does anything look familiar to you?"

The old sailor breathed deep through his nose, lowered his hands. Tears didn't come, but the threat remained.

"Nothin'," he said. "Ev'rythin'. It all kinda looks the same here, one tree just the same as the other. A bush is a bush."

Ailyssa sighed, too, and he noticed her chin droop toward her chest. Whatever'd been givin' her hope were fadin' fast and it caused an ache in his heart. He knew so little about this woman, but the idea o' her losin' faith weren't somethin' he wanted to see, and the urge to keep it from happenin' overpowered him.

"Ivy's got to be here somewhere. Last I saw her, a crack o' thunder scared her into callin' out her brother's name, then she took off runnin' without explanation."

"Her brother?"

"Mmm hmm, Thorn what I told you about."

She raised one hand and rubbed her short hair on the side o' her head closest to him. He weren't in any way surprised to note flecks o' dust and dirt shimmerin' in the sunlight when she did. It frightened him to guess what he might find crawlin' in his own hair and beard.

"The missing Small God," she said, voice but a whisper. He didn't suspect she intended the words as an accusation, but hard not to take them as such.

"I tried to keep him safe," he said, lookin' at his feet. "I did my best."

She lowered her hand, touched his thigh. "You did, Horace. It's not what I meant."

"What did you mean?"

"The thunder; I remember hearing it, too. Just once."

"Yep. Only the one."

"And then she said his name and ran off."

She paused in her speakin', but it seemed to Horace Seaman she intended to say more. He raised his gaze from his scuffed-up boots and watched her features. Her eyes darted from one spot to another as if she might've been lookin' at things, although he realized she couldn't see nothin'. It continued for more'n a few heartbeats, her lips movin', too, carryin' on an unheard conversation what she didn't mean for him, anyway. When the lip movin' and eye flittin' stopped, she turned to face him. Though she directed her head toward him, her blind eyes had no ability to find his, the effect o' her starin' his direction rather'n peerin' at him a disconcertin' thing. Her expression gave an impression o' sadness.

"I believe your friend Thorn might be dead."

Her words might've been fingers what sank themselves into his chest to grab his heart and give it a good, tight squeeze. He opened his mouth and closed it a couple o' times like a fish gulpin' to breathe, because he thought he should respond, but no sounds emerged. The lone thing his body took upon itself to produce was those tears he'd been fightin' against. Now they came whether or not he wanted them to, leavin' him nothin' to do but try his best to keep them quiet and hide his cryin' from Ailyssa.

"I'm sorry, Horace. He was important to you, wasn't he?"

He pressed his lips together because his mouth weren't goin' to do him no good; the painful knot cloggin' his throat refused to let words pass through, no matter what.

"It's why Ivy reacted the way she did. She must have some kind of connection with him."

She turned her head away from him and more tears flowed into his scruffy beard, as though her unseein' eyes upon him gave reason for them to stay in hidin'. Her gaze swept across the forest, like any person havin' a look at the trees and brush, and he wondered if sometimes she had her sight, at least a little. He meant to ask her, if for no other aim than to distract himself from the idea he'd lost his friend, but she stopped him from doin' so when she stood suddenly.

"I think I know where she went. Come on."

She held out her hand, expectin' him to take it. He hesitated, the exhaustion what'd made him sit on this log settlin' into his bones with the grief about Thorn, makin' it so he never wanted to move again. If she weren't here, he might've slipped off the rottin' thing, settled on the ground, and curled up in a ball until the moss grew right o'er top o' him.

She tugged on his hand, unwillin' to let him give up. The old sailor stood, his reluctant knees poppin'.

"Let's go," she said and led him away, toward the green wall glowin' in the distance.

—◦◦◦—

She moved her feet as though directed by an invisible guide—as unseen as everything else around her. Leaves slapped her arms and legs, none of them registered by her eyes. The seaman trailed behind her, and she heard his struggle to keep up, felt bad to push him when he so obviously wanted to grieve the loss of the Small God; the certainty about the significance of his death invaded her like a hostile army bent on taking over the kingdom. The metaphor wasn't so far from the truth.

Without knowing how, her feet found a path free of obstruction and hindrance. Other than the branches and foliage brushing her limbs, no logs or stones presented themselves to trip over, no impedance emerged to slow their travel. How did Goddess' influence appear and disappear so quickly? Might it be she tested Ailyssa at every opportunity?

Truthfully, her faith had waxed and waned more often than she cared to count since her expulsion from Olvana. Many times it had deserted her. Yet Goddess returned to her to offer guidance again and again. Even if she chose not to return her sight, she continued guiding her steps as she made her way through the forest with the sailor in tow. Ailyssa experienced no fear of stumbling or running into the trunk of a tree, such was her renewed conviction in Goddess' touch upon her.

And her confidence in knowing how and where to find the Small God whom Horace referred to as Ivy shone brightly in her chest, filling her with warmth and hope. Though she saw nothing but the empty whiteness clouding her vision since that day in the gardens, she sensed a path laid out before her, one she could follow—she might even do it quickly if not for the old sailor slowing her pace.

She thought to tell him to hurry, but doubted the ability of her words to make him move faster. The poor fellow had been through so much, and she suspected he hid more—things he hesitated to reveal to her. She didn't know what they might be and assumed it didn't matter, but she experienced a measure of discomfort in putting her confidence in someone she knew so little about, especially a man. She'd been raised her entire life not to trust men.

But these were desperate times, not only for her, but for everyone.

She continued through the forest, Horace trailing behind her as she navigated the perceived-but-not-seen trail. The path bent and curved, presumably leading them past and around obstructions. Birds chirped, leaves rustled, the sailor exhaled ragged breaths; Ailyssa pushed on.

Time and distance melted together, taking with them her perception of how long they walked this way or how far they'd traveled. The temperature may have cooled minutely, perhaps meaning afternoon turned to early evening, but of this, she couldn't be sure. The exercise of walking kept her warm, bringing perspiration to her skin beneath her robe. Horace didn't speak, because he sensed her surety or because the effort made him too short of breath to find his voice. If he didn't clasp her hand in his, she might have believed she'd left him behind.

One thing she noticed as it changed: the blank chasm around her started to fade. Vague shapes floated through the void, at first nothing but white shadows, impressions more likely made by imagination than vision. She fought the flutter of excitement tickling in her gut, but it became more and more difficult as the shadows and impressions rectified themselves into actual figures.

When the initial smudge of color flickered in the chalky wilderness, she stopped in her tracks.

Her sight was returning.

VI - Trenan - Ghosts

*T*HE HORSE CAME TO a stop and Trenan raised his head, opened his eyes. The sudden daylight blinded him and shut them again. When did he last gaze upon the world? The answer eluded him.

When next he cracked his lids, he scanned the surrounding area, recognized nothing. Where he'd come to, how he arrived, and why, remained mysteries. He stroked his horse's neck, then wiped his hand across his brow.

Breathing hurt. His head pained him. His ass felt as though a hard saddle had pressed it for more sunrises and sunsets than any man could stand to sit a horse. He inhaled, winced at the pain in his ribs, tasted the threat of rain on the air.

And he remembered.

The bitter tang of orange came to mind first—the remnants of whatever cursed magic the black priests had cast on his warriors. Their loss struck him next, preventing any relief over having survived.

The prince.

The master swordsman's heart jumped in his chest. He had a sense of having climbed onto this mount, but what of his son? Did he also escape? He twisted in the saddle, jerking around to look behind him and nearly overbalancing and slipping off.

With the second horse's lead attached to his, the animal had halted a pace to the rear. Teryk lay against the steed's neck, arms dangling.

Trenan dismounted, heart pounding in his ears. His knees gave way beneath him and he tumbled to the ground, landing on the shoulder without an arm. Pain jolted across his upper back and he bit down on his teeth to keep from crying out; he didn't know if they were alone, or who might be nearby. Though fog crowded his brain, instinct told him not to risk attention.

He rolled onto his side, positioned his arm beneath him and levered himself up. The horse upon which Teryk lay danced aside a step, startled by the scuffling; Trenan caught the lead in his fingers to make sure it didn't bolt.

"There, there," he said, struggling to keep his voice even and calm the animal. The hammering of his heart inside his chest and the knot in his stomach did not reflect his outward demeanor.

The horse steadied, and he moved past, making his way to the debilitated prince. He raised his hand, hesitated before touching him, sure he'd find his flesh cold to the touch, life gone from his body. With the princess dead, he didn't think he possessed the capacity to go on if Teryk passed, too. Ishla would never forgive him.

He sighed out the air in his lungs but paused before drawing another, steeling himself, and extended his arm until his fingers touched the prince's cheek.

Warm. He lives.

Relief overcame him, clogged his throat, brought water to his eyes. Hand still on the young man's face, he let his head droop and allowed tears to squeeze out between his lids. One followed the path of his eyelashes; it hung from the end of them before plummeting to the dirt at his feet. A second ran down the side of his nose, another along his opposite cheek. He wiped them away, wondering about the last time he'd cried. As a child, and a few nights after losing his arm, but no other times in his memory.

What's wrong with me?

He raised his eyes skyward. A cluster of birds glided past high above, their dark shapes outlined against the blue stretching out beyond them. As he turned his gaze away, he thought he glimpsed one of them immense compared to the others; he didn't look back—likely a trick of the tears blurring his vision.

You've never worried you'd lost a child before.

But it wasn't only that. The fate of his warriors weighed; the prospect of losing Ishla's love—even a love he'd never have in person—shrank his heart to the size of a pea. Nothing had ever affected him this way before—not the loss of his arm, not the birth of a son circumstances left him unable to admit to having fathered, not the deaths of countless foes and friends over the course of a violent life.

He returned his attention to the prince. What had come to pass couldn't be changed, but he might yet influence Teryk's. He leaned closer.

"Teryk. My prince." The young man showed no reaction. "Son."

The speaking of the word aloud tightened his throat again, brought more tears threatening at the corners of his eyes. He sniffed hard, swallowed, ashamed of this unaccustomed emotion.

Trenan put his hand in front of the lad's face, testing for the waft of breath flowing from his nose and mouth, and found it, the flow shallow but rhythmic—an excellent sign. With a finger, he brushed hair away from his forehead. His eyes remained shut, but he noticed them moving beneath his lids, darting first one direction then the other—dreaming. The tension in the master swordsman eased. The temptation to shake the boy, wake him from this slumber to make sure he'd incurred no damage from whatever the dark priests had left behind almost overcame him. He gripped Teryk's shoulder, but stopped himself. A body and mind repaired themselves best when they rested. He let his arm fall to his side.

The concept of needing rest explained how he came to be...wherever he found himself. He'd passed out from the fumes, miraculously escaping the devastating effect they'd caused in the warriors of Ikkundana, and the horse carried its unconscious rider away from the danger. Whether the steed did so out of instinct, or he'd prompted it to, eluded him, but it didn't matter. They'd escaped with their lives.

Trenan stepped away from the prince, redirected his attention to their surroundings.

Brush and trees lined the dirt track. Judging by the foliage and the sun's position in the sky, he suspected it might be the same path he and his soldiers had traveled on their way to the Green, but the mist cluttering his brain made certainty difficult. Likely a hundred tracks which appeared identical to this one criss-crossed the kingdom.

He took three steps toward the brush on the right-hand side of the road, scuffing his feet in the dirt and raising a dust as he moved. Rain had fallen during their trek to the Green, the sheets of water turning the path to mud. If he now followed the same track, the sun should have dried its surface and left behind at least a few vague impressions of hoof prints. He detected none.

The downpour may have lasted long enough to wash them away.

Nothing definitive in either direction. He continued to the border between dirt road and forest, careful of his steps. It didn't appear anyone traveled the path much—tufts of grass grew at irregular intervals, which he'd have found beaten down and choked out on a well-used track.

The brush at the edge of the trail buzzed with countless bees collecting pollen from pink flowers or stealing juice from plump berries. He thought of plucking some juicy fruits for himself, but the idea of putting them in his mouth and swallowing them made his stomach lurch. Whatever he'd inhaled remained in his system enough to keep his body from wanting him to eat.

The possibility of imbibing sustenance abandoned, he glanced both directions along the path. Ahead, the track stretched out for a while before disappearing around a corner. Its surface lay empty but for the tufts of grass and the odd stone strewn across it. In the other direction, the trail ran straight, vanishing in a distant haze. Trenan squinted, trying his best to decide if heat, distance, his mind, or something else caused the indistinctness.

The dust raised by black priests pursuing us.

The master swordsman breathed in and out heavily between parted lips, took two paces along the path in the direction they'd come. It gave no sign of what the cause of the obscurity might be. He stared, concern creeping into him with each passing moment. Instinct dropped his hand to the hilt of the sword dangling at his waist. But what good was his weapon when the warriors chosen by the Goddess and trained by him had disappeared in the priests' wake?

This is no place to make a stand.

He strode to his horse, fingers brushing Teryk's shoulder as he passed in an unaccustomed gesture of caring. He reached his steed, grasped the saddle horn and placed his foot in the stirrup but stopped before mounting, his attention usurped by an out-of-place sound drifting to his ears.

The master swordsman jerked his head to the right, looking over his shoulder at the spot at the edge of the track where he'd stood moments ago. At first, he saw nothing unusual—bees buzzing from berry to bloom, leaves agitated by a wan breeze, everything ordinary.

Then he spied the face peering at him from behind a bush, the features mostly obscured. His breath caught in his throat. How had he not seen this man before?

His foot found the ground again, his fingers on the grip of the crownsword. He took one step toward the intruder, yanking half the length of his steel from its scabbard as he moved. His heart pounded against his ribs and saliva filled his mouth near to the point of overflowing. The muscles in his arms and legs tingled, but not because he expected an attack to come. Thumping chest, overactive salivary glands, stimulated limbs—his fight-or-flight instinct desperately encouraged him to flee.

He experienced fear.

He swallowed hard, forcing the bitterness of fearful spit down his throat and parted his lips to speak.

"Who...who's there?"

His voice quavered and shame prickled heat in his cheeks; he moved no farther forward, waiting for a response from the man hiding in the brush. Trenan held his breath, worried that, should he inhale, he'd detect the bitter orange scent again.

The face reacted to his behest by moving from behind the covering of leaves, coming to a spot where he clearly saw the man's features. The master swordsman tilted his head. Somewhere deep inside his consciousness, he recognized a familiarity in the fellow, but found himself unable to place it. He hadn't seen the faces of the priests responsible for the disappearance of his warriors, but knowing so did nothing to relieve the threat of knots creeping into his limbs. His brows dipped, his lips pursed, then realization dawned.

Many seasons had passed since he'd gazed upon this man. He didn't know his name, nor anything about him. Not his age, his family situation, what he believed or didn't believe.

The face of the first kill made by Trenan's hand.

The master swordsman stumbled away a step, Godsbane sliding into its sheath. Warmth drained from his cheeks; his breath stuck in his chest.

How can this be?

But how meant nothing. With black priests close, the memory of their magic lingering in his mind, and the princess left dead in a meadow, his thoughts seemed not his own. He swallowed hard, attempting to dispatch the unfamiliar taste of fear along with his spittle, but the uncomfortable feeling remained. He gripped the saddle's pommel again, reinserted his foot in the stirrup and boosted himself onto the steed, teetered on the edge of overbalancing and tumbling off the other side.

The master swordsman grabbed the reins, steadied himself. The height afforded by being on horseback returned some of the confidence he'd grown used to. He pulled on the lead, guiding the animal toward the spot where he'd seen the fellow.

At first, he thought the dead man had fled. No face peered at him from between broad leaves, at least none he saw. Trepidation and concern began to drain from him, then he spied the impossible visage again, ten paces farther along the track, but not so far he didn't recognize him as the same person.

But he appeared different now. His hair lay flat on his forehead, stuck in place by brown and crusty blood. Purplish circles ringed his eyes, his lips parted in a skeletal smile. He stared without blinking. He'd gone from looking like a young soldier's first kill before he died to how he must have looked by the end of the battle.

Trenan's mount whinnied and stamped its front feet, agitated by the dead man's presence. The horse's discomfort increased its rider's disquiet.

As the master swordsman watched, the blood plastering the fellow's hair to his forehead changed color from brown to red, from dried to fresh. A fissure opened in his face, running from the crown of his skull, between his eyes, ending at his mouth. His tongue lolled free.

I killed him by splitting his head open.

A memory of how it had felt to end his first life returned. The seasons had turned the thirteenth time for him. He shouldn't have been with those warriors and fighters as they marched to engage the landing party from the Leeward Kingdom, their ship put to shore near Brookbridge, but he'd managed to hide from those who cared. When he found himself part of the fight, getting exactly what he'd longed for—a chance to prove himself a man—he had no choice but to take the invader's life.

The way his head had split beneath the edge of his blade had surprised Trenan. As much time as he'd spent honing his skills with the weapon, he wouldn't have thought he possessed enough strength to cleave a man's skull in two. Or perhaps a skull broke open with more ease than he'd imagined.

After ending the fellow's existence, he stood over him, staring at the blood-covered cheeks, the crack between his eyes, the pink-gray brain matter leaking out of the wound. Overcome by what he'd done, he decided to never forget this face—not the broken version he peered upon at the end, but the living visage full of life and possibility.

As he stared at the handiwork of a sword long snapped in two and melted down, wielded by the strength of an arm no longer attached to his body, he realized his failure. Despite the prayers he said each time he went into battle, the mercy he begged for his fallen foes, the reverence he claimed to have for the gift of life, he'd forgotten the first man a weapon he'd held brought to his end.

And so he came back to haunt him.

Gripping the horse tight between his thighs, Trenan reached behind to check the knot tethering the prince-carrying mount to his own. His fingers shook, and he stopped before testing it, closed his hand into a fist, then opened it, flexing his digits wide. The quiver remained. He spat a curse from his lips and completed his task, ensuring a connection secure enough to hold.

When he turned back, the dead man had emerged from the fringe. He stood at the side of the dirt track, the blood from the wound flowing over his cheeks, down his neck, disappearing beneath the leather chest piece he wore over a forest-green jerkin. A dark patch showed on the front of his plain brown pants where his bladder voided itself upon his death. The small patches of skin showing through the streaks of red looked cold and white.

Trenan's gut coiled and lurched as the man raised his arm, pointed at him, the long-dead finger accusing him. Desperate, he glanced over his shoulder, tempted to reverse the horses and flee the way they'd come. To his eyes, the murky horizon appeared larger, closer. He imagined dark dots at its base, the distant shapes of murderous priests coming to slay the prince and take his life.

He shifted in the saddle, rotating toward the man, found he wasn't alone. Other men gathered around and behind him, a few on the other side of the track, three dozen to Trenan's estimation. Blood and gore were common amongst them; many missing limbs, a few eviscerated, two without heads. Wherever skin showed, it glowed white and bloodless. Eyes stared, blind and dead. Severed fingers, broken teeth, chests laid open.

And the same sense of familiarity Trenan recognized in the first man he identified in some of these living corpses.

A chill galloped up the soldier's spine, chattering his teeth together until he bit down hard, the muscles in his jaw flexing and knotting. Beyond these impossible figures from his past lay their path of escape, but did following it mean fighting his way through the throng of dead warriors?

Do I have to kill them again?

His breath squeaked in his throat and sweat dampened his brow. His bowels squeezed tight and the urge to piss caught him off-guard; he clenched hard and quick to keep from wetting himself like a frightened child.

What the fuck is wrong with me?

Whatever the priests had left behind in their wake had made him a shadow of the renowned master swordsman, but he couldn't let it stop him. He may have failed the princess, but he represented Teryk's last chance for survival.

He drew his tongue across his lips, sighed his chest full of air, and expelled it with a loud huff. His hand reached for his weapon, fingers fumbling to find purchase. When they did, he pulled the crownsword free, its weight many times greater than what it ought to be. His arm shook under its mass as he struggled to keep it from falling from his grip.

With his heart beating faster than he could ever remember it doing, Trenan set his heels to the horse and advanced, ready to pass through the gauntlet of dead men.

VII - Teryk – Healer

*D*ARKNESS SURROUNDED HIM, BUT he retained slight awareness of the world outside. Not like when a dome of sand covered him, blocking out everything.

When was that?

He sensed movement, a meager breeze on his face, an up-and-down gait beneath him. Warmth pressed against his chest and arms, though the sparsity of sound struck him. Was this death, or the edge of it? Was sight taken from him, never to return? The thought of opening his eyes crossed his mind, but he took no action to attempt it. If he could no longer see, he didn't wish to find out. If this was to be his end, then he wished it over; he was unsure why he should want it so.

"Don't you recall?"

The words drifted to his awareness as though carried on an autumn wind, coming from all directions at once but from nowhere, as well.

"Who's there?"

A sliver of white floated before him, small, or perhaps distant. The blackness made it impossible to tell what it appeared to him, or its distance from him. Teryk concentrated on it, trying to recognize something about it—its shape or size, features, anything.

"Do you not recall what happened?"

The question set his mind reeling, as though someone had spun him too many times and left him dizzy and nauseated. With naught but darkness around him, he had nothing on which to steady himself. The vertigo continued, and the sliver of white grew.

"Do you remember the lies? The treacherous knife? The blood?"

The words hit him hard—a storm's wave slamming against the shore—and he remembered other things. Not lies or knives or blood, but being amongst such waves, floating atop the ocean, monsters, a foreign beach. How did it fit?

The pale fragment grew bigger, closer. A face. He didn't recognize it, and its unusualness struck him. At first, he didn't realize why, but it soon came to him it was hairless—no hair on its head, no eyebrows, nothing.

"Who are you?" His voice shook with equal parts nausea and fear.

"Most call me the healer, though it is perhaps not the most exact of titles." The lips on the face didn't move with the words, their faded pink holding steady, but he understood it was this—person? Thing?—which spoke to him.

"What do you want?"

"Why, to heal you."

The sense of movement continued beneath Teryk; he concentrated on it, attempting to use its rhythm as a touchstone to yank him from the whirling maelstrom of his mind. The vertigo eased; the nausea abated. A second patch of white appeared, smaller than the first; a hand held out toward him, unnaturally long fingers splayed.

"But you must remember."

More memories returned, but nothing to do with what the face spoke of. This time, he recalled a river, a secret room, a scroll. Mixed amongst these he saw another person, a young woman. It swirled before him an instant before recognition broke.

Danya.

The realization triggered a landslide. Juddah, Ailyssa, the inside of the barn. He remembered the trip to the Green and, finally, everything that happened there.

"No."

Even in his head, it came out but a whisper. The feelings of movement, the brush of wind on his cheeks disappeared, buried under an avalanche of emotion. If he possessed the ability to shed tears or lash out in anger, he'd have done so.

"It's not your fault," the unmoving face said. "So much manipulation, so many lies for so long. What else could you do?"

"It was me," Teryk replied. "I'm the one who stabbed her. I'm the one who killed Danya."

The hand stretched out closer to him, or what might have been him if he consisted of something more than blank darkness. He wanted to recoil from the lanky fingers but lacked the ability to do so in this dreary, hopeless place.

"The skinny man gave you the knife. The one-armed gave you reason. How can you accept responsibility for doing what anyone would have done, given the circumstances?"

Teryk flexed his hands, felt tacky liquid on them. The blood of his sister. His friend. The only person who'd loved and supported him his entire life, whenever he needed her, no questions asked. Blood he'd spilled in anger and resentment. A life he'd taken out of jealousy. The only life he'd ever taken. The one life he'd never want to end.

"Why didn't they tell me?" His words quaked, tears he couldn't cry in this lightless world imminent. "If they'd told me the truth, none of this would have happened."

"They didn't want you to find out because they wished this to happen. Wanted you to kill her. Trenan demanded your sister's blood on your hands."

"But why? He loved her as if she—" His words broke off and the white face loomed closer in front of him. Other memories nipped at the edge of his mind. "As if she was his own child."

"But she wasn't. You were. That meant she was the firstborn. Their lies stole your destiny from you. Took your sister away."

Through the swirl of rawness, a memory coalesced. Another time in a dark place like this, after a fight left him near death. The colorless face had been there, too, hidden beneath a cowl, the hairless, sexless body disguised by a black robe. He'd been healed then, but at what price?

"What do you want of me?"

"I want the vengeance you deserve."

The face before him and the memory converged, two white ovals overlaying each other until they became the same.

"I know you."

The faded pink slash of lips curled at the ends. "We have met. Another paid the cost to save you when you needed it."

"If you have such power, why don't you seek vengeance for me?"

The grim smile spread. "It's not how it works. I cannot give or take away for myself. Always the price must be met."

"And what is the price?"

"Speak your desire and you will find out."

Teryk's life danced through his mind, both the one he lived and the one left unlived. He watched himself grow and change, saw how different it might have been if the king was his sire, or if he'd known Trenan to be. He wondered briefly if the thoughts belonged to him, or if the so-called healer planted them in his head to sprout like a fungus, a mold inserting itself into the crevices of his subconscious mind. How could he realize the difference?

"You are unsure for now," the white face said, ghastly smile fading. "But you will know soon. You will see what must be done."

The pale oval diminished, as though the healer moved away, shrinking in the distance. The up-and-down gait returned beneath Teryk; the caress of a breeze found his cheek again, and the face became but a colorless smudge before disappearing completely. Everything went dark again—for an instant or for a season; he didn't know.

Eventually, a splinter of light forced its way into the black, tiny but dazzling. It expanded steadily, blinding him until he adjusted to it and recognized he'd opened his eyes.

A dirt track stretched out before him, lined on both sides by trees and brush out of which peered faces he'd never seen. Blood splashed many of them, pain and suffering marred every one of them. Teryk realized the sight should have frightened him, but it didn't. He redirected his gaze along the lead tethering the horse he sat to the one in front of him, guiding him along the road, then to the broad back of the one-armed soldier seated upon it.

Trenan.

The healer's words echoed in his head:

"Their lies stole your destiny from you. Took your sister away."

Teryk wondered what the price the healer spoke of might be.

VIII - Evalal – Fireball

*T*HE BALL OF FIRE passed too close over her head.

Evalal ducked, sensed heat against the side of her neck as the falling star whizzed by above her. She didn't judge it near enough to warrant moving out of its way, but reflex took over. The sound of it rushing through the air assaulted her ears, and she turned to follow its trajectory, forgetting the creature so recently stalking her. It was long gone, now the least of the threats to her.

The falling star streaked over the short space and hit the green wall. The earth shook. Verdant sparks shot into the sky, turning the night into a field of green stars instead of white. A boom rumbled through the air and Evalal winced, raised an arm to protect her face.

The star lay against the veil high above the ground like a spoonful of oatmeal flung against a wall by a child. She lowered her arm, gaze holding fast on the glowing spot. Its glow diminished bit by bit, and she took a tentative step toward the Green. Without thinking, she tightened her grip on the small knife she held, directed its tip in front of her.

The light flickered and dimmed, resembling the guttering flame of a candle, while slipping its way down the glowing wall. Streaks of green lightning shuddered across its surface like veins beneath translucent skin. She thought of the princess lying dead behind her, veins emptied of blood, her life stolen from her.

Goddess' plan.

Might this be part of her design, as well? She'd placed the Small Gods in the sky, banished them for abandoning her. But the power to dispel evil and the ability to control it likely weren't the same thing. If Goddess manipulated those who watch from above, why let them return at all? Why put them through this and allow the princess to die?

Evalal swallowed hard, forced the concern from her mind. The glow continued its slow path along the front of the veil, its brightness weakening with each passing breath. She took three more steps toward the wall, hesitant to leave Danya's side but drawn to the fading light.

When the afterglow extinguished halfway down the blockade from where it hit, the rest peeled itself away.

And the form of a man tumbled to the earth.

Despite her trepidation, Evalal rushed forward, already within earshot as the shape struck the ground with a sickening crunch of bone. Tall grass, nearly invisible in the dark, brushed against her legs. Worry over what might lurk amongst those blades visited her mind and disappeared as quickly as it came. A man had fallen from the sky; small animals skulking and hiding before her footsteps became a relative inconvenience in comparison.

She pulled up short three long paces before reaching him. Part of her wanted to continue on, to fall to her knees beside him and administer the healing aid she'd been taught since her memory began. Her teachers had instilled the desire to be of assistance deep inside her, ingraining it in her being, but common sense prevailed. She leaned forward for a better view, her body half turned, ready to flee should it prove necessary.

The man lay twisted at the waist, one arm pinned beneath him and both his legs canted at a near impossible angle. With this cursory examination, she recognized three broken limbs, at the very least, though she guessed much worse. She relaxed halfway, certain his state precluded any chance of this fellow jumping up to attack her. A good chance he'd do nothing ever again.

Evalal took one step toward him, then another. He wore no clothes of any kind, not a stitch of cloth covering even the most private parts of his body. Fine, dark hair dusted his limbs, a coarser mat of it upon his chest, running down his belly and farther.

She'd never seen a naked man.

The hair grew thicker where his legs came together, but its thickness and the angle of his hips prevented her from seeing more. She possessed a vague idea what might be there; it wasn't a secret kept from them. She'd heard about other of the Goddess' sects using men for procreation, though not the temple of the Mother of Death. Between the unwanted children dropped off at their door and the babes the Mother produced herself, the rest of them remained as pure of body as they did of mind and spirit.

Other sisters whispered rumors about what she'd find.

Not just of what might be inside the pants of a man, but of those who left the order because they enjoyed what it did for them. This concept lay beyond Evalal's imagining. Men had their purpose in the world, but it had little to do with Goddess and her followers.

Curiosity brought her a step closer.

Her eyes adjusted to the change in light, the brightness of the falling star having left her partially blinded when its glow disappeared. Now she'd become accustomed again to the shine of the moon and the muted radiance of the veil, enabling her to see more readily. The mystery remained, and she took another step, leaned closer.

She glimpsed pink flesh. At first, she assumed it merely the skin of his thigh but, if so, this was an extra flap at odds with the rest of him. Instead of being part of his legs, it appeared pressed between them.

A tickle rose in the bottom of Evalal's belly and she realized her breath grew short, quickened, as though she'd run to arrive at this spot. Or like she experienced fear. Neither was the case. Deep down, she knew he should be fearful; here lay what might be one of the banished Small Gods returned to the world, prophesied to bring the end of man. But as she gazed on his broken and naked body, she saw no danger.

Another step. She crouched, squinted, leaned in.

It resembled a thumb, longer and wider than her own, but likely not much larger than the man's own. It did not finish with a nail, though, and the skin upon it appeared wrinkled and veiny, the sort of flesh found on someone noticeably older. She couldn't be sure, but she considered it might be soft to the touch.

She raised her head, glanced over both shoulders, craned her neck to peer to where the princess lay. With nothing unusual or distressing to cause her alarm, she returned her attention to the man before her.

The shadows cast by the moon shining over her shoulder and the dim luminescence of the veil made it difficult to tell whether or not he drew breath. She thought she saw shallow movement in his chest; in other moments she doubted it. She spent a handful of heartbeats concentrating on trying to discern the truth but found her attention wandering. Her gaze slipped along his torso. She told herself she might see his breathing moving his belly, yet her observations moved lower until her eyes settled again on the misplaced thumb.

It's not a thumb.

The tickle in her belly replied, expanding both up into her chest and down toward her groin. She shifted her position, but the movement caused the sensation to expand.

He must be dead. Nobody survives an impact so severe. Or the fall.

She considered putting her fingers under his nose in search of air finding its way in and out, but she hesitated. If he lived, she didn't want to put her hand near his mouth and his one good arm. How would she protect Danya's remains if he captured her or hurt her?

I should return to the princess.

She shifted again, and the tickle in her belly spilled downward, startling her. She'd encountered such an agitation before; they taught the sisters from an early age how to give themselves pleasure. Some even helped each other, though Evalal never experienced any touch other than her own.

What did some enjoy so much about this man-thing they chose to forsake Goddess?

Is it magic?

It didn't seem so. Something magical wouldn't appear so shriveled and insignificant. So...plain.

And yet it ignited the tingle in her abdomen spilling into her loins. Some kind of bewitchment?

If he's dead, his skin will be starting to cool.

Her training in the art of healing told her not enough time had passed for flesh to grow cold. The insulation provided by muscle and fat retained warmth long past the point the heart stopped beating, blood stopped flowing, and awareness ceased in the mind. But what other choice did she have to determine if he yet lived?

Thus justifying what she knew to be a questionable act, she lifted her hand, realized it still gripped the dagger Teryk had used to kill his sister. She switched the knife to the other, reached toward the fallen man. Her fingers shook. She curled them into a tight fist, opened it again, flexed her palm. A heavy sigh found its way in through her lips and she leaned forward a little farther, a little farther.

Two fingertips brushed the man's thigh.

Evalal jerked her hand away. She'd enjoyed the prickle of the hairs on his leg, the warmth of his flesh. It didn't prove him alive, but it might. She reached out again.

All of her fingers touched his thigh. It wasn't this part of him the sensation warming her belly and lower encouraged her to explore, but it was all she could bring herself to do. The muscle beneath the skin felt firm but slack, exactly as expected from someone unconscious, or dead.

She slid her hand down by the width of her small finger, moving it closer to the place where his legs came together. The excitement expanded into her chest, but it took on a unique aspect. Instead of the invigoration of anticipation, she worried someone might catch her doing something she shouldn't be doing. But a remote place like this lacked anyone to see, offered nobody to punish her for circumventing a vow. Partly true, she realized.

Goddess sees everything.

The voice in her head belonged to the Mother of Death; she'd listened to the woman speak the words so many times in her life there could be no doubt. The thought quelled the feeling in her chest, forced it toward her belly, lacing a sliver of sadness and disappointment behind. Never again would an opportunity like this present itself.

She didn't remove her hand.

Evalal inclined her head, inhaled through her nose. Night's smells—better farther from the rising odor of the deceased princess and the looming smoke of the incinerated dead man—calmed her. She lowered her chin, directed her gaze toward the fallen man's face.

His eyes were open.

The girl froze. She searched her memory, attempting to recall if they were this way before. She'd allowed the mysteries of a male she found to distract her, leaving her unable to remember whether they'd been closed or if they stared skyward as they did now. Her hand lay upon his thigh, forgotten as she struggled to return to herself.

He groaned.

Evalal tumbled, scrambling away from him. The sound he made sounded small and strangled, in no way threatening, but it proved the warmth of his skin meant he yet lived. And she'd been caught.

Her heels dug into the ground, pushing her away, until she stopped and pushed herself to stand. She stared at him for the space of five heartbeats, and another pained moan crossed the air between them.

Evalal ran to the princess, fell to her knees at the side of her fallen companion, and prayed for forgiveness.

IX - Trenan – Lucidity

TIME SMEARED LIKE A child painting with his bare hands upon a canvas. The way the colors mixed and combined so it became impossible to tell one from another, so did the hours and days that passed.

Trenan had no recollection of how he'd gotten away from his grisly past surrounding and threatening him, how he made his escape from the place. Did mere moments pass, or did the sun set and rise again? Had it done so more than once? Godsbane nestled in its scabbard, gray clouds hid the sky.

And what of Teryk?

He swallowed hard, the insignificant amount of saliva his mouth conjured scraping the inside of his arid throat. With fingers gripping the saddle horn tight enough to blanch his knuckles white, he shifted to peer over his shoulder. His gaze trailed along the horse's flank, found the lead fastened to the rear. It stretched out behind, showing the other horse following, but did the prince sit atop the steed?

He sighed, shivered, raised his eyes.

Teryk sat straight in the saddle, looking like a man recovered from whatever ailed him. He grasped the reins in his left hand but did not stare ahead at the road. Instead, he cocked his head to the right, a serious look creasing his brow.

"Who are they?" he asked without diverting his eyes. The master swordsman followed the young man's gaze to the side of the dirt track.

The dead men stood at irregular intervals, some of them mostly hidden in the brush, only their faces showing, others standing in the open at the edge of the fringe. Trenan didn't need to remember any of them to recognize them as people he'd killed. He wanted to run away from their wounds caused by his sword, from the loss gleaming in their expressions because of him, but they held his attention. None of them moved, other than their eyes following the horses and riders as they passed.

"I took their lives," he replied, his tone flat and voice barely more than a whisper. "I prayed for mercy for them."

"Your prayers didn't work."

The accusation in Teryk's statement shocked him, wrenching his gaze to the prince. The young man continued staring at the living corpses lining the edge of the road, his expression shifting to one of pain, torment.

"Are you okay?"

Had Trenan been the type to count heartbeats to mark the passage of time, he'd have found it flexed and pumped blood through his veins fifteen times before Teryk turned his head—it seemed a very long while. His son's eyes fell upon him, though the lad's expression gave the impression he didn't see him, his gaze instead penetrating him, staring beyond him. The master swordsman wondered what he saw. The distant horizon? What the future held? The past?

"I murdered my sister," he said, ending the elongated pause. "I killed Danya."

Trenan released his hold on the saddle horn, fumbled for his reins without looking and slowed his horse, prompted it to stop. Teryk's mount did the same and the master swordsman turned in his seat, his back hurting with the movement. He gazed at the prince, his heart aching but also pounding with the memory of his sister's face gone porcelain with blood loss. His son's gaze returned from wherever it had disappeared to, settled on the master swordsman's. Devastation shimmered in his eyes, rimmed them with wetness.

"It wasn't your fault." Trenan wanted to reach out, put his hand on the prince's shoulder to offer comfort, but too much distance lay between them. "You weren't of your right mind. The black priests—"

"Didn't kill her. I did."

"They—"

"I understood what I was doing. Finding out I wasn't the firstborn of the king—that she was—felt as though it destroyed my life. I blamed her."

His gaze trailed away, returning to the faces at the side of the track, and Trenan looked aside, too. A portion of the dead men wore expressions twisted with agony, some fear, a few appeared peaceful.

"It's you I should have blamed."

For the second time, Teryk's words jolted Trenan's attention from the ghostly gallery watching them pass. He jerked his gaze to the prince as a lump the size of his heart rose in his throat, threatened to choke him. He attempted to swallow around it, parted his lips to speak, but Teryk interrupted.

"Why didn't you tell me? None of this would have happened if I'd known."

Steel and ice weighed his words, and they slammed into Trenan's chest as though launched from a slingshot. His mouth opened and closed three times, each time with an intention of speaking, but the knot in his throat and the dryness of his tongue prevented him. What could he say? Teryk wasn't wrong.

"It's your fault Danya is dead. You should have told me the truth when you found out about the scroll and the prophecy."

Trenan forced some saliva down his gullet, squeezing it past the lump with a squeak he heard in his head. It tasted bitter and acidic, the flavor of failure and loss. He closed his eyes, breathed in slowly, deeply, expanding his chest to its fullest before exhaling and opening his lids again. He found the prince staring at him and nearly lost his resolve, something which had never happened to him.

"How could I know you'd go running off to fulfill a silly prophecy? You didn't tell me you were going or seek my advice."

"You've known me my entire life," Teryk snapped, his voice rising in volume. "How did you not know? You raised me."

The pressure in the master swordsman's chest expanded, shooting pain along his arm. In that instant, he was thankful he sat a horse because, if standing, his knees might have given way. He wanted to respond, to speak words to make things better, but this time it wasn't his mouth failing him, but his mind. Nothing came to him, no excuses to give. He was the boy's father; he'd raised him like a father should, but neglected to act like one because he never thought it his place to do so.

Look where it got us.

He hung his head, relieved not to see his son staring at him with disdain, though he sensed the prince's eyes upon him. All the turns of the seasons he'd spent as a soldier—most of them, every decision his to make—and he'd never hesitated. Until now. Sitting on a horse in the middle of a dirt track with his child needing his support, he didn't know how to proceed. Should he say something? Embrace him? Put his heels to his steed and continue on their journey? Perhaps if Trenan was raised by a father to serve as an example, the right course might be plain; his own sire's solution to everything included the whip, the rod, or the fist.

Rather than doing anything, the master swordsman stared at his lap. Waited. Part of him hoped for the dead men to emerge from the forest and converge on them. At least then he'd have a sense of the correct action to follow.

"I was there when you lost your arm."

At first, Trenan thought he must have misheard the prince. He raised his chin, half expecting to find a bloody axe in the young man's hand. No weapon, but his expression threatened to spit daggers at him.

"What?"

"The battle when an axe took your arm. I was there."

He shook his head. "You weren't born yet. I—" He hesitated, unsure if he should finish his sentence. The prince's expectant look convinced him to do so. "I didn't lay with your mother until after I lost it."

Teryk cringed, the muscles in his jaw bulging beneath the stubble lining his cheeks. His nostrils flared, and his eyes narrowed. Trenan gulped, wishing for the opportunity to take the words back.

"I was there," he repeated. "When you and she determined your lies."

The master swordsman was unsure whether he shook his head again, or if it simply hadn't stopped. "No, you weren't."

"I was there when the Small Gods raised the veil, and when Goddess dispelled sin from the world. I saw the fall of the Pillars of Life and the death of the priestess Rak'bana. I sank with the Whalebone and touched the black sand of the Land Across the Sea."

The master swordsman stared, vaguely aware of his mouth falling open. What curse had the black priests cast upon the prince to cause him such delusions? He knew they'd changed him, but he'd hoped for Teryk to come through the experience unscathed.

"Teryk." The next word fell from his lips without his intention of speaking it; he realized what the effect would be as soon as it landed in the air. "Son."

"Don't call me that!"

Trenan flinched, the sharpness of the prince's tone sinking deep into his chest, wounding him in a way he'd only been wounded once before. The first time, it had come from this young man's mother, though the harm had been through necessity and no fault of hers. He looked away, unable to continue seeing the hurt and anger in his son's face.

"How could I have experienced all those things, been shown so much, and not be the prophesied? How can I not be the firstborn, destined to save the world?"

Breath shuddered in and out of Trenan's chest. He attempted to stop his body from shaking, but to no avail. His nerves and muscles took on a life of their own, ignoring the wishes of his brain. The shiver deepened; his teeth chattered. Silence reigned between them as the sounds of the forest and the creatures it contained carried on. Birds chirped and fluttered, wings beating the air when they flew past. Insects buzzed, rodents scuttled, leaves rubbed against branch and bark. A chill rose on his skin and he raised his eyes, though he avoided meeting the prince's gaze.

An inky cloud drifted in front of the sun, blocking its warmth and casting a shadow across the day to match the one creeping into Trenan's heart. A fat drop of rain plopped on his horse's nose; it nickered, shook its snout. More drops followed, the first few pattering on the ground, their small impacts kicking up puffs of dust thirsting for the moisture.

Trenan tipped his head back, let the droplets land on his cheeks, his lips. They should have brought him relief, invigorated and refreshed him. They didn't. A weight filled his body like wet sand dumped into his limbs and torso until it threatened to burst them like overripe fruit. No matter how hard he tried, he fell short of filling his lungs with a satisfying amount of air, failed at clearing his mind enough to figure out what to say or decide what to do.

When he next looked, Teryk no longer sat upright. He'd sagged against the neck of his horse, arms drooping as they did before he'd spoken. His eyes were closed, and saliva glistened at the corner of his open mouth.

"Teryk?"

No reaction. Trenan let go of the reins, reached across the space between them, and grasped his shoulder, gave him a shake. He didn't respond and the master swordsman wondered if their conversation happened, or if it might prove a figment of his imagination like the dead watching from the roadside.

He lowered his chin, found his eyes pulled to the side of the road and the faces of the deceased men staring out between dampening leaves, branches bouncing under the impact of the droplets of rain. Blood glistened and ran from ghastly wounds he'd inflicted, tinting the drizzle with a light pink hue. In that moment, he became certain the reason the victims of his sword and hands had gathered along his route was because his own time drew near. A lifetime of violence in the name of a king and kingdom approached its end. They'd showed up to collect him.

He glanced sideways at the young man seated on the horse behind him and to his right and wondered if his death might happen at the hand of his own son.

X - Evalal – Growth

*S*HE NOTICED THE FIRST green tendril the second sunrise after the star man hit the wall.

Evalal hadn't moved from the princess' side since, splitting her time between prayer and staring at the broken heap lying at the foot of the veil. She slept when her body gave her no choice, drank water from a wineskin left behind by the weapons merchants. Whether they'd meant to do so, she couldn't guess, but she thanked Goddess when she discovered it.

The growling in her stomach refused to cease.

At first thought, when she saw the tender shoot, she wondered if it might be edible. Part of her training as she grew up at the temple included recognizing herbs and other plants usable to a healer, but she'd not yet learned to discern other flora—those suitable for eating from those inedible. For that reason, she did not pluck it at once and jam it into her mouth. Despite her resistance, her gaze kept finding its way to the thin and curling stalk.

The deathly scent emanating from the princess' corpse had forced Evalal to move away, shuffling her bottom across the ground and through the grass while staying as close as possible. Now she moved closer again, holding her breath against the heart-wrenching odor. She leaned in, examining the shoot.

The plant grew to the span of her arm, delicate spade-shaped leaves dotting its length. From what she remembered of plants, its rate of growth expanded far beyond what one might expect in such a scant time. Perhaps it was present all along but, in her distraction over the death of her companion and the Small God plummeting against the wall, she'd not seen it.

She stole a glance over her shoulder, suddenly and inexplicably sure of finding the man risen from his crumpled heap and crossing the space toward her. Her suspicion proved fancy. With her head turned away, she exhaled the stale air from her lungs and inhaled a breath tainted by the stink of rot, making her stomach roil.

When she pivoted toward the shoot, it appeared to have grown longer. She raised an eyebrow, leaned forward and set her palms against the ground, lowered her face to within a hand's-breadth of the plant. With her eyes, she traced along its path, following its smooth surface to its source.

It snaked between blades of grass, over a heart-shaped stone, beside Danya's leg, under her knee. Evalal crawled around the princess, moving past her feet and being careful not to set her palms on any of the patches of dried blood on the ground near her. Once to the other side, she located the growth emerging from beneath her, corkscrewing its way along her thigh until disappearing.

She gasped and gulped an inadvertent mouthful of putrid air. Her body reacted without her consent, her throat and chest spasming. She turned her head and retched, heaving and choking but expelling nothing more than saliva and bile. Its bitterness stung her tongue, and she spat to clear the acrid flavor. Sweat dampened her brow and her palms. She went to wipe them on her thighs and realized she'd put her hands in one of the dried patches of blood. Flakes of brown stuck to her flesh, the last remnants of the princess' life, and she gagged again, wiped them on a patch of grass.

She stayed hunched over until the reaction passed, drawing quick breaths between her teeth as though they'd filter the smell and taste of her companion's death from the air. They didn't, but she became accustomed; what choice did she have?

With the sweat on her forehead nearly dry and the convulsions shaking her body subsiding, she faced the princess again, staring at the spot where the plant began: the pouch attached to Danya's belt.

"The Seed of Life."

She didn't intend the words to whisper between her lips, but couldn't stop herself. It didn't matter; the only person near enough who might hear her speak lay crumpled at the foot of a shimmering green wall. A man who, so far as she knew, cared not about her or the seed, if he yet lived.

Without intending to, she bent her body forward, lowering her head closer to the pouch. A movement within the soft doeskin bag caught her attention—a tiny shudder, hardly noticeable. She considered the agitation a trick of the light or her rumbling hunger causing a hallucination until a delicate frond emerged from the pouch's opening. Her eyes widened, but she kept herself from inhaling the rank air.

As she watched, the leaf unfurled like a waking body stretching. A length of stem pushed out into the open. Another petal followed, and more stalk. Before long, the shoot measured as lengthy as the space from her wrist to her elbow, the plant moving snake-like, wending its way to the ground.

Evalal shook her head. She exhaled through her nose, turned her face away to draw a breath. When her gaze returned to the pouch, a third runner poked out of it.

A surge of excitement grew in her chest. Never did she need proof of Goddess, her love and intent, but if ever a time came for confirmation, this was it. And what else caused something to grow at such a rate but the Mistress of the World? Evalal's heart swelled, filling with joy despite the death arrayed on the ground before her, the threat lurking in the forest and in the sky. Tears welled in her eyes.

Maybe this means the end of Danya's life had purpose.

She pushed away from the fallen princess, allowed herself to fall to the grass, facing skyward. In the daytime, the menace of the Small Gods remained hidden. She supposed it possible they continued streaking across the firmament, finding their way to this world to wreak havoc, but they now loomed less of a danger while sunshine caressed her cheeks and she sensed Goddess so nearby.

Evalal sighed, closed her eyes, and smiled.

—✦—

Another sunset. Another night crawling past dotted with falling stars and snatches of sleep littered with nightmares.

As much as she enjoyed lying on the ground with the sun shining on her face during the day, Evalal did her best to avoid gazing toward the sky when the moon rose and the stars emerged. The bright pinpricks of light with the long tails speeding across the night frightened her. The constant, needy growl of her stomach sapped her strength. Lacking food and energy did little to instill courage as she lay in the dark, waiting for sunlight to return.

What if it doesn't?

She'd thought of counting the stars falling from the sky but decided she didn't see the point. Did it matter to her if twenty fell or two hundred? Either way, she remained here, with the princess, until Goddess showed her she needed her somewhere else. One star had fallen against the veil; none of the others truly meant anything to her.

Unable to find sleep again, Evalal sat up, groaning with the effort as her belly complained yet again. She'd contemplated foraging for sustenance, but a cursory survey of the grassland near her yielded nothing palatable. Finding food meant traveling up the hill to the forest and leaving Danya unattended. While the possibility of plump berries and tender, edible shoots tempted saliva to her mouth, the memory of the predator lurking in the grass held her to her spot and her promise.

She sighed, the inhalation of stale air catching in her throat and prompting a fit of coughing. Despite her best attempt to quell the attack, the rough hacking exploded through her lips and rolled across the quiet field, bounced off the veil to echo back at her, its volume multiplied. By the time it reached her ears again, it became a dozen stranded young women barking up their lungs. When the disturbance passed, she pressed her palm to her mouth, listened to see if any other sounds might follow.

At first, she detected nothing but the distant song of night birds, the chirp of crickets. After a few heartbeats, she perceived a rustle in the grass, gentle but distinct, and then her gut rumbled, drowning out the sound of everything but her own breath.

Evalal shivered, though it wasn't cold. She shifted, wondered if she'd find the strength to defend herself and the princess if the animal which had stalked them the night the man fell from the sky returned. Doubtful, but she didn't have to let the beast know.

The grass rustled again, distinct and close, startling Evalal. She jumped, put a hand flat on the ground to keep from tipping over. The other fist clenched the thin knife Ive had given to Teryk, but her arm lay at her side, conserving the bit of strength she might summon.

"Leave us alone," she called out at the night, intending her words to be a harsh warning, but they came out as more of a strangled wheeze.

She breathed deep, barely noticing the stink the day's warmth had raised in the princess. Amazing what a person can become used to. She cleared her throat.

"Get away from us."

This time her throat and mouth operated in the manner she intended. Her admonition rang into the night, her belly growled its agreement, but the rustle came again, closer. The sound lacked the threatening growl of the last beast which stalked them, but she realized whatever hid in the tall grass meant to make them its meal.

Evalal raised the hand holding the dagger, her undernourished arm protesting the decision. She held the small weapon in front of her, helpless to stop the quaking and using every bit of her energy to keep from dropping her lone source of defense.

Rustling.

The curtain of grass at the edge of their beaten-down haven parted and a tiny nose poked through. Evalal tensed, awaiting an attack. Her throat tightened, and she fought to control tears from coming. How did she end up here, about to give up her life to protect a dead woman?

A gray head followed the snout, then a compact body covered in sleek fur, and finally a bushy tail held straight up in the air.

A squirrel.

It took three scampering steps toward her and stopped, sat up on its hind legs, nose twitching, its gaze darting side to side, a nut in its mouth.

With a relieved sigh, Evalal lowered the knife. Her throat unclenched, and she laughed a nervous chuckle bordering on turning into tears if she let it. She shook her head.

"You scared me, little fellow."

She'd seen squirrels before—outside Draekfarren, precious few trees grew in the Horseshoe, but they all seemed to house a family of the small creatures. Never had she been so near one, though. Darker lines of fur ran along its gray back and down its tail, its wide eyes glimmered in the moonlight. How silly she felt for shuddering and shaking without knowing what hid in the grass.

The animal darted forward a few more steps before stopping just out of her reach, settling on its haunches again. It took the nut from its mouth—an acorn, she saw now—with its tiny front paws and held it out and up, extending it toward her. A gift.

Stunned, Evalal stared at the creature. She'd never seen or heard of a wild beast acting in this manner. When she didn't react, the squirrel shuffled closer to her, stretched the offering out farther and higher. It made a chittering sound.

Hesitant, she reached out and accepted the tree nut between her thumb and finger; the animal stood resolute until she took the gift, then it scurried away, disappearing into the meadow at the same place where it appeared. Evalal stared after it, watching the tops of the grass part before it until the movement disappeared from her sight. She held the acorn up in front of her eyes, turned it over between her finger and thumb.

The squirrel had removed what she'd have called the acorn's cap and cracked the nut open for her as though understanding she lacked the strength to do so herself. A fissure ran along its hard shell from top to tip. Her mouth watered at the thought of the tender meat inside. She inserted the point of the dagger into the crevice and twisted. The acorn split the rest of the way, and her stomach gurgled with anticipation.

The two halves of the shell tumbled to the ground, forgotten the instant she freed the innards of the tree nut. She popped the nutmeat between her lips, chewed and swallowed so quickly she couldn't have described the flavor. Her belly rumbled with approval, a sound which devolved into a demand for more. With it so devoured, Evalal wished she'd taken more care in consuming it, savoring its essence and texture and prolonging its effect; she didn't know when her mouth might experience the pleasure of food again.

The wait turned out to be shorter than she expected.

Little time passed before the squirrel—or perhaps a different one—showed up with a second acorn. With this one, she took her time, enjoying the sustenance it provided. The flavor hadn't yet cleared her tongue when the next offering came: another acorn. Then a deer mouse carrying a red berry. Evalal hesitated—she still found difficulties telling the difference between the edible ones and those poisonous to humans; some even caused death. She held the fruit in her hand for a moment while other creatures visited, each dropping an item of food on the ground before her: more acorns and berries, green plants, two varieties of fungus.

This is not from the animals. This is from Goddess.

For the first time in longer than she dared recall, a smile found its way onto her face. She pushed the fruit between her lips, pressed it against the inside of her cheek with her tongue until the flesh broke and its juice leaked out. Both sweet and sour flavors filled her mouth, and she closed her eyes, letting the fluid mix with her saliva, enjoying it as though it was the first berry she'd ever ingested...or the last one. She heard the sounds of other animals delivering their offerings but did not open her lids, trusting none of them came to cause her harm.

Goddess loves me.

She swallowed and her heart swelled.

XI - Trenan – Fighting the Dead

*T*WICE THE SUN ROSE and set without sleep, without food. The only water sating his thirst fell from the clouds above, ran down his forehead and along the side of his nose to his lips. During that time, he never once glanced at Teryk seated on the horse behind him. He knew he followed—the splashing of the animal's hooves in the puddles on the road told him so. Though curiosity and worry gnawed at Trenan, he kept his gaze forward, allowing an occasional drifting to the sides of the track.

The dead men remained.

He didn't think he saw the same face more than once, but rain and fatigue made it difficult to be certain. Each appeared a different person, but they shared one thing in common: they'd died by his hand.

How many have I killed?

He knew soldiers who kept count, the act striking him as both disrespectful and morbid, so he'd never partaken in such self-indulgence. Besides, if he'd done the same, he'd have lost track long ago.

He shifted in the saddle, his ass slipping on the slick, wet leather. His fingers tightened on the reins as he righted himself. To his right, a mother and her child stood at the roadside, the little one's face a mask of red the rain couldn't wash away. Blood soaked the woman's dress from an unseen wound in her torso. Trenan thought this woman and her boy likely lurked in a dark, forgotten corner of his mind, biding their time, waiting for an opportunity such as this to emerge and remind him of what he did to them.

Without meaning to, he jerked his gaze away, directing it over his shoulder where he glimpsed the prince.

Teryk slumped, leaning against his mount's long neck. Passed out from exhaustion and hunger? Sleeping? Dead?

Trenan faced forward again. He realized the need to stop at some point. The fear he'd carried with him since Teryk's accusation—real or imagined—eased after seeing him incapacitated, but worry for his life replaced it. The possibility his son had expired occurred to him, but the line of lost faces watching as they passed stopped him from doing anything but riding toward Ikkundana, or Woodsel, or the Horseshoe, whichever he reached first.

Clouds hid the sun, though he lacked the recollection of how to use it to determine direction, anyway. He understood the possibility—and that he should know how—but the actuality of it eluded him. At night, he refused to raise his eyes skyward. Someone had once warned him to keep watch for danger found in the dark firmament, but he couldn't bear to see the streaks of light burning their way across the night. Truthfully, he wasn't sure why; it brought relief when the rain came, turning the sky overcast and hiding the stars as indiscriminately as the sun.

And the faces remained.

The farther they traveled, the more he recognized them and their accusatory stares. He'd killed them. In self-defence, in the king's name, in anger. Every one of these men—and many women and children—had died violent deaths at his hand. Some by the sword and other weapons, others by his bare hands.

Try as he might to keep his gaze directed ahead, the invariable curves in the road, his peripheral vision, and morbid curiosity combined to make sure he saw they remained watching him, taunting him, accusing him.

Threatening him?

The throng of long-dead warriors stayed to the sides of the path, never appearing on the dirt track. He thought to see if they followed in his wake, but he didn't want to any more than he wanted to raise his eyes to the sky at night. Not only might he find an army of those he'd killed, he worried about finding the haze hanging in the air, closer than before, the black priests in pursuit.

The rain will have settled the dust.

The thought did nothing to ease his anxiety. Every breath he drew, he imagined the faint odor of burnt orange rind wafting out of the forest or down from the sky, perhaps rising from the road, or carried on the breeze from the dead watching him pass. Whatever caused the scent kept him dulled. Once, he'd have faced the dangers head-on, drawn his sword, hollered threats he intended to carry out. But now his weapon remained sheathed, his voice quieted by unease. He gripped the reins too tight, breathed too shallow.

By the time the drab, gray day darkened as the sun readied itself to set behind the clouds for the third time, Trenan's eyelids did their best to slide closed despite his efforts. His head nodded forward until his chin bounced against his chest. He jerked it up again, snapped his eyes open only to have exhaustion overcome him again and again, the nodding and jerking to wakefulness repeated over and over.

He released his grip on the reins, slapped himself across the cheek. The snap of flesh against flesh rang out, beaten down by the falling rain. The sting on his skin flashed into his brain and he did it again, harder. A tooth cut into his lip, the tang of blood springing to his tongue. He fought against gagging and shook his head at his throat's reaction. How often in his life had he tasted his own blood? More than most, and he'd never reacted like this. He spat, used his sleeve to wipe away the line of bloody dribble left behind on his chin.

The road stretched on ahead, distance smudged to near obscurity by rain and darkness. He squinted. Did he see movement? His eyes darted to the side, toward the faces peering from the brush.

Still there.

The coppery flavor in his mouth curled, and he spat again. As he turned his head to do so, he inadvertently peered along the road behind them. No army of the dead followed and, if the haze remained, rain and darkness blended it into the night. Instead, the prince caught his attention.

Teryk sat straight on the horse again, both hands gripping the reins, his awareness directed to the front, though he didn't appear to see Trenan looking at him. Water ran from his hair, across his forehead, onto his stubbled cheeks; he made no reaction to the drops pattering on his head and face other than to blink them from his eyes. Acrid bile rose into the master swordsman's throat, and he struggled to choke it down.

With the countless men he'd fought and killed in myriad battles and skirmishes, the true bite of fear had never sunk its teeth into him. He'd always known one day his death loomed somewhere in his future—it visited everyone eventually—but the thought of it never made him hesitate or gave him pause. The first time he'd experienced it was because of his own son.

"Teryk?"

Despite the pale faces staring at them from the side of the road, the master swordsman reined his horse to a stop and slid out of his saddle. His boots splashed on the muddy road, throwing a dirty spray onto his legs. He grasped the bridle of the prince's mount, ensuring it stayed calm with the dead peering from the verge of the forest, though he wasn't sure he'd remain so himself. If he kept his back to them, he could pretend they didn't exist.

"Teryk."

He dragged his fingers along the horse's neck, stroking the animal as much for his own good as for the beast's comfort. The prince did not respond. Trenan reached out to touch his arm, but hesitated. The last time they'd interacted, Teryk had glared at him with hatred burning in his stare. Remembering stayed Trenan's intent; he wasn't sure he possessed the fortitude to bear the disgusted expression, the loathing directed toward him again.

His hand hovered halfway to his son, a tremor shaking his fingers. He curled them into a fist, flexed them; an inhalation brought cool rainwater into his mouth along with the air. After swallowing, he released his breath, and grasped Teryk's wrist, shook it gently. The horse snuffled, blowing air from its nostrils to clear away the water streaming out of its mane and down its long snout. While Trenan's attempt to rouse the prince produced no effect, the horse's sound appeared to shake Teryk free of whatever trance gripped him. He angled his head, directing his gaze toward the soldier standing beside his steed.

The urge to look away tightened the muscles in Trenan's neck, but he held fast, staring up at his son. Emotions mixed in the master swordsman's chest and stomach, threatening to spread to his limbs, paralyze him: hope and elation because the boy's expression held none of the enmity of the previous time, but also worry and fear. Where the prince's eyes had gleamed with hostility and dislike, now they appeared empty—of recognition, of emotion, of life. If it weren't for the bloom of color in his cheeks, he might have been another of the dead come to haunt Trenan for his sins.

"Are you all right?"

He continued staring. He didn't blink, nor did his mouth move. Water dripped from the end of his nose and onto his arm in a steady rhythm, its patter lost amid the rest of the rainfall. Trenan waited for a reply, pulse racing. If Teryk responded with accusation and hatred, he thought his heart might break open and spill blood from his eyes and ears, leaving him to bleed to death in the middle of nowhere, his life washed away by the interminable night's rain.

But the prince did not answer his mentor's query. After an interval seeming to drag on for a lifetime, he redirected his gaze along the road ahead, staring at nothing, recognizing nothing.

Trenan breathed a sigh it embarrassed him to admit signaled his relief. As much as he didn't wish his son ill, a lack of response proved preferable to many alternatives.

He lifted his hand from the young man's arm, took a step away from the horse, his foot splashing in a muddy puddle. He stopped. The prince sat with his shoulders slumped, head sagging. Trenan wanted to do more for him, support him as his father, but what? He'd been the one who caused the prince's grief and anger.

What will Ishla think when she finds out?

She'd be devastated. The prospect of her holding him responsible for her daughter's death and her son's near-comatose state left him cold, but she might blame herself, too. If she did, he couldn't imagine her being able to live with herself. His life was grim enough without her to love; how much worse off he'd be if she didn't live at all?

Trenan shuddered, and a stream of rainwater ran along his back, increasing his chill. He looked at his feet, the muddy puddle water lapping at his boots as droplets of rain splashed into it, gradually expanding its coverage of the ground, and shook his head. He must keep Ishla from finding out what happened. Not seeing either of her children again was a punishment she didn't deserve, but at least she couldn't blame herself.

We can't return to Draekfarren.

He nodded to himself, looked up again. The prince straightened in his saddle, lifting his chin from his chest and standing in the stirrups to peer along the road ahead. Trenan pivoted, feet splashing, but his own horse blocked his view from discovering what Teryk saw. He took one step away before he froze.

They'd crept from the brush and the edge of the forest in silence, their dead steps making no sound in the sodden grass or on the muddy road. In his concern for the prince, for himself, for Ishla, he'd forgotten the specters of the slain men watching from the shadows. Another mistake a veteran soldier should never make.

"Damn it."

He spat the curse from his mouth like a piece of rotten food as once unfamiliar—now recognizable—fear flooded into him, setting his limbs tingling with numbness. Out of instinct, his hand fell to Godsbane's hilt, and he pulled the sword, extended it before him. Steel whispered against leather; most times when he freed his sword thus, the sword's voice spoke to him of victory, calmed him, reassured him. Not today.

Drops of rain bounced against the silver length of the blade, dripped from its sharp edge. Its tip wavered. To Trenan, a foe threatening him with an unsteady weapon gave him certainty of dispatching the fellow. But none of the dead men held swords; their threat wasn't against his body, but his soul.

He stalked away from his horse toward the group, each of whom he'd killed once before. His mind whirled and spun, leaving nausea to rise from his belly into his throat. Every attempt to swallow it made it worse. His heart thumped and raced; sweat coated his palm, combining with the rain and threatening to loosen his grip on the sword's hilt. His knuckles turned white with the effort of holding it, the tendons in his hand ached.

With ten paces remaining between him and the grisly group, he halted. He searched his memory, attempting to recall when, if ever, his body and mind had reacted in this manner to a fight in the past. No instance came to him—no nervous sweat, no fearful heartbeat, no tenseness and worry. In his recollection, he'd experienced a calm assuredness, knowing victory lay ahead.

But he'd never fought dead men; only created them.

He bit down on his teeth and exhaled hard through his nose. He intended to stalk toward the group, return them to the graves whence they'd come, but his legs refused to carry him forward. His feet stayed in place as though spikes pinned them to the ground. Behind him, a horse blew rain from its nostrils, shook its head, the sound startling him and making him jump with surprise. He twisted, making sure the prince remained where he'd left him.

The horses—Teryk seated on one—stood in the same spot as when he'd crept away. Instead of experiencing relief, Trenan shivered; how his life had altered in such a brief time. The days spent sparring with Teryk and his sister, training the siblings, seemed both like yesterday yet also so long ago. As though time contracted upon itself, sandwiching his life into a tangled mess, its bits and pieces impossible to tell one from another.

When he returned his attention to the gathering of animated corpses ahead of him, he found them closer. They'd advanced to five paces from him, making no sound as they moved. He shuddered, wiped rain from his brow and raised the sword that now weighed as much as a man to him. His shoulder knotted; his arm shook. He opened his mouth to howl a war cry at them intended to instill fear, but a vague croak emerged and embarrassment crept into his cheeks. In his mind, he realized his son was in no condition to experience his failure, or taste disappointment, but it affected him nonetheless.

Trenan leapt forward, swinging Godsbane at the nearest of the group of men. It included a fellow missing his left arm below the elbow where, one time in a season past, the master swordsman's weapon had cut clean through it and into his abdomen. Even now, a loop of his innards poked through, glistening with wetness.

The sword's sharp edge sliced through the fellow's neck, but Trenan spun wildly as the blow encountered no resistance. He stumbled three steps toward the verge where road and forest met, boots splashing in puddles and barely keeping his feet beneath him, arm waving. Godsbane slipped from his grip, clattered to the ground.

Steadied, he pivoted to face the throng, his breath coming in short, sharp pants, mouth tasting of blood. He must have bitten his tongue or the inside of his cheek without realizing he'd done so. He spat, gaze darting between the group of dead men and his blade lying on the road two paces away. None of them made a move toward him, though each watched with wide, unblinking eyes. Not the surprised expression of a child, but as if they possessed no lids to close.

Trenan crouched and reached for the weapon without taking his gaze from his adversaries. His fingers brushed the track, drawing troughs in the mud. None of his foes moved; they observed him fumbling around blindly and held their ground. He dared to glance away, found the sword and gripped its hilt, stood and hefted it.

They were closer still, an arm's length distant. Trenan bellowed—more in dread than intending to startle his adversaries—and swung the blade in a wide arc. It cut air and nothing else. He swung it the other way, then back again, his eyes closed in the manner of a frightened child. His chest constricted, realizing how he acted, allowing fear and disgust to usurp so many seasons of training and experience. He tried to stop himself, to force his lids open and his arm to cease swinging, but to no avail.

A sound came to his ears, high-pitched and desperate, and it took a moment to realize it wasn't the voice of once-dead men being wounded and killed again, but the cry of his own throat. He clamped his mouth shut, cutting off the scream so he heard nothing but the huff of his effort-filled breath and the hammering of blood in his temples.

He opened his eyes as he swung the sword yet again, experienced the same lack of resistance. It spun him and he let it, intending to use the opportunity to make sure the prince still sat the horse behind him. He did, but Trenan misjudged the distance between himself and Teryk's mount. The tip of the crownsword contacted the animal above its right front leg, the sharp steel biting into its flesh. It reacted, screaming and rearing, its sudden action catching both men by surprise. Teryk reached for the saddle horn but missed and somersaulted backwards out of his seat. Trenan stumbled and toppled to the ground, landing hard, his armless shoulder slamming against the road and jarring his spine. He gritted his teeth at the pain as shards of light flashed in his vision. Breath wheezed from his lungs, and he lost his grip on Godsbane. Muddy water splashed into his face, particles of dirt finding his eyeballs and entering his mouth. He coughed and blinked, pushing with his feet to move away and avoid being trampled by the pained and frightened horse.

He heard the prince hit the road near him, a whoosh of air as the impact knocked the breath from his lungs. Raindrops hammered the ground, splashing in puddles and beating against Trenan's armor, the sound filling his ears.

He scrambled around, rolling onto his back, mud squelching beneath him. The dead men loomed, blood and pus dripping from old wounds, brain matter and intestines glistening, strings of saliva dangling from shattered jaws. Trenan kicked at the nearest of them, watched his foot pass through without effect. The pain in his shoulder turned into searing agony, and he screamed.

Out of instinct, the master swordsman reached across his body, put his hand to the wounded shoulder. His fingers came away bloody.

Kicking his feet to scramble away from the men he'd killed once before, Trenan jerked his head to the right, shocked by what he'd found.

Instead of a scrape on the armless shoulder he'd grown accustomed to in the time since he'd lost his limb, a short, bloody stump protruded from his torso. The master swordsman's eyes widened; his mouth gaped. He gulped a mouthful of air into his chest, heaved it out again. This was how his arm had appeared after an enemy lopped it off while he protected the king. Later, the royal surgeon had removed the stump to prevent infection, leaving an empty spot where once he'd possessed a limb.

How—?

Men he'd killed ages past, a stump removed long ago.

In his fall, Godsbane had slipped from his grip. He cast his gaze around, searching for a glint of light on its blade to reveal its resting place, but he saw only the feet and legs of spectral warriors returned from the grave to seek revenge. They crowded him and he realized their brows didn't drip with rain as his did, their clothes weren't sopping. The precipitation passed through them in the same way his sword had.

They're not real.

The thought made sense, but he resisted accepting it. Teryk had seen them. They'd stalked them from sunrise to sunset to sunrise again, implacable, unrelenting. They couldn't possibly live in his mind and nowhere else.

I've already killed them.

In his life, he'd wondered if his actions one day might have consequences. Certainly he realized he'd never be a man to die from old age, but concern for his soul in the afterlife sometimes surprised him. He didn't truly believe in having a soul, or in the existence of a place men went after death, but neither was he convinced both were lies. He'd thought occasionally of living with a modicum of caution in case there proved a price to pay, but duty kept that from being a possibility.

Trenan struggled to draw another breath, but his chest proved unable to do so. His legs quit moving and the muscles in his body knotted and twisted. He collapsed to the road, aware sloppy mud would find its way into the wet and bloody wound, sticking to it, working into his system to cause infection. For an instant, he forgot the dead men gathered around him, their grisly wounds, their accusatory stares. He'd killed them to protect the kingdom, to save himself and others. It was his duty to do so, and he'd do it again if he had the ability.

But he didn't.

He lacked the strength to breathe, never mind defend himself. After a time, he pulled his gaze away from the bloody stump, returned it to the threat of his foes hovering over him. They'd parted, allowing another figure to join them. At first, what he saw confused him. This wasn't a soldier slain by him, though he'd met the man on the battlefield and seen him die.

He stood over Trenan, a baleful smile upon his lips and an axe dangling from his grip, its edge smeared with blood and tissue. His eyes burned, and a laugh rolled from his throat; the warrior who'd taken the master swordsman's arm all those seasons ago.

And he wore Teryk's face.

The specter reached a hand out toward the master swordsman, and panic flashed through him. He renewed his effort to scramble away, and the dead soldier's lips moved as though he meant to speak, but no sound emerged. Trenan heard nothing but the rain, the splashing of Teryk attempting to regain his feet on the muddy road.

The ghostly man's touch found his forearm, fingers grasping, tightening. He felt them. Gooseflesh overtook his arm, a tingling filled his limb as if he'd slept on it wrong and woken to pins and needles as it sorted itself out. It spread up through his shoulder, across the top of his chest, into his neck. It restricted his throat to the size of a pin hole, so breath struggled to find its way through. The sensation gripped his heart, squeezed it. His mouth opened and closed, opened and closed, gulping for air, and attempting without success to cry out in terror.

He attempted to jerk away, but the corpse's grip held fast. Others moved in, hands reaching, fingers grasping. Some of them found his shoulder, his neck. A man with no legs gripped his leg. The uncomfortable sensation filled him and then Trenan lay pinned to the ground, eyes wide, face lifted toward the sky.

The instant before the world went black, the rain clouds parted and a streak of white light tore across the night.

XII - Evalal – The Fallen

*E*VALAL WOKE WITH THE warmth of the sun on her cheek and hunger
rising again in her belly.

She didn't open her eyes immediately, though her body felt truly rested
for the first time in a long while. A memory of the parade of forest animals
bringing her food came to her and she smiled. Appreciated as it was, the
rumbling in her stomach had returned while she slept.

First she stretched, pleased to note energy had returned to her limbs,
then she opened her eyes.

Though none of them blocked the sun which had somehow climbed
high into the sky while she slept, wisps of cloud scudded the blue
firmament. Evalal propped herself up on her elbows, a vigor she hadn't
experienced in days finding its way into her. She breathed deep, fresh air
rejuvenating her lungs. While she would normally have been pleased at the
lungful of breath tingling her chest, the absence of the smell emanating
from the princess' remains shot a bolt of panic through her.

Something has taken her while I slept.

She jerked upright, spun to the right, her buttocks scraping the ground,
and saw only grass and the veil. Disoriented, she blinked, realized she had
turned herself around in her sleep, and pivoted the other direction.

Danya's remains still lay where they'd been since Teryk plunged the knife
into her throat, but what Evalal saw brought her to her feet.

Thin green filaments wound around the corpse of the princess. They
didn't cover her completely—there was enough space between them to
see a woman was within, and they hadn't wrapped themselves around her
head—but the rapidity with which they'd sprouted and grown left the girl

stunned. She approached her fallen friend, knelt beside her as she had done so much since the dagger had pierced her throat.

Delicate leaves sprouted as she watched, fine lengths of plant that unfurled and stretched toward the sun. Evalal shook her head, awed by the sight. It kept her attention for a while as tendrils positioned themselves, covering more and more of her flesh. She might have stayed there the entire day, enthralled and mildly worried by what she saw, but the loud and rolling complaint of her belly interrupted her.

She stood, wishing she hadn't eaten all the berries, acorns, and other small delicacies the animals had brought. Perhaps one of the mice or squirrels had dropped a bit of food; if she looked, she might find something to sate her aching gut.

With a hand on her stomach in an ineffective attempt at settling it, she cast her gaze upon the flattened grass surrounding her. The parade of forest creatures bringing sustenance the night before had worn a noticeable path in the grass—the most likely place for her to discover a bit of food which had been dropped and forgotten. She followed it, bent at the waist. Her heart jumped when she spied a smooth, hard-looking surface amongst the blades of grass and stooped to grasp it. When her fingertips touched it, she realized it was merely a stone.

Disappointed, she picked it up anyway, straightened, and turned to her left, intending to cast it away so it wouldn't fool her again. She cocked her arm but stopped before throwing the rock. Instead, it slipped from her fingers and thudded to the ground by her feet as she stared.

In her worry about the fate of Danya's remains, and then her wonderment over how the shoots originating from the Seed of Life had grown, she hadn't noticed the pile of foodstuffs heaped at the edge of her area. Acorns, berries, leaves and roots. Each different food formed its own stack, meticulously organized as though by a highly organized cook.

The stone forgotten, Evalal hurried across the space separating her from the opportunity to break her fast.

She dropped to her knees in front of the neat gatherings, knees skidding on the ground, and reached first for the berries, grabbing three at once and jamming them all into her mouth at one time. The acorns and other tree nuts were already shelled for her and she scooped a handful into her mouth before she had even swallowed the sour-sweet berries. A squirt of juice and hungry saliva ran from the corner of her mouth and she wiped it away on her shoulder. She scuffled sideways, reached for a handful of tender shoots and leaves, trusting that the animals Goddess sent would only bring her items which wouldn't be a cause of illness.

As she collected a handful, she noticed more items left behind and stopped, hand raised halfway to her mouth, bits of green foliage poking out between her fingers. The joy over feeding slipped out of her.

The heap catching her attention wasn't as large as the others—at least, it wasn't made up of as many individual bits. But the items composing it were considerably larger: two squirrels, a rat of some variety, and a rabbit.

All had been killed with great efficiency. No blood caked their fur; one might have mistaken them for sleeping animals. Evalal couldn't help but wonder if any of them had been the ones she'd seen bringing her food the previous evening. Her heart shrank at the possibility at the same moment her belly gurgled in the anticipation of meaty juice upon her tongue.

But did Goddess expect her to imbibe the raw flesh of these tiny sacrifices? The thought made her feel queasy until she noticed that the forest animals had taken this into consideration, as well. Beside the carcasses lay two large stones, perfect for creating sparks, and a gathering of dried grass, kindling, and larger chunks of wood. By this time, she'd seen enough not to be surprised by the working of Goddess.

Instead of staring in wonder, Evalal retrieved the dagger and set to cleaning her meal and lighting a fire.

———

Her own belly full and satisfied, Evalal fashioned a plate out of a large, flat leaf and gathered a selection of nuts, berries, and the last few bits of meat on it. She stood holding it on her flat palm as she stared across the waving sea of grass toward the shimmering veil.

The occasional clouds dotting the sky when she woke had expanded, hiding the sun and casting the world in gray relief the color of a faltering mood. She'd said a prayer over the wildlife sacrificed to provide her nourishment, the thanks relieving her of all but the smallest sliver of guilt, and that last bit had disappeared the instant the first bite of savory meat touched her tongue.

The contentment and energy brought to her body by filling her belly should have lifted her mood for the rest of the day, but a thought kept returning to her. No matter how hard she tried, she couldn't put it out of her head.

The man who hit the wall.

She'd been trained as a healer from her earliest memory. When she had no food and was worried for her own survival, it had been easy not to think about the man lying broken—perhaps dead, but maybe not—at the foot of the veil. Once her own safety was secured, though, her learned instincts turned to the suffering of others.

"But he's a Small God," she said aloud.

Her voice didn't crack this time as it had the last time she bothered to speak words. The nourishment provided her had energized not just her limbs and mind, but her throat as well. She took one step forward, her foot passing from the flattened area she'd begun thinking of as hers into the long grass surrounding her and the dead princess. For an instant, she expected to encounter resistance, as though she crossed an unseen boundary not meant to be broken, but this wasn't the case. Long blades caressed her leg and nothing more.

She swallowed, saliva clicking in her throat, and inhaled through her nose. The breeze carried with it the scent of honeysuckle from somewhere unseen.

"He's probably dead."

It seemed the most likely scenario. Part of her experienced relief at the possibility, but it also stirred up guilt in her chest. The opportunity to be of true assistance and aid to the poor fellow had come and gone the night she saw he still lived after slamming into the wall. The sun had risen and set a number of times, and he'd had no water. If he was now somehow still alive, his bones and tendons would have started knitting themselves together in entirely the wrong ways. If he survived, he'd do so as a mockery of his former self.

Evalal shook her head. What was his former self? He'd hung in the sky, a pinprick of light, for the turning of more seasons than she had the ability to comprehend. What had that been like for him? Might he have learned a lesson from such a punishment? Could he have dedicated himself to a new way of being instead of returning to his former ways?

She nodded to herself. "People grow and learn," she said.

She pressed her lips together and started across the clearing. At first, the man was nothing more than a dark spot against the verdant curtain, its dim light seeming to brighten as the daylight dimmed. As she got closer, the spot became a smudge, then a heap, and finally a shape. She stopped with only five paces left between them, her heart racing.

Though her memory proved a bit hazy, she thought he still lay in the same position she'd left him a few sunrises before: limbs still twisted, face still directed toward the sky. She couldn't tell if his chest rose and fell with breath, the distance between them still too great for her to pick up such nuances.

What does Goddess want me to do?

So much of what had happened to her and Danya since they left the temple had felt so directed, as though Goddess peered over their shoulders, guided them whenever there was any doubt about their path. As much as she hated losing the princess whom she'd begun to think of as her friend, she knew it was a part of Goddess' plan, just like everything else. But this was not so clear. Was she meant to help this man? Leave him to die?

She crept forward two more steps. The hand extended before her cradling the makeshift platter quivered, but she realized the answer to her questions. If he was dead, Goddess' will be already done. If he yet lived, she had a duty as one trained in the healing arts, even if she was but a novice. The decision made, steadiness returned to her hand. She took one more step and crouched beside him.

His cheeks and forehead were devoid of color, his lips cracked. Her gaze moved down from his face to his chest; she carefully kept her eyes from moving lower, still experiencing shame over the curiosity she'd succumbed to the first time she'd been this close to a naked man.

At first she detected no movement and a moment of relief washed through her, but it proved short-lived.

His chest rose and fell, the movement slight and rapid but there, coming from nowhere as though he'd been holding his breath to see what she'd do. Only then did she realize she'd been doing the same. She released the air from her lungs slowly, allowing it to escape between her lips, then inhaled again.

The man bore an odor, but not the rotting flesh stink the princess had emanated before the seed's shoots enveloped her. This was the scent of a body fighting to heal itself but losing the battle. In her training, she'd been exposed to inflammations, infections, gangrene and recognized its pungency and what it meant.

If she didn't help the man, his death would soon come, and it would be both painful and horrific. Another clear sign from Goddess.

Or was it? Why would she want a Small God, banished so long ago, to survive?

Why would she allow the princess to die?

The voice belonged to the Mother of Death, the words spoken and their meaning as clear as if she stood behind Evalal whispering in her ear. She wasn't meant to understand the machinations of Goddess' doings; her place was simply to carry out what needed to be done. The bigger picture may never be clear to her, but her one small piece—no matter what it might entail—had to be accomplished or Goddess' puzzle wouldn't be complete.

She sighed again and took a berry from the leaf-platter, held it over his parched lips and squeezed it until it broke open and juice flowed between her fingers. The first droplet hit his chin, the liquid's dark color appearing like blood on his pallid skin. The second drop landed on his lips; she thought she saw them quiver.

No more juice flowed from the broken berry, so she tossed its husk aside and picked up another, repeating the action. This plumper bit of fruit yielded three droplets of nourishment, every one of them finding his lips, draining between them into his mouth.

She put the flesh of the berry into her own mouth, chewed it until it became near to paste, then took it out between her fingers. She put the masticated berry to his lips, pushed it through, and jerked her hand away as though she'd come close to touching fire. An excited thrill vibrated through her. In her life, she'd done little anyone would consider daring, living as she had in the temple and spending her time doing Goddess' bidding. Any danger and excitement her life had held came after she met Danya.

The moment of excitement fled, squeezed out by grief. She glanced over her shoulder toward the flattened grass where she'd left the princess, but saw nothing beyond the sea of grass. She hadn't noticed the wind picking up as it had, its gust waving the tall stalks, the path she'd taken to arrive at the fallen man swallowed up as though it had never existed.

Will her remains be safe without me?

After what had happened the night before, she suspected she wasn't the only one watching out for the care of the princess. Plus, the flora wrapped around her seemed to serve to quell the odor of her decomposing body. If there was no scent to attract predators, she should be safe.

Evalal faced the man, took another berry from the leaf. Only three more remained. She'd also brought some nut meat and bits of cooked rabbit, but it didn't seem there was any chance he might be able to chew what she gave him. She already worried the berry flesh she'd put in his mouth might be too much.

As before, she pinched the small fruit, squirting the juice onto his lips. This time, the pink and white tip of his tongue responded, finding its way out to recover a drop of wayward fluid. The man lump in his throat rose and fell as he swallowed, then a rattling breath found its way into his chest.

Evalal stood and took a step away. He was in no shape to be a threat or cause her harm, but she decided care was the best course of action. She knew she was here to protect the princess—such as that was—and that was her first priority.

A drop of rain spattered against the veil and tiny bolts of green lightning spider-webbed across its surface. The man's lips moved. Evalal bent closer, noted that one of his eyelids had opened a crack, the other gummed shut by blood and disuse. Another droplet of rain landed on the back of her hand. More movement of his lips.

Is he trying to speak?

She dropped to her knees again, set aside the leaf-platter and the food remaining on it. With caution, she leaned closer, a panicked alarm sounding in her head despite the man's obvious incapacitation. She chastised herself silently. What kind of healer was she to be frightened of a man thus broken?

Evalal pursed her lips and leaned close enough only the space of three fingers separated her ear from his mouth. At this distance, she heard the gasp of his inhalations, the rattle of his expulsions of breath. These were the sounds of a man in pain, desperate for relief, possibly near the end of his life. How could she deny him whatever small comfort she might offer to keep his last time from being nothing but torment?

She waited for what seemed like a long time, listening to the sound of his labored breathing, the increasing patter of rain on her back, the veil, the grass. The green wall hummed minutely—something she hadn't noticed before—and crackled like a tiny fire each time a raindrop struck its surface.

These other sounds distracted her enough she almost missed it when his mouth moved again and he spoke.

"Water."

⎯⎯

First she had to find one of the broad leaves similar to the one she'd used for the platter. It would have been easiest to use that one, but she'd left it on the ground beside the man and didn't want to return to him until she had the water he so desperately needed.

The task of finding a suitable leaf proved more difficult than she expected. Not only did it need to be the right size to hold a suitable amount, but it had to be free of tears and holes, as well as pliable enough to form into a bowl without ripping. Searching for it and thinking about how she would use it to collect the rain now falling more steadily made her realize how her own thirst had developed.

From where she stood atop the hill at the edge of the forest, she had a clear view over the meadow to the veil. The flattened patch of grass where the princess lay stood out in stark contrast to the rest of the grassland, though, if she didn't know it, she'd never have guessed the remains of the princess would be found there. The green shoots from the Seed of Life had all but encased her, the nourishing rain thickening them and bringing blossoms along their length. Toward sunset from there, the man lay against the wall, unmoving. Would he still be alive when she returned?

Evalal plucked a large frond from a bush, setting its branches rattling and droplets of rain that had collected on it splashing off. She cupped the leaf in her palms, bent it as gently as she could, her breath held. Too many had already torn to be thrown aside and her patience was wearing thin. She not only wanted to bring water to the poor man, she also wanted to return to the princess to see what was happening to her.

The leaf proved more elastic than the others she'd found, its surface pliable and willing to be manipulated. With a breath of relief, she turned and started down the hill, leaf in hand and cautious excitement flickering in her chest at being able to return to Danya as well as help the man.

"Small God," she reminded herself and suppressed a shiver.

She pushed her way through the grass, the leaf pressed against her chest, keeping it flat to prevent any rips or tears, and soon arrived at the flattened patch of grass that had practically become her home. She knelt beside the verdant mound that had been the dead princess not so long ago and held the leaf extended in front of her and up, cupped in both hands to catch the rain.

As droplets pattered against the surface of the leaf, each one seeming to dry the inside of her throat, she stared past its edge at where the princess lay.

The once delicate shoots had grown in thickness to the size of rope. They looped around and around Danya's remains, hiding almost all of her within but for two fingers protruding between the stalks and one foot which remained uncovered. Its leaves had become the size of Evalal's palms and flowers bloomed at regular intervals, each bunch of differing colors as though they all belonged to different plants. She'd never seen anything like it, not even in Goddess' garden at her own temple or any of the others she'd visited during her lessons. Her training in herbology was by no means complete, but she'd never heard of a plant capable of growing so many different colors of blossoms.

The soft padding of raindrops against leaf changed to the plunk of water landing in water. Evalal lowered the leaf cup, peered over its edge. She was pleased to find it had filled to half its capacity so quickly. Her first thought was to raise her hands again, fill it to the brim, and take it to the fallen man, but the dryness in her mouth prompted a different decision.

She brought the edge of the leaf to her lips, puckered, and tilted it as she sucked thirstily. The cool rainwater spread across her tongue and the inside of her cheek, quenching the fire of her thirst. She swallowed it, relief washing down her throat. It was barely a mouthful, but it satisfied her needs, nonetheless. The last few drops drained from the leaf and she closed her eyes, savoring the feeling it brought. For an instant, it seemed she could forget the state of the world, the dead princess, the identity of the man lying at the foot of the veil. In that moment, there was the satisfaction of water in her mouth, the scent of rain, the beauty of the flowers blossoming on the Seed of Life's vine.

Then the water collected in the leaf was gone. She opened her eyes again and her gaze fell immediately to the exposed foot poking out from the green cocoon. Her heart shrank. Her head sagged. Would the world ever be right again? The days of learning in the temple, frolicking in Goddess' garden, worship, love, seemed so long ago.

Evalal stood, her limbs heavy. Danya's remains would be safe without her at her side; the Seed of Life would see to that. It would be better for her to collect rainwater closer to the man so she wouldn't spill it on her way to him.

She crossed the meadow toward him, leaf held out before her. Rain stuck her hair to her skull, ran down her neck. A moment before, she'd felt thankful for it and its ability to slake her thirst. Now she wished it would end and allow her to dry.

When she reached the man and knelt beside him again, leaf held out like an offering, she distracted herself from her thoughts by examining the mythical curtain stretching out both directions and up toward the sky. How many of Goddess' followers could say they'd seen this example of their deity's power? Few, if any.

Raindrops sent flashes flickering across its surface. She did her best to find beauty and awe in the combined display of nature and magic, but struggled to find her way past the heartache and loneliness creeping into her chest, finding its way into her muscles and bones. What she wouldn't give to be at the temple. It was an honor to have been chosen by the Mother of Death—by Goddess herself—to be the princess' guide and keeper, but she hadn't realized how alone she would end up being.

She closed her eyes, unsure if it was rain or tears running down her cheeks.

Did this loneliness explain her willingness to aid a man whom Goddess had seen fit to banish from the world? To put herself in danger? Helping him might even be a threat to the world at large, yet here she was collecting rain to offer him nourishing water. Were these the acts of a person of her right mind?

Evalal chewed her bottom lip. She'd been so sure this was what Goddess wanted of her, but now doubt crept in. Perhaps it was her own agenda that drove her. But if it wasn't what Goddess wanted, surely she'd step in and prevent it, stop her before it was too late.

Frustrated, she opened her eyes and lowered the leaf to peak over its edge. The makeshift bowl had filled almost to the top. The time had come to make her decision: give the water to the injured man and hope it was

Goddess' will for her to help him, or keep it for herself and leave him to die, hoping that was her deity's intention.

"Guide me, Goddess," she whispered.

The broken man groaned in response. She'd hoped for something more definitive, but this would have to do.

His eye was open a slit as before, his cracked lips parted. The tip of his tongue came out of his mouth, searching for the small drops of water it could reach. Evalal had failed to keep the princess alive, but she might be able to help this man.

She brought the edge of the leaf close to his mouth, sloped it slightly so a thin stream of rainwater dribbled over the lip. It splashed against his lips and the lump in his throat bobbed as he struggled to get it down his throat. He managed to raise his head ever so slightly, the cords in his neck tightening with the effort, so Evalal brought the leaf closer until it touched his bottom lip, tipped it farther.

He sucked at the water, pulling it into his mouth. Some spilled out the side, but he seemed to get most of it down, drinking with desperation until the leaf-bowl was empty. When she moved it away, he relaxed the muscles in his neck and his head settled on the ground. A fat drop of rain spattered against his eyes causing him to squint, blink it away.

Evalal rested on her haunches, the empty leaf drooping between the thumb and fingers of one hand. She watched him as he licked his lips, swallowed the last remnants of the water she'd provided. The black cloud in her head and heart lifted. Suddenly she was no longer alone, no longer a useless piece of an unknown puzzle. Her presence here had value and worth, reason.

She reached to her left, set the leaf on the ground beside the one she'd used as a platter earlier in the day. When her gaze fell upon it, she stopped, tilted her head.

It was empty.

Gone were the last few berries, the bits of rabbit, the nut meats. She scanned the ground nearby, searching for signs that some animal had come and taken the foodstuffs for itself. She saw nothing to indicate that had happened.

But if it wasn't an animal...?

The thought didn't have an opportunity to complete before the answer revealed itself.

The man pulled his arm from beneath him, unfolded his legs, and stood.

XIII - Horace – Followed

*H*ORACE WEREN'T SURE WHEN the sounds o' the forest returned—the squawk o' some birds and the songs from others, the buzz o' insects, the creepin' o' unseen animals hidin' in the brush; it'd taken a bunch o' time after escapin' from them pasty white fellas what wanted to eat them. The smells'd always hung in the air, and it took thankfully fewer steps to get away from the coppery scent o' spilled blood.

If the ol' sailor lived the rest o' his life without havin' to take a whiff o' the godawful odor again, it might be too soon.

Ailyssa's hand gripped his, pullin' him along as they made their way through thickets o' trees, around impassable brush cloggin' their path, o'er hills and fallen timbers. It struck him she were movin' with the confidence o' someone with eyes what peered at ev'rythin' lyin' before them, but she said nothin' and he didn't ask. Truth told, exhaustion's fingers dug so deep into his bones, he weren't sure his mouth'd work if he gave it a go. So he let her lead, wishin' all the while for a chance to sit himself down to rest his weary legs or, better yet, hopin' for a few minutes to close his lids and refresh his tired brain.

But she led on, a woman on a mission, her pace unrelentin', only slowin' when he faltered too far behind—most often when goin' up a hill. It were just as they got to the top o' one o' them hills—really no more'n a slope, but in his state, every mound came out a mountain to Horace—when a movement caught his eye. At first he dismissed it as a forest creature gettin' close to find out who be traipsin' through their home. He gulped frightened saliva, put his gaze on Ailyssa's back.

Ten more paces farther after clearin' the top o' the rise, he thought he spied another, this one at the far outside o' his vision. Though reluctant to do so, he turned his head. By the time he got his neck cranked in the right direction, weren't nothing to see but tree trunks and leafy greens. He opened his gob to say somethin' to Ailyssa, but his earlier worry proved true: nothin' sprang forth but a croak as if a toad'd built a home in his throat.

He tried conjurin' up more saliva like what he swallowed not so long ago, but his mouth refused to play along. Instead, he attempted plantin' his feet and draggin' his companion to a halt—didn't work, either. Ailyssa tugged harder and gave him some encouragement.

"Come one, Horace. We're getting close."

Gettin' close? Gettin' close to what?

To death, maybe. Or to somethin' eatin' them.

He continued allowin' her to pull him along, because he didn't have much choice. His eyes flickered side to side quick enough with each stride he worried they might work their way outta his head and pop out onto the forest floor, lost amongst dead needles, lichen, and fallen leaves. With his luck, he'd step on them himself and end up as blind as the woman.

But she ain't so blind now, is she?

For an instant, he wondered why she hadn't told him if it were the case, but he forgot the thought as soon as he spied another leaf move. Whether caused by wind or the brush o' a furry head, he couldn't've guessed. When he stared at the spot, weren't nothin' to observe but a bush what looked like all the other bushes. He sucked his bottom lip into his mouth, fought the urge to chew the soft flesh.

Now other leaves trembled and shook; not where he were lookin', but always at the periphery o' his vision. Enough outside his view to prevent him from bein' sure they actually moved. Each time, they ceased under his attention. His heart fluttered against his ribs like the hardly seen movement o' the fronds, tension built in his limbs makin' followin' Ailyssa more and more difficult. Sensing his reticence, she tugged harder, eatin' up her own strength to keep him movin'.

Somewhere behind them, a branch snapped, the pop amplified by his growin' fearfulness and the forest's relative quiet, startlin' him. If the woman leadin' him heard, she gave no sign. He craned his neck to see but, like ev'ry other time, weren't nothin' but the forest what they'd passed through, though he were startin' to think them trees were closin' in, crowdin' them, maybe steerin' them a particular direction. Even in his current state, he dismissed it as his imagination—a forest didn't care where they went.

Did it?

Once more, Horace opened his mouth to say somethin' to his companion. Another croak, a gurgle. He closed his chops, swirled his tongue around the inside tryin' to create some lubricant, then licked his lips and prepared for the task once more. Before he got his jaw to perform the chore, Ailyssa halted.

She released his hand from her grip, raised her arm. One finger uncurled from her fist and stretched out, pointing through the forest to their port side.

"Look," she said, soundin' a bit breathless herself.

A green glow found its way between the tree trunks and bush leaves, squeezin' through every crack and crevice. The woman started walkin' again, amending her path to take them toward the shimmerin' veil.

—◦◦◦—

Her sight hadn't returned completely—the forest remained shapes without detail, just enough for her to navigate, like walking on a gloomy night with a sliver of a moon to light the path; the white haze lingered over most of her vision, the shapes dark, the opposite of night.

Until the green glow.

No mistaking where the brilliance came from; the luminescence beckoned her.

Why they should make their way to the veil, she didn't know. All she could do was follow the instructions seemingly whispered directly into her being and hope for the best, hope it wasn't misguided, misinterpreted emotion guiding her. Or some malevolence taken hold of her.

Behind her, the sailor increased his pace and effort upon seeing the green glow, but his exuberance lasted a short time before he lagged again, pulling on her, slowing her. She wished for the opportunity to stop for rest, but the force driving her wouldn't allow dalliance. More than once, she considered letting go of his hand and forging on alone, but the thing keeping her from respite also kept her fingers laced with his. Whatever she was meant to do, this was how it was supposed to happen, and with whom.

"I think somethin's followin' us."

Horace's words found their way into her ears, but didn't register in her mind at first. They might have been an insect buzzing near her head, or a bird singing high overhead—background noises for ignoring rather than the words of a companion to be heeded. When he dug his heels into the ground, pulling her to a halt and threatening to tip her from her feet, she faced him.

He stood close, and she made out his features almost as clearly as if her vision had returned—the first time she'd seen his face. Worry creased a brow already marked with the lines of age. His gray hair stuck out past his ears in the way of a man who kept his locks cut short but necessity had forced him to neglect them for an extended period. A twig hung unnoticed by him from his beard; she had to stop herself from giggling at the sight because it amused her, but also because she saw it at all. If she hadn't had the good sense to stifle the laugh, his expression would have done so for her.

He leaned closer to her and whispered: "I think somethin's followin' us."

Any mirth fled from her. Reflexively, she plucked the twig from his beard, dropped it to the forest floor to join a myriad of similar detritus, and peered over his shoulder, scanning the woods at his back. Without the green glow of the veil, anything more than a few paces away dissolved into white haze and vague lines, suggestions of shapes. Horace didn't move, his watery blue eyes fixed on her as though he hoped to see whatever she did reflected in them because he didn't want to look for himself.

At first, she spied nothing but the mostly straight lines of tree trunks, the curves of leaves. Enough time passed for her to consider telling him he was wrong, his fancy was getting the best of him, when the trembling of a branch caught her eye. She shifted her head toward the subtle movement, unsure if she'd seen it or if her own imagination had gotten the better of her. Her heart turned into a caged bird, wings fluttering against the bars of her ribs, desperate to get free even as her breath ceased being drawn.

The forest seemed eerily quiet beyond the hammer of her pulse in her ears. No rustle of leaves or scampering of tiny feet, no birds singing. Horace's stomach growled, reminding her of the days since either of them last consumed anything other than shoots and berries. Ailyssa squinted, her eyelashes framing the branch she'd seen—or thought she'd seen—move. The air in her lungs turned stale, burned, and she exhaled, drew a fresh breath between parted lips.

The limb shook again as though it waited for her act of breathing as permission to do so, but this time she watched it happen, leaving no doubt about the veracity of the movement. The leaves trembled again; a shape appeared from behind it.

A small and thin creature, the haze of her vision turned it into little more than an impression: a foot, a narrow calf, a skinny thigh. A hint of a colorless leg outlined against a colorless background.

Ailyssa's heart jumped into her throat. She leaned away, pulling on Horace's hand, hoping for the sailor to understand her with no need to speak. His feet held fast to their spot, stubbornness or fear rooting him like the trees surrounding them, as though he'd become part of the forest. She glanced at his face, saw his eyes searching hers, the barely contained panic reflected in them. In that moment, she wanted to comfort him, to take away his fears, to lay him down to rest, and to feed him until his belly was stuffed full. But this wasn't time for any of that. This was the time for but one thing, and she put a word to it, forcing it up past the knot clogging her throat.

"Run!"

XIV - Ishla – Dansil

THE TIME BETWEEN THE knock and the door opening wasn't enough for Ishla to bid the person on the other side to enter. As such, she'd already guessed who came to interrupt her in her chamber before Strylor stuck his head through the crack.

"My queen, the king requests your presence."

The muscles in her jaw bunched as she grated her teeth. How many times did she have to tell this oaf to await her permission to come in before he entered? If he continued this way, he was likely to catch her changing, or bathing—exactly why he ignored her? Being queen's guard was less a job to Strylor and more an opportunity.

"Inform his majesty I am busy right now and will attend him when I am able."

The soldier pushed the door open and stepped into the room. As usual, his eyes found their way up and down her before he spoke again.

"I'm told it's important." He shuffled his feet side to side, scratched his ass as he so often did. It made her wonder if the man ever bothered to bathe.

She stood from her divan, setting aside the item she'd been holding—a picture drawn by Danya in her youth, a child's depiction of the family standing in the garden on a sunny day, light glinting on the golden crowns they each wore.

"What could be so important as to interrupt my rest, guard?"

"A rider, my queen."

Her breath caught. She parted her lips to ask what kind of news the messenger brought, but it could only be one thing. She came out from behind the divan and made her way toward the door. Strylor stepped aside and held it open for her to pass through, then followed, closing it after them and undoubtedly gracing her backside with his lecherous gaze. She didn't care. If someone carried word of her children, of Trenan, she needed to hear it.

The queen's guard's weapon and armor clanked as he hurried to match her pace; she ignored the sound, her mind racing through the possibilities. What if she walked in and found Trenan had returned with both Teryk and Danya? Of course she'd embrace them, but could she prevent herself from reacting in the same manner to the master swordsman's return? She'd quelled her emotion for so many turns of the seasons, yet it got no easier. She worried over him as much as she feared for the safety of her children.

"Where is he?" she asked over her shoulder.

"Meeting room."

She nodded to herself and took a left down the next corridor, Strylor clanking along behind her. She truly had been taking a restful day when he interrupted her and, in her hurry to leave and find out the news, she hadn't stopped to don shoes. Her bare feet whispered on the carpet. At the end of the hall, she mounted the stairs, each stone riser cold on her soles, but the feel of it meant as little to her as the noise of the man following her. What if Trenan returned with one of her children and not the other? Or none?

A knot formed in her chest, rose into her throat; she swallowed hard to suppress it. No point getting upset when she didn't know what message the rider carried, and she had it under control by the time she reached the top of the stairway, where she stopped. A moment later, Strylor pulled up beside her. He took a deep breath, as though keeping up to her on the curving flight of stairs proved too much for him.

She glared at him for a heartbeat. "What do you know?"

"Nothing, my queen," he said, shaking his head too enthusiastically by far. "One of the king's men came and told me to fetch you."

Her lip curled at his use of the word—'fetch' her, as though she was an object to be gotten, a thing tossed for the dog to retrieve. As she peered at the queen's guard, she supposed at least half the description was correct.

"He said nothing to you?"

"Just to bring you because someone has news. He didn't say what, wouldn't've told me if I asked."

"And you didn't ask?"

He looked away. "I did. He wouldn't tell me."

This, she believed. Satisfied, she spun from him and proceeded along the hall, the soft touch of carpet returning to the soles of her feet. The meeting chamber lay ahead on the right, its location noticeable by the two armed guards standing outside it. When she approached, they each offered a shallow bow. One of them tapped his spear against the thick wooden door, then they both stepped aside. It swung inward, opened by an unseen hand. As Ishla crossed the threshold, her mind continued sorting through possibilities—her children, Trenan, Osis.

But she saw none of them as she found her way to the center of the chamber. She first looked to the table at the front of the room where her husband always sat, but his chair was empty. Instead of his usual spot from which he presided, Erral stood by the window, peering out into the courtyard, hands clasped behind his back. Ishla took a step toward him, lips parting to ask about the news, but both forward movement and question ended when she noticed the man standing next to him. One person she hadn't thought she'd find here upon being summoned by the king.

Dansil.

The onetime queen's guard stared at her, his expression an unreadable mix of discomfort, embarrassment, and glee. She froze, unsure how to interpret his presence. He'd departed with Trenan to search for her children, and it appeared he'd made his return alone. Ishla's belly cinched tight.

"Dansil?" Strylor exclaimed from behind her. "When did you get back?"

No one acknowledged the current queen's guard's words; they didn't even cause his friend to remove his gaze from the queen.

Nothing happened for the space of ten heartbeats, and Ishla knew this to be an accurate count, for she experienced every thump in her throat and at her temples. If the pause drew out any longer, the incessant pounding of her own heart might have made her scream at them to inform her what news he'd brought, but the king spoke before she felt compelled to voice her frustration.

"Tell her." His tone emerged flat and free of emotion; he didn't turn from the window.

Dansil's eyes darted toward Erral, then back and, in the space before he opened his mouth, a chill ran up Ishla's spine. She understood his hesitation meant whatever message he brought wasn't good.

"Trenan tried to kill me," Dansil said. He paused again, as though he expected an exclamation of disbelief from the queen, or perhaps words of support. She offered neither. If anything, she wanted to grab him by his shirt front and shake him until he gave her news of her children. When he didn't receive the hoped-for reaction, he continued.

"Last time we saw the princess, she wore one of the red robes of the Goddess, the ones they dress the ill in, so I suggested we should make for Ikkundana—the city of the sick."

He paused again and canted his head, as though asking Ishla if she followed along well enough. She gritted her teeth and crossed her arms in front of her chest.

"Before we arrived, Trenan stuck me with a dagger while I slept." He shifted and pointed toward a spot on his lower back. "Think he poisoned me, too, because I was right out of it for days. Don't remember arriving at the forsaken city. Woke up in a dark room after gods knows what they might have done to me."

The queen's eyes narrowed as she wondered why, if Trenan intended to kill him, why did he take him to Ikkundana, a place equipped to heal the wounds of a man suffering from a stabbing? Why not leave him behind to bleed to death? She didn't bother voicing the question, instead waiting for him to continue, to get to the point.

"Not long after I woke, I heard horses leaving the city and saw a procession led by Trenan. I broke out and followed them. And can you guess where they went?"

He waited again, and this time Ishla's impatience refused containment.

"Will you tell me your fucking news?" she snapped.

Dansil looked as though she'd slapped him. He swallowed hard, hooked his hands on his belt and continued; the queen noticed the fingers missing from his left hand. She was sure he'd possessed all ten digits before. Was this a wound Trenan had inflicted upon him?

"They went to the Green, your majesty."

A chill prickled along the flesh of Ishla's arms. Behind her, Strylor fidgeted as though the words made him uncomfortable, leather creaking and sword tapping against his thigh. Erral remained at the window, unmoving, hearing the tale for a second repetition.

"And Danya?" she prompted.

Dansil nodded. "Aye. The princess was there. And the prince, too."

He delayed again, his propensity for dramatic pauses driving the queen to the edge of rage, but this time tempered by hope. He'd seen both of her children, so maybe the news he dragged out for the sake of a story might be good after all. She drew short breaths she quickly released, their rapid nature enough to make her light-headed; she put effort into slowing her air while she waited for him to continue.

"But they weren't the only ones."

Another pause. Ishla's hands curled into fists. "Who, Dansil? Who else attended them?"

She watched the man lump in his throat rise and fall as he swallowed. "Black priests."

Coldness returned to her skin, a gray haze fogged the edge of her vision, and she took a step to the side to steady herself. This time, the soldier didn't linger before continuing.

"They were there for a sacrifice, Queen Ishla. I saw it with my own two eyes. Trenan himself plunged the knife into Danya's neck, then they left her to bleed to death while he and his friends hightailed it out of there, the prince in tow."

She opened her mouth, though what she might have intended to say escaped her, so she closed it. The gray around the edge of her vision expanded as pressure pushed against the inside of her head. She did her best to breathe, but her lungs refused to draw enough air to satisfy her; her throat tightened until it no longer allowed breath through. Her eyes darted toward the king, but Erral remained at the window, his back to her as it had been through Dansil's tale.

He knew what he was going to say. But he did nothing.

Ishla's legs turned to water, and she dropped to her knees, the first tears of many to come spilling down her cheeks. Her daughter was dead, her son missing, all because of the man she loved.

How could he?

The king pivoted from the window, directing his attention to his wife kneeling in the middle of the meeting room but doing nothing to offer her comfort.

"I will send a task force to find the murderer," he said in an emotionless tone. "And bring Trenan here to face his punishment."

Ishla's chest tightened around her heart. How could this be? Trenan had treated both Teryk and Danya as though they were his own, and she knew he loved her from afar all this time. How could he take the life of someone he cherished?

The tears came in earnest and Ishla rested on her haunches, raised her hands to cover her face as her chest heaved. She did her best to contain the sobs ripping at her breast, but they proved too much to hold and her mother's grief broke through her fingers in a long moan. Through a blur, she saw Dansil and Erral watching her. No pity showed on the king's features, no anguish of his own, no emotion but anger.

He knows.

"Queen's guard, do your duty and escort the queen to her chambers."

She heard her husband speak the words, but they meant nothing to her. The world around her meant nothing to her. She barely noticed Strylor's hands on her waist, helping her to stand. He directed her toward the door, out into the corridor, everything happening as if in a dream. Haze and fog shrouded all, the only thing real to her the pain in her chest where she'd once kept her heart.

Her son missing. Her daughter dead. The love of her life to blame.

XV - Trenan – Rescue

*S*ENSATION RETURNED, BUT NOT the uncomfortable pins-and-needles tingling which had filled him before he lost consciousness. Icy rain pattered on his cheeks, splashed in puddles beside his head. Someone gripped his shoulder, shook him and said his name.

"Trenan."

If not for his recognition of the voice, the master swordsman might have stayed wherever he was, waiting for death to claim him and relieve him of the troubles of his life. Instead, he opened his eyes.

The man looking down at him did so with equal parts concern and confusion.

"Osis?" Haze crowded Trenan's thoughts, but he recognized his compatriot, though he didn't understand how he came to be here. "Did I kill you, too?"

The soldier's brow creased. Trenan watched water drip from the end of his nose, the droplet lost amongst the falling rain.

"What do you mean? What's happened, Trenan?"

The master swordsman sat up, the movement setting his ears ringing. He jerked his head first one way then the other, scanning the road, the brush at the edge, the forest beyond. If the tortured and lifeless faces haunting them remained, they'd gone into hiding. A measure of relief washed through him, but he realized he couldn't tell Osis about them. If he did, his long-time friend might think he'd lost his mind.

"Nothing," he replied, then stood with less grace than normal, extricating himself from the mud puddles collected on the track. Once on his feet, he attempted to wipe dirt from himself, his also dirty hand failing miserably.

Osis took a step away and regarded the master swordsman. Trenan wondered if the soldier was assessing what might have happened, or if he awaited instructions from his superior. The question lasted but an instant before other concerns came to his mind.

"The prince." He stopped smudging mud across himself and looked around. "Is Teryk all right?"

"He is," Osis replied. "At least, he appears uninjured. Beyond that, it's hard to know. He hasn't spoken a word."

Trenan sighed and nodded once as his eyes found the young man. He stood with the group of riders who'd arrived with the sergeant-at-arms, a thick cloak thrown over his shoulders to protect him from the rain. He faced away from them, staring off into the forest.

Does he perceive the dead ones even though I don't?

Trenan followed his gaze: tress and brush, trunks and leaves and darkness. No ghostly faces, no accusatory glares, no glistening wounds. If he spied anything, whatever it may be was invisible. He shuddered, then remembered Osis scrutinizing him.

"Water down my spine," he said with a nervous chuckle. "Been wet for days."

"Aye, we all have."

Trenan started toward the prince and the group of soldiers and Osis followed, their boots splashing in the rivulets of rainwater flowing along the middle of the road. He recalled telling the sergeant-at-arms to return to Draekfarren, but did he tell him to gather more men to join in the search for the royal siblings? His memory failed him. So much had happened since they'd parted ways.

The last time we saw each other, the prince was missing and the princess alive.

A recollection of Teryk inserting the knife into his sister's neck flashed across his mind and bile rose in his gullet. He turned his head, bent at the waist, and retched, the foul- and bitter-tasting fluid disappearing in the muddy flood. An instant later, Osis' touched his shoulder.

"Are you all right?"

Trenan raised his hand and nodded but did not straighten. More nausea threatened, so he waited. His throat convulsed again, he gagged, but nothing more rose from his stomach. He spat, wiped his mouth on his sleeve, inhaled a shuddering breath.

"I'll be fine." He coughed, spat again. "Perhaps a wineskin?"

Osis called to one of the other soldiers to bring the master swordsman a drink.

What's wrong with me?

Never in his life had Trenan experienced such a reaction—to anything. He'd seen more death than most, absorbed and doled out torture. His sword had split men in two from skull to tail bone, he'd watched babies being born, assisted surgeons perform their duties—including seeing the amputation of his own stump. Gangrene, infection, dismemberment, disembowelments. Nothing did this to his gut.

What did the priests do to me?

A soldier arrived bearing a wineskin, offered it to the master swordsman. Two more breaths and his gorge returned to its rightful place; he grabbed the skin, squirted a mouthful of its content between his lips. The fruity taste of wine overwhelmed him, but he held the fluid in his mouth, sloshing it around his tongue and the insides of his cheeks before spitting it out. He took another swig and handed it to the fellow who brought it, this time swallowing the liquid. It burned the inside of his throat as it fouled its way to his empty belly.

It didn't sit well in him. If rainwater wasn't streaming down his face, he knew he'd find clammy sweat on his brow; if he tried to hold his hand steady, he'd fail. Osis patted his shoulder, drew him along again toward the group of soldiers and horses. Trenan followed, gaze darting between the distracted prince and the dark verge of the forest. Still, he spied none of those risen from the grave to stalk him, but he feared they might return.

They arrived at the others and Osis escorted him to a horse. It surprised the master swordsman to find it the same one he'd been riding since they'd left the Green—Yoli's steed; he'd expected it either to have fled or been slain by the dead. He ran his fingers along the wet hair on the horse's neck, patted it. Resting his hand on the animal—such a familiar and comfortable action—brought him minor relief, but also made him recall another gesture that never failed to bring him confidence.

He lowered his hand to the scabbard dangling from his sword belt but discovered it empty. He thought his blood might congeal in his veins and he jerked his gaze over his shoulder toward where Osis found him lying in the road. Teryk was not of his right mind, his sister dead, and now he'd lost Godsbane—the symbol of the king.

"The crownsword is safe," his friend said, noticing and interpreting his distress.

Trenan nodded. He thought to ask for it, or another sword, but abandoned the idea. For the first time in his memory, he didn't think having a weapon close at hand capable of relieving him of the tension and concern knotting his muscles and bringing an ache to his back. Without a word, he grasped the saddle horn, put his foot in the stirrup, and heaved himself up onto the horse. His brain spun with the movement and he gripped the pommel hard while it settled, then realized Osis had spoken. He shook his head to clear the gauzy sensation and peered at his compatriot.

"What did you say?"

"What of the princess? Did you have any luck tracking her down?"

Trenan stiffened again, thoughts and memories racing through his mind. He stared at the sergeant looking up at him from where he stood beside the horse, but he didn't see his friend. Instead he saw Danya lying dead in the grass outside the Green, and black-robed priests, Goddess warriors, the prince's blank expression, the bright tail of a star shooting across the sky. Had Osis and the others seen it, too? Did they understand what it meant?

What do I tell him?

Telling the truth likely meant his own death. While he deserved the punishment due, what would it mean for the prince? How would knowing what happened affect Ishla? He drew his tongue over his lips, tasting cool rainwater and the salty sweat of his newfound cowardice. Beneath his worry for Teryk and his mother, another unfamiliar discomfort brewed, tugging at his mind.

He didn't want to die.

"Trenan?"

The master swordsman shook his head, an action he imagined Osis would take as an answer but which he did to loosen unpleasant thoughts. He cleared his throat, gone dry as old parchment despite the recent gulp of wine to wet it.

"We didn't find her," he said, the lie scraping along his esophagus.

Instead of berating him for not succeeding in his assigned duty, or accusing him of failing the king's orders, Osis nodded.

"Then we continue."

He spun on his heel, boot squelching in the sopping track. The master swordsman shivered, imagining them arriving at the scene of Danya's murder, finding the princess' decomposing corpse, the girl Evalal perched on the ground beside it. Evalal—witness to all. Her words could put him to death.

"No," Trenan said, the word quiet and rasping. He coughed and repeated himself. "No."

Osis stopped, poised with the toe of his boot in a stirrup and his hand on the saddle. He looked over his shoulder at his friend, raised an eyebrow. "No?"

"No," Trenan said again. "We didn't find the princess, but we found someone who did."

He paused, suppressing a shiver, and Osis waited for him to continue. The master swordsman's mind raced. Lying was not something he did; he'd never thought of keeping the truth of Teryk's birth a lie—secrets are different things from deceits.

"Fellick and Ive," he said. The untruth felt right, believable. "The weapons dealers. We ran into them and they'd seen Danya. They told me she headed toward Draekfarren."

The instant the last words left his mouth, he regretted them. While traveling any road in the kingdom, one expected to encounter merchants, but telling Osis the princess was heading to the Horseshoe might prove a mistake. It meant they wouldn't find her dead at the foot of the veil, but what would happen when she never returned to her family?

At least they won't know the fault lies with me. Or Teryk.

Likely, they'd never discover what happened to her. Punishment still awaited Trenan for his failure, but he'd keep his life, something which seemed far more important now than ever before.

"And you think they spoke true?"

The master swordsman pursed his lips, nodded curtly once. "They had no reason not to."

His gaze darted past Osis, to the one other witness to what had passed: the prince himself. Men of the king still surrounded him, but he'd raised his head, his stare fixed on Trenan, burning into him. Had he overheard his lies?

He blames me.

The sergeant-at-arms boosted himself onto his horse, wiped rainwater from his eyes. He looked from Trenan to the group of soldiers gathered around Teryk and back again. His expression showed nothing. He held the master swordsman's gaze for a moment before nodding.

"You are in command, swordmaster. If Draekfarren you say, then Draekfarren it be." He prompted his horse to the right, facing the others. "Mount up. Let's put some mud beneath our hooves before we stop for sleep."

Trenan drew a deep sigh between his lips, held it for the space of a few heartbeats, then let it slowly out through his nose. He scooted side to side and forward and back in the saddle, in search of a comfortable position, but found none; during the hazy, half-forgotten ride from the veil, he'd developed a sore on his backside and hadn't detected it until now. With each movement, it shot pain into his buttock, a minor torture reminding him that, though he might have averted punishment and death for the time being, they likely lay in his future.

The master swordsman put heels to horse and began the journey home, gaze held straight ahead lest he find dead faces continuing to mock him from the verge. His eyes found the prince's slumped shoulders, his hanging head. Concern twinged in his gut, though he couldn't tell if he felt it for his son or himself.

What will he say if asked about his sister?

Trenan shivered, blamed it on the rain running along his skin, but he knew better: fear trembled his spine.

Will it come down to him or me?

The thought tied his stomach in a knot that threatened to rise into his throat, bringing wine-tinged bile with it. He swallowed hard. He must talk to Teryk, make him understand what was best for both of them; that was the only choice which made sense.

I have to make him see.

The group of soldiers trotted away, leaving the Green and its secrets farther behind.

XVI - Evalal – Rebirth

THE MAN STOOD TO his full height, towering over Evalal, and she fell onto her buttocks, staring up at him. In that instant, she wondered how she'd thought of him and the others like him as Small Gods. When they appeared as pinpricks of light in the sky, flickering in the night, impossibly distant, it made sense. But, now he loomed over her with the threat of violence and death in his hands and on his face, the sobriquet seemed ridiculous.

Fear vibrated through the girl and she pushed her feet against the ground, scrambling to escape. The heels of her boots cut divots, pushing aside grass and dirt until they found purchase and her backside slid away from him.

The man glared at her, his expression blank yet threatening. His mouth opened and closed as if he stretched the muscles in his jaw, making sure it worked; a pink tongue snaked across his lips, wetting them. His shoulders rose and fell, sinew rippling beneath skin so pale it might have glowed had it been night. He took a step toward her.

Fear exploded into panic, filling Evalal's limbs with fervent energy. She rolled onto her front, pressed herself up on her hands, and got her legs under her. Her feet slipped at first, throwing her to the ground, but the second attempt proved successful; she shot forward and away from the man who fell from the sky.

Her heart pounded, clammy perspiration glazed her forehead. She reached up and pushed her hair out of her eyes, resisting the urge to look back as she moved, mind racing. What could she do to protect herself from him? The distraction proved costly—her feet tangled, and she fell. She twisted her body at the last second to land partly on her shoulder and partially on her chest instead of her face. The impact sent a lightning bolt of pain through her and knocked the air from her. She rolled onto her back, gasping to find her breath. Tears streamed, smearing the shape of the man striding toward her into a near indistinguishable blob, white against the shimmering green veil.

Her feet churned the earth, legs attempting to propel her away from the encroaching threat, but the lack of air to energize her and the fear tightening her muscles offered merely failure. As she struggled, he came closer, closing the space between them with slow, dogged steps. The nearer he drew, the more difficult it became to draw breath. When two of his long paces remained between them, Evalal fell back, chest heaving, and threw both her arms in front of her face.

She closed her eyes, clenched her teeth, and ceased trying to inhale air into her lungs. If a few of his blows could end her life, what was the point in wasting energy on breathing now?

Though her heart pounded in her ears, the girl heard the footsteps of the man who fell from the sky as his feet trampled dry grass. One step brought him almost to her. A second, so close by her, and she tensed every muscle in her body, awaiting the pain. A third stride, then the sole of a foot tamping the earth a fourth time, quieter now, moving past.

Evalal eased the tightness in her tendons and opened her eyes. Without thinking, she drew a breath, and this time coaxed a gulp of air into her chest. She lowered her arms, cocked her head.

The naked man moved another three paces while she recovered, striding past her without a second glance, ignoring her as though more important things than relieving her of her life required his attention.

The princess.

Evalal gasped her lungs full of air, the action sending pain across the top of her chest and through her shoulder where she'd hit the ground. She rolled onto her side, gathered her legs beneath her, and struggled to her feet. This was why she'd stayed behind, why Goddess chose her. Protecting the resting place of the princess mattered more than anything, more than everything. She couldn't let her be disturbed.

She stumbled forward, her fumbling, pained gait faster than his shuffling strides; she needed but a few heartbeats to catch up to him.

Then what?

She had neither the time nor space to formulate a plan; Evalal overtook him in six off-balance paces, reached out and grasped his forearm with both hands, and dug her heels into the ground. He dragged her two more steps, as though he didn't realize her presence, before shaking his arm the way a horse might flick its tail to shoo a fly. A small gesture, but it proved powerful, and sent her stumbling away, barely maintaining her equilibrium to keep from tumbling once more. Not so much as a peek in her direction.

Evalal breathed through clenched teeth, the fibers of her muscles tingling beneath her flesh. Part of her mind told her to flee, to save herself, but her entire life had brought her to this point. Every bit of her training, faith, and belief, everything the Mothers had taught her from the moment the birth woman had deserted her at the Mother of Death's temple, led to this. She forced the urge deep inside herself, gathered her energy and strength, and lunged at the man who fell from the sky once more.

This time, she caught him in the mid-section, wrapping her arms around his waist. She drove hard with her feet after she struck him, hoping to send him off balance. Pain lanced down her side from her shoulder and chest, but when the impact made him stumble, her satisfaction soothed it.

Stumbled, but didn't fall.

He stopped, tilted his head and looked at her as the annoyance she must have been to him. Evalal stared up at the blank threat in his eyes, her heart beating hard as she gripped him around the waist, refusing to let go despite the gesture's futility. They remained like an out-of-place statue until he grabbed her by the front of her robe with both hands and lifted her. She struggled to maintain her grip, but her fingers slipped and he pulled her away, held her before him as though he toyed with a doll.

Light flickered, a piece of the star he used to be shining in the depths of his eyes, mesmerizing her. Evalal's mouth fell open as she watched the white sparks. Had she ever seen anything so beautiful? She thought to raise her hand, tempted to touch it, but her arms hung at her side the way she dangled uselessly in the man's grip.

With no more warning than a grunt of effort, he tossed her aside. Evalal inhaled a startled breath as she hurtled away from him, arms waving to right herself. She struck the ground with a thump and a pop, her arm snapping beneath her.

Agony burst through her, worse than any she'd felt in her young life. She rolled over, cradling the injured limb against her. Tears streamed from her eyes, staining her cheeks. Everything disappeared but the pain. The sun and sky smeared to a blue and white smudge. Blood thumping in her ears overcame any other sound, and the throbbing in her arm made the ground pressing against her spine as unnoticeable as if it didn't exist.

A sob escaped her throat as she rocked back and forth to comfort herself, the entire world around her swallowed up in the excruciating torment of the broken bone. Her breath came in ragged gasps between sobs and moans, each rise of her chest sending fresh agony along her arm. In the recesses of her mind, hidden beneath the pain, she understood she had something important to be doing, but she couldn't bring herself to pay attention to the thought.

With the injured limb held against her, she propped herself up with her other arm, hoping not having the broken bone resting on her when she breathed might give her relief. It didn't; the effort of holding it up proved as painful.

Evalal sat for five heartbeats, head hung, tears flowing, mucus running from her nose onto her lips. She lifted her good arm, drew it across her face, smearing the cloth of her robe with salt water and snot alike, but also clearing her vision. She raised her chin from her chest, blinked away fresh tears, and gazed along the path cut through the tall grass by a man who had fallen from the sky.

"No," she whispered, and pain flared.

She ignored it, leaned forward, and began crawling after him, her injured arm held against her. She'd failed in stopping him before, when she possessed two healthy arms, so it seemed near impossible now, but she needed to.

Somehow.

Each time Evalal lifted her good hand off the ground—bits of grass and rocks stuck to her palm—and put it down again, it jarred her broken limb. Tears flowed despite her efforts to stop them; they blurred the man ahead of her, making it difficult to tell how far away or how near Danya he was. She pressed on, no idea what to do when she reached him, but knowing she must try.

The princess may be dead, but her role was long from over.

She lifted her hand, put it down, repeated the action, her knees dragging along the ground behind her. Blades of tall yellow grass brushed her face, some of it dry and rigid enough she wondered if it might cut her. Maybe it wasn't only tears staining her cheeks. She followed the path made by the man she pursued, avoiding the grass, but sometimes it appeared it reached for her, grasped for her as she passed. She tucked her chin toward her chest.

Even with her eyes directed toward the ground, she didn't see the sharp rock hidden beneath the compressed grass. Her palm found it, she shifted her weight onto it, and it sank into her skin. Evalal cried out and, before she stopped herself, lifted her hand, overbalanced, and pitched forward.

Bright stars of pain flashed in her vision as she landed on her fractured arm. Another scream escaped her throat, and she rolled onto her back. Her eyes were open, but she saw none of the blue sky hanging over her, its unending expanse disguised by tears and a haze of agony. She closed them tight, bit on her lower lip.

Beneath her, the ground rumbled.

Slight, but noticeable, ongoing. She held her breath and concentrated on it, using it to distract herself from the torture of her arm and now her palm. The pain didn't disappear, but she got through it, forced herself to sit up. A forearm already wet with tears and snot found its way across her eyes, clearing her vision enough to make out more than just shapes.

Above the tall grass, she spied the flowers and vines growing over the princess beyond the man ahead of her, but her faulty depth perception left her unable to discern how far before he reached Danya.

The rumble grew and Evalal turned in time to see the first buck leap from the meadow. It plowed into his side, hitting him with its head, square between its antlers rather than goring him. The two of them fell in a heap, hidden from her sight by the grass. The tall blades shivered and shook. She stretched her neck, ignoring the pain, but saw nothing; she scrambled to her feet.

The man who'd fallen from the sky levered himself from under the big deer, grasped its antlers in one hand, its snout in the other, and twisted. The snap-pop it made reminded Evalal of her own bone breaking, bringing nausea to her gut. Sour saliva filled her mouth as he dropped the sagging animal, but other creatures emerged before he reoriented himself and continued toward the princess' final resting place.

A squirrel scampered out of the grass, its claws digging into him as it climbed his leg. Evalal wondered if this might be one of the same squirrels which had brought her sustenance when she needed it so badly. Her lips moved in prayer for the animal's safety. What hope did such an insignificant thing have against someone who so easily threw her aside and downed an angry buck with the flick of his wrist?

Red dots stood out against the man's white flesh as the squirrel avoided his first swipe at it, making its way up to his torso. It wasn't so lucky the second time as he snatched it in his hand, squeezed hard, and tossed it away.

Evalal's heart sank, but Goddess and her minions weren't finished.

More small animals rushed him: squirrels, rabbits, a weasel, rats and mice. They darted in and out, nipping at his feet, avoiding his swipes and kicks. He'd catch them and throw or kick them away, but two replaced each one he stopped. Evalal crept closer, wondering if she had a part to play in this; the forest creatures threw him off his intended course, but they didn't do any real damage. She took another step, and a second stag leapt from the grass, surprising her.

The man must have seen it at the last instant because he twisted away, one point of the animal's antlers piercing his flank instead of the full rack eviscerating him. He turned with the impact, kept his feet beneath him, and grabbed the deer by the neck, swung it around as the antler tore at his side. Hope sprang forth in Evalal's heart, the sight before her distracting her and reducing the pain of her broken limb to an almost-manageable ache.

He tossed the stag to the ground like anyone else might a much smaller animal, raised his hand and plunged it into the animal's chest. Evalal gasped. He pulled it free, bright red blood covering his arm to the elbow, and discarded what she assumed must be the deer's heart into the tall grass. Her gorge rose into her throat and she struggled to fight it.

The man stomped the earth, crushing a mouse beneath his sole. A bird dove from the sky, grasping at his face with its talons, but its small size and unfamiliarity with the maneuver made it easy for him to bat it aside. The poor thing fell to the ground in a heap of feathers beside the first fallen deer.

More animals came at him; he dodged the next charging stag, turning its inertia against it. He squashed rats, downed birds, tore rabbits and squirrels in two, his face remaining blank and emotionless even as blood splashed across it. These insignificant lives meant nothing to him, just like Evalal's had no value. The lone thing of consequence to him was reaching the princess. What would he do when he got there?

He will end what the Seed of Life started.

She shuffled closer as more animals emerged to meet their deaths, but her arm flared with pain, felt as though it weighed more than it should. Another deer—the largest so far—charged him, but he struck it with his fist between the eyes as it reached him. He stepped aside as it fell to the ground, limp as a sack of vegetables. The corpses of beasts piled up around him, so many the attackers stumbled over the fallen, making it easier for him to defend. An eagle swooped out of the sky; he caught it by the leg, smashed it against the earth.

"No!"

Evalal hurried her pace as much as her broken arm dangling at her side allowed her. She didn't have the energy to cradle it to her chest to protect it. Blood trickled from the palm of her other hand, dripping from the tips of her fingers. The army of animals defending the princess thinned. A few gave up and turned tail for the forest, the rest died beneath the fists and feet of the man from the sky.

When the attack abated, he stood in one place for a few heartbeats. Cuts and gashes marked his skin, along with the pinpricks of claws, the bite marks of sharp teeth. Blood oozed from them, but he didn't appear to notice. His shoulders rose and fell three times, taking time to catch his breath, then he continued at the same maddening pace as before, each implacable step carrying him nearer his goal.

"No," Evalal cried again, hurrying despite the agony it caused her.

It took her twelve painful strides to catch him. Not knowing what else to do, she leaped onto his back, throwing both her arms around his neck. Her broken limb screamed, made her want to let go, but she held on, using it to help press her other against his throat, hoping to squeeze the life from him.

Her attack caused him to stop, distracted, but caused no more effect. He reached up with hands bloodied by his own wounds and those he'd inflicted on the animals, grabbed her by the shoulders of her robe, and flipped her over onto the ground in front of him.

Her spine hit and more pain exploded inside her, from her arm or another fresh injury; she couldn't tell and didn't care.

This will be the end of me.

Goddess had given her a task, and she'd not only failed, she'd been the impetus of her own undoing. If she'd killed him when he first fell, instead of nursing him, helping him heal, the princess would be safe, and she would live on. But she'd made those mistakes and deserved her fate.

The man glared at her with the same blank expression boiling with an incredible threat of violence despite holding nothing at all. His hands curled into fists, he raised his arms above his head.

Evalal closed her eyes, whispered a prayer, and waited to die.

XVII - Ishla – Mourning

*I*SHLA STARED OUT THE window, but her tear-veiled eyes saw nothing of the courtyard, buildings, and streets beyond. Even if she registered what they gazed upon, she wondered if her lamenting brain would have recognized them for what they were. All it knew was her children.

And Trenan.

She drew her forearm across her face, wiping away more tears. How her body continued producing them was a wonder; it had barely given her a break since Dansil's declaration of the master swordsman's murderous treachery.

How can it be true?

She recalled Trenan treating her offspring as if they both belonged to him. He'd loved her in every possible way under impossible circumstances. Gifts that showed up hidden about her chambers from time to time had come from him, not from her husband. She'd kept them all, stashed away from the world, brought out in secret when she needed a reminder of love, an escape from what it was to be married to a king. How many times had she fantasized about giving up one for the other?

She turned from the window, crossed the room to her bed and knelt, bent forward until her ear brushed the floor, and reached under. Her fingers skimmed the wooden crate tucked away beneath; she stretched farther until she grasped the edge, then pulled the container toward her.

Sitting on the rug, she peered at the top of the box without moving the lid. Inside, she'd find dried flowers, a heart-shaped rock, unsigned notes written in an awkward hand—some, proclamations of love, others sincere but clumsy attempts at poetry. A bracelet fashioned by a local craftsmith, a shell from a faraway beach. Memory after memory of a love destined to fail other than on one night and in stolen glances. A love doomed from the start had now seen the last flicker of possibility extinguished.

Ishla rested her hand on the lid of the crate. Part of her ached to open the box, sort through the memories, bask in what might have been. Another part wanted to upend the container, dump its contents on the floor and stomp them to dust. Under both lurked the temptation to hide it under the bed, forget about it until she found out the truth for herself.

Behind her, the door handle rattled. The queen inhaled a startled breath, looked up from the box as the door opened. She jammed the crate back where she'd gotten it, smoothing the skirts of her dress out of habit before wiping the tears on her cheeks away with her hands. A heartbeat later, Erral stepped across the threshold.

The king's gaze swept the room before finding her standing beside the mattress. One eyebrow rose as though he'd ask her about this, but then he must have thought better of it. He strode halfway to her and stopped, a full six paces away from his wife. He didn't move, simply stared at her, and the grief and sadness tightening her chest threatened to become rage.

Why didn't you do more? How could you let this happen?

She wanted to scream the words at him, but bit her lower lip instead. Her anger served no purpose now.

"I've put together a platoon of men. They leave in the morning."

She took a step away from the mattress, breathed a deep breath in through her nose, attempting to settle herself. "What will be the duty of this platoon?"

"To find Trenan and bring him here to answer for his actions."

Her hands curled into fists and her lips pressed into a thin line. One more step his direction as she fought to compose her voice, as both rage and anguish threatened to usurp control.

"And what of the prince? Shouldn't finding our son be paramount?"

"Your guard says Trenan has him." He waved a dismissive hand. "Find one, find the other."

He turned from her and took two steps toward the door, as though their conversation was finished. No comfort offered, no further explanation, no discussion about what allegedly had come to pass. She advanced the same two paces to follow him.

"You don't believe him, do you?"

The king stopped, did nothing for the space of four heartbeats, then pivoted to look over his shoulder at her.

"Which part?"

"All of it. The black priests, Trenan." She hesitated. "Danya."

"What reason does this man have to make up such lies?"

"You do. You believe him. How can you?"

Erral spun toward her, anger painting his brow. "How can I not? This is hardly the first of Trenan's transgressions against my crown."

They glared at each other and Ishla felt the air in the chamber grow cold, as if ice flowed from his stare. She swallowed hard, fighting against the tears rimming her eyelids yet again.

"What do you mean?" she said, keeping her voice quiet to stay in control.

"Do not suppose me stupid or obtuse, woman. I realize Trenan coveted things belonging to me. I have eyes."

Things belonging to me.

Her gut twisted, both at his apparent knowledge of her transgression and his choice of words. Was that how he thought of her? As a thing that belonged to him? Under other circumstances, she wouldn't have risked pushing him further—sometimes, comments are best left unsaid. But this wasn't other circumstances; her daughter was dead, her son missing, and Trenan being blamed for both.

"What things, Erral?"

He glared at her; rarely did she use his name instead of his title except in intimate moments; even when it was just the two of them, he preferred she didn't. She watched how it bothered him show on his face.

"My children, for one."

"Your children?" Her voice skipped up in register and volume. "You were too busy being king to be their father. Someone needed to raise them."

His lip curled. "It was his job to train them, not to act as their sire. And we both know that's not where his yearnings for parts of my life ended."

She stomped across the carpeted floor, closing the space between them until less than an arm's length remained. Being so close was a danger should he strike her for what he might consider insolence, but she couldn't stop herself. She inclined her head so their eyes met, uncaring if he should recognize the disdain she so clearly felt.

"What do you mean, my king?" The last words dripped with sarcasm. "Say it."

The muscles in his cheek bulged and the cords in his neck stood out as he used his self-control not to lash out. She held her ground, daring him, heart thumping against her ribs as her body wondered if he'd hit her while her mind didn't care.

"Enough," he said, squeezing the word out between clenched teeth. He took a step backward. "My men leave in the morning to bring Trenan to answer for what he has done."

He turned from her and went to the door, rested his hand on the handle for an instant before facing her again.

"Rest assured, Ishla, he will be held accountable for everything."

The king pulled the door open and stepped through, slamming it behind him. Ishla stood staring at the doorway, at once both seething and thankful for the rage distracting her from her losses. But the distraction didn't last long. How could anything keep all that had happened from her mind?

It returned to her in an avalanche, the force of it sending her stumbling backward until her legs contacted the bed. She sagged onto the mattress, but this time, no tears flowed from her eyes. She stared at her hands in her lap, an agonized moan threatening to escape her throat, but she fought it, struggling to keep emotion from overcoming her, leaving her incapacitated. This wasn't the time.

She raised her chin, glowered at the closed door. The man who'd brought the news—Dansil—had been her guard before he left with Trenan. She realized the two of them didn't get along, though she didn't understand why, but was it enough for Trenan to kill him? Enough for him to lie and blame Trenan?

Or to deceive them about Danya's death?

What if she's not dead?

Ishla stood, energy flooding into her body. Dansil had brought with him no proof of the princess' demise or Trenan's guilt, merely his word. Erral may believe it, but she did not have to. But the king had other reasons to punish his master swordsman, reasons he'd known but kept to himself for...how many turns of the seasons? Whether the former queen's guard told lies or not was irrelevant to the king; he'd find Trenan and likely kill him.

I have to find him first. I have to find out the truth.

She cast her gaze about the chamber, knowing she wouldn't discover anything reasonable for a journey. Everything in here belonged to a queen.

But suitable travel garments were the least of her worries. She didn't know where to locate Trenan, how to get there, or what to expect when she did. She crossed her arms and tapped her foot, grateful for the distraction from despair, hopeful it had been misdirected in the first place.

But how...?

It took but a moment for the answer to present itself. Where it came from, she didn't understand. The solution wasn't something she'd have considered at any other time. But it presented itself to her as clear as the sun on a cloudless day. She nodded, deciding it the right decision, then set to figuring out clothing to wear to hide her identity while four words echoed in her head.

The Mother of Death.

XVIII - Horace – Small Gods

*F*UCK ME DEAD.

Ailyssa's hand tightened on his and she pulled hard enough he worried she might've wrenched his arm right outta its socket. Its jerkin' caused him to stumble, but he kept his feet beneath and followed her because what other choice did he have?

Horace possessed not the slightest idea what'd set the woman off, made her take off runnin' at once after yellin' out the word. He did his best to peer o'er his shoulder at what might've spooked her but saw nothin' and felt glad for it. He weren't sure his poor ol' sailor's heart'd take much more o' what the woods offered up. At least when he floated atop the mysterious depths, standin' upon the deck o' one boat and another gave him safety.

Until he'd gotten knocked overboard. And then the God o' the Deep ate his ship.

Forest. Sea. Each had their evils. What Horace hankered for right then were a roof o'er his head and a mattress under his ass.

A wide leaf slapped him across the face as though it meant to smack him outta his thoughts, and it did. He sputtered and wiped dew drops from his brow, trained his gaze at the path along which he were allowin' a blind woman to lead him. The absurdity o' this choice struck him, but he couldn't change it; she gripped his hand too tight to pull away, and his legs lacked the energy to overtake her and blaze the trail himself. He resigned himself to bein' led from whatever'd given her the desire to flee but, when he realized what direction she'd picked for them, he considered it might not be the best o' choices.

"Hey," he said, the word comin' out more breathless than he intended. "Hey."

If Ailyssa heard, she made no sign o' doin' so. She continued pushin' through the brush, avoidin' thickets what might've proved too dense while side-steppin' even the skinniest o' tree trunks as though she had no problem seein'. Horace stretched his neck, strugglin' to peek past her and figure out if she might've gotten her vision back, but the green glow ahead o' them and gettin' closer with each step made him think maybe she hadn't.

"Ailyssa. Stop. The veil."

She kept goin', pullin' him along. He attempted to wriggle his fingers free from hers, but she weren't havin' none o' that, so he began draggin' his feet to slow her; didn't work, either. The sightless woman plunged through a tangle o' branches and leaves, raisin' her arm to protect her face but not warnin' the ol' sailor about the snap-back he received. A branch caught him square in the mouth, makin' him twist his neck to get away from it. The taste o' blood washed across his tongue and, with his head turned tryin' to recover, he glimpsed a flash o' pale flesh amongst the greenery behind them.

They found us.

He imagined the faceless things with their indentations for eyes and red smears where their mouths should be. Did they smell them? Usin' their non-existent noses to follow them all this way?

Panic speedin' his heart, Horace looked past his companion again at the impenetrable veil what they'd soon find themselves trapped against at the mercy o' those blood-thirsty things.

The green wall loomed ahead, its glow castin' an eerie light across the forest, its hue turnin' the greenery more verdant and givin' most ev'rythin' else a sickly tone. It seemed impossible to Horace to guess exactly how much distance lay between them and it. His own vision blurred, his legs grew heavier, becomin' pillars beneath him which took every bit o' effort to keep them movin'. He stumbled, caught himself. His heart jumped into his throat at the possibility o' them beasts catchin' him, rubbin' parts o' his body against their mouthless faces. He touched his hand against his mouth and it came away bloody. He swallowed, tastin' it.

"Ailyssa."

The word slipped out no more'n a whisper, but she must've heard it, for the woman halted. The ol' sailor skidded to a stop behind her, noticed her head tiltin', her nose close to touchin' the mythical veil what, not so long ago, Horace'd considered a tall tale. And now here they found themselves practically pressed up against it, with savages what wanted to tear them to pieces and eat their flesh sneakin' up on them.

Leaves and branches shook behind him, the noise as loud to his ears as the thunder and wind o' a third-season storm upon the open sea. Ailyssa's grip loosened on his hand and he pulled it free, his knees failin'. He slipped to the ground, foldin' up on himself. Part o' him wanted to look up and see how close the creatures followed, find out how many beats remained before his heart's final pump, but he didn't. What would be the point? What could he do with such a brief period? Make atonement? Ask forgiveness for the wrongs he'd committed? Gaze at another person one more time? Only the last held any sway, but it weren't enough. He sank down until his ass settled on the damp forest floor, raised both his arms in front o' his face, coverin' his head, and awaited his terrible fate.

The brush rustled and shook, and it seemed to him the ground may've quaked beneath him. He squeezed his eyes shut so tight his noggin began hurtin'. His jaw ached with the effort o' clenchin' his teeth. At any instant, he expected a sharp claw to find him, penetrate his skin, burstin' the sack what was his body to spill his life's blood all o'er the dirt and moss on which he sat.

When a touch found his forearm, it startled him and made him jump as though it'd been a talon piercin' his flesh. He gasped a breath, his tight throat turnin' it into a frightened wheeze. He cowered away, the veil buzzin' behind him where his shoulder brushed up against it. The hand remained, but no claws dug into him. Instead, the cool fingers caressed him.

"It's okay, Horace Seaman."

The tender voice might've been music to his ears. The ol' sailor lowered his arms, slow and cautious, and opened his eyes until he peered into the face in front o' him with its smooth, gray cheeks. He stared for a moment, swallowed hard.

"Thorn?"

The thin lips struggled into a sad smile and he realized his mistake. He sighed.

"Ivy."

She nodded, lifted her touch from his arm and offered her help. He gawked at it for a few beats o' his heart, mind wanderin' for an instant to his lost friend, then he slid his hand into hers. She pulled, both firm and gentle, and helped him to his feet. As he rose, towerin' o'er her, he peered past her at the forest beyond.

And then hundreds o' Small Gods gathered behind her.

Horace's jaw dropped open. He spied far more o' them than before and wondered how he hadn't realized they followed them and not the scary, pasty things he'd suspected o' stalkin' them. He looked from his left to his right, turnin' his head slow as he scanned the gray-skinned fellas, their sizes and shapes varying only slightly from one to the next. When he finished observin' them, he found Ailyssa starin' at him, a smile on her lips and moisture sparklin' in her eyes. He stared at her for a few heartbeats before she leaned closer.

"I can see," she whispered, attention remainin' fixed on him. "I think it's because of them."

Her gaze flickered to the gatherin' o' small ones around them, but then returned to him. For his own self, Horace didn't look away. When her eyes found his again, she blinked, and a tear tumbled out, leavin' a wet and shimmery path down her face. Her smile broadened, and she raised a hand, set it against his cheek.

"This is the man who saved me."

Her words raised a sudden knot to his throat as though her mention o' it brought back ev'rythin' what'd happened since he first saw her and the hairy creature. She held her palm restin' on him for a few heartbeats and it might've been longer if not for Ivy tuggin' at his sleeve. They both redirected their attention toward the Small God gazin' up at them.

"Come."

She twisted her head to peek o'er her shoulder and took half a step. Without words or an agreement to do so, both the ol' sailor and the Barren Mother followed her. She led them through the underbrush, away from the green barrier, as the others o' her kind began movin' toward it. After ten paces, they passed through the advancin' line o' small gray men; probably not ev'ry one o' them was male, but he didn't have the time nor the inclination to be checkin'.

Horace craned his neck to look at them Small Gods what not so long ago he wouldn't've believed existed, yet here they was, in the pale flesh. He got but a glimpse before havin' to concentrate on his footin' lest a creeper grab hold o' him and send him tumblin' to the ground. He counted eighteen more steps before Ivy brought them to a stop.

"What's happenin'?" he asked, raisin' his gaze from watchin' his path to focus on the small woman.

She didn't respond with words, instead puttin' a finger o' one hand to her lips; she lifted her other arm and pointed. Horace turned, the heel o' his boot grindin' in the peat underfoot. His eyes met Ailyssa's as he did and he saw hers still glistened with thankful tears, but an expression o' wonder had added itself into the mix. They held each other's gaze for an instant before completin' the rotation to bring them to facin' the glowin' green curtain again.

Lookin' at it threatened to give the ol' sailor a shiver up his spine. But now he saw more reasons for shiverin'—the group o' small, gray people had formed a line in front o' the veil, stretchin' out forever in both directions. Their backs faced him and, so far as he knew, they might be standin' with their noses pressed against the magical barrier. He glanced toward his companions, but they both remained mesmerized by what were goin' on before them. Goosebumps crawled along Horace's forearms as silence overtook the forest; birds ceased chirpin', bugs stopped their buzzin', even the wind died off, leavin' leaves danglin' and inanimate.

It reminded him o' his last day standin' on the deck o' the Devil, not too long before he near got ate by another kind o' god. The memory made it impossible to fend off the shiver any longer. It quaked up his spine, chatterin' his teeth together inside his closed mouth when it got to his head. He inhaled a lengthy breath through his nostrils and would've sworn the forest's scent had turned to oceany brine.

His gaze found its way to the barrier and the gray ones arrayed out before it. The scene had changed slightly: each of Ivy's kind had raised their arms out to their sides. They wasn't close enough to each other to touch, but not more'n a fly might've squeezed through the spaces between the tips o' one finger and the next. They stood without the slightest o' tremor amongst them.

And then the sound began.

It weren't an indistinct noise what built—no buzz growin' into somethin' more. The chant started all at once, though Horace'd noticed no signal from any o' them, nor thought any could've seen such a sign had it occurred, facin' into the barrier as they was. It started nonetheless, emergin' from nowhere in a language what he'd never heard and held no hope o' decipherin'. Ailyssa's hand crept into his, the feel o' it so familiar after spendin' so much time tryin' to find their way around the forest. Her fingers squeezed his, but he knew she didn't do so to attract his attention—seekin' comfort from his touch, or offerin' it to him through hers, maybe both.

No matter—weren't nothin' comfortin' to him now, and he weren't in no place to give it as the chant continued and the ground rumbled beneath his feet. Emerald lightnin' flashed across the barrier, makin' him flinch. He managed a glance toward Ailyssa but, if she'd noticed him bein' startled, she gave no sign. Her gaze were glued to the scene before them, fixed and unwaverin'.

The deep green streaks zig-zagged along the surface again and again; Horace wondered if the chant made by the Small Gods were what caused it, or if somethin' else. He set his jaw, tensed his muscles, doin' his best not to let the irregular bursts make him jump, but without success. Each time it crackled along the barrier, his body jerked as though it were attached to him.

It near knocked him off his feet when the impossible happened.

XIX - Evalal - The Fall

I'M SORRY, MOTHER. *I failed you.*

The moments before death came for her stretched out, mortality tricking her, making her not want to die despite the renewal awaiting her on the other side, despite her surety she would soon suckle at the breast of the Mother of Death.

Forgive me, Goddess.

She'd seen the seasons turn but five times when the Mothers explained her life's role to her. A simple task, and her preparations for it had begun right away, her youth spent in study and training. But where did it get her? The seemingly straightforward duty laid out for her ending in failure and the end of her life imminent at the hands of a giant, naked man. The preparation and education meant nothing in the face of meeting a Small God fallen from the sky.

I should have done better for you, Danya.

Evalal's body remained tensed, awaiting the death blow at any instant, as her mind strove for an answer for how this might have gone differently. What could she have adjusted to make sure she completed the task of keeping Danya safe? Where did she stray from the path intended for her by Goddess and the Mother?

Why hasn't he killed me?

Too much time had passed. She considered prying her eyelids open to see if he'd changed his mind and resumed his trek toward the fallen princess, but they refused to do so. Before she convinced the muscles in her face to do her bidding, a breeze touched her cheek, brief and cool, like someone releasing their breath against her; there for half an instant, then gone. A sound accompanied it—the rustle and crunch of a foot treading upon brittle grass.

Her lids loosened, curiosity getting the better of fear, and one opened a crack. Light streamed through, blinding her at first, but she knew it meant the hulking man no longer loomed over her, blocking the sun. She opened the other eye, peered at the space where a Small God fallen from the sky had stood.

Evalal struggled up onto her elbow, her broken arm aching. She scanned the area between her and where Danya lay. Yellowing grass separated them and, above it, she saw bright flowers on the ends of tall stalks, vines twisted around them offering support. Streaks of red splashed across some places, and she spied the carcasses of animals who'd given themselves to preserve the princess and the Seed of Life's work. Nowhere did she see the pale flesh of a man. She spun to look the other direction; the action made her stomach lurch as pain shot through her wounded limb.

He'd covered half the distance between them and the barrier cutting the world off from the Green beyond, moving faster than she'd seen him. She unfolded herself, a knot in her leg tied by the strength of fear cinched in her thigh. She ignored it, hobbling to her feet, concentrating on keeping her balance. It took a few heartbeats for her body to correct itself, loosen up enough for her to stand without more than normal effort.

She squinted after him, wondering what had distracted his attention from her. The sinews in his back and buttocks flexed and released as he crossed the small expanse of grassy plain, his focus ahead as though he'd forgotten her and the princess. Evalal took a step after him, wobbled on her knotted leg, steadied herself, took another stride, then another. The tangle in her muscles sorted itself, and she increased her pace, cradling her arm against her stomach. Curiosity drove her even as she thought she might be better returning to the mound, protecting Danya should the fallen man change his mind and return to destroy her.

He stopped short of the veil, four or five paces remaining before he would have touched his nose against it. She took three more steps before halting herself, the length of fifteen horses between them. She didn't want to catch up to him and chance incurring his wrath, nor get so close as to prevent her from bolting should he refocus his attention on her.

His body went rigid, muscles tightening, bulging beneath his pale skin. He stood mimicking a statue until he turned his head first one way then the other. She stared at his back, her own body tensed and ready to flee should he face her. But what had drawn his scrutiny?

Evalal pried her eyes away from the man who fell from the sky, hesitantly satisfied that whatever he spied might occupy him long enough for her to discover what it was. Her gaze trailed over the tops of the blades of yellow, found the spot against the veil where he'd come to rest when he crashed. Nothing appeared out of the ordinary. She glanced at him—he still peered straight ahead.

She looked to his landing site again, thinking something about the grass had captured his regard, or an item he'd left. But she didn't recall him having anything with him and, naked as he was, he'd had no hiding spot. A moment later, a movement caught her eye.

It wasn't the swaying foliage or a stray forest animal—they were dead, had fled, or keeping their distance. This movement originated on the far side of the green wall, its significance muted by the glowing barrier. Evalal squinted, slid forward another step. The outline of a human form?

She took a second slow pace, then a third. Her eyes flickered from the shape to the man's back, ensuring he hadn't moved or turned to face her. He hadn't; he appeared as unaware of her presence as before. Her gaze returned to the spot, couldn't find the silhouette again for an instant, then it rectified itself.

A head. Two arms, two legs. A body of slight stature, and unclothed, light-skinned.

The girl sucked a surprised breath, the air whistling between her teeth. Her mouth flooded with saliva and she swallowed it away.

The figure raised its arms to the sides, its angular chin tipped upward, but it wasn't alone. Similar figures stood to either side of it in the same pose, each of them standing close enough to the other their outstretched hands appeared to be a finger's breadth from touching. Now she was aware of them, they became easier to see, and Evalal realized there were more of them. Many more.

The line of small beings stretched to the edge of her vision in both directions.

Their heights varied only slightly from one to the next, as did their overall size. Easy to mistake one for another. These—creatures? Men?—were what had captured and held the man from the sky's attention, and Evalal understood who she looked upon.

The Small Gods.

No matter who told the tales or how many times she heard them, a vast chasm lay between the faith of knowing and the reality of seeing. Her jaw slackened, mouth falling open. She wanted to move closer, get a better view of these creatures she'd heard about but never seen, could never be sure existed until now, but fear outweighed curiosity. She preferred to have said a sense of duty to the princess kept her from moving, but she knew it wasn't the truth—the pale-skinned man's presence prevented it.

He continued ignoring her, his gaze sweeping along the green barrier, observing the small men on the other side. Evalal looked at him in time to see the muscles in his legs and buttocks flex as he moved forward, striding toward the veil with purposeful steps. A streak of verdant lightning flashed across its surface, silent but bright, diverting the girl's attention once again.

Another followed, traveling the same path as the first, then others in other places. Each ran skyward from the ground, shimmering over the smooth veil before disappearing. More followed, traveling the opposite direction. One formed in front of her, starting out a circle before two arms shot out to the sides, one streaking windward, the other leeward. The green veins of light burned impressions upon her eyes as they shot away from her to disappear. She wondered if they might go on forever.

Each streak flickered and disappeared in silence, no clap of thunder following each tongue of lightning the way it did during the storms of third season. Only the rustle of the wind in the grass disturbed the quiet until the man who fell from the sky pounded his fists against the magic barrier.

They thumped against it, sending spider webs of light crackling across its smooth plain, their sound a stark difference from the silent lines she thought created by the creatures standing on the other side.

He struck it again, a third time, sparkling and popping. A hum began, low at first, more a feeling in her chest than a tone in her head. It swelled until it became the buzz of a distant cloud of flies. The lightning grew thicker, more frequent, and the man paused in beating the wall to cover his ears. He leaned back, opened his mouth, and let out a loud groan—the only sound she'd heard from him since he'd begged for water. Not even when teeth or antlers penetrated his flesh did he make a noise.

His cry drew out, as though he thought the noise might deter the mounting din of the hum and buzz. Where did it come from? The barrier itself?

Evalal looked away from him, peered through the translucence of the green wall at the small figures on the other side. Their positions had not changed—arms held out, heads pitched back, eyes raised toward the top of the veil—except for the three in front of the man. This trio lowered their chins to stare at their adversary, and she saw their thin lips moving. She wondered if they spoke to him—if he heard them through the barrier—or to each other, until she realized their mouths moved in unison, the three of them forming the same words over and over again.

Chanting.

He removed his hands from his ears, hammered against the wall again. His fists and forearms struck with the sound of thunder, emerald arteries extending from the spot in all directions, snakes escaping their nest. The ground rumbled beneath Evalal's feet, a tremor, but enough to startle her into repositioning herself. She stared, mouth open, eyes flickering from pale man to the paler figures behind the green wall.

The air felt thick, difficult for her to inhale, sound traveling through it more slowly. She raised her good hand to the front of her face, wiggled her fingers, the actions slowed by the viscous air. The man fallen from the sky pulled his hands away from the barrier, his movement similarly muted, then brought them against it.

The speed at which he moved didn't appear enough to do more than hurt a fly, but the thunder crashed again. Veins appeared; this time they weren't snakes fleeing, but cracks which started and stayed. He struck it again, and the cracks turned to fissures. Once more and they became chasms.

Evalal realized she still held her hand in front of her face and let her arm drop. The hum and buzz grew to a constant moan, the sound of wind blowing in haunted woods. Thunder crashed again, the ground shuddered. Panic gripped the girl, and she stumbled away a step. Her gaze darted along the fabled barrier, its once serene surface now a mess of cracks and breaks like a pottery bowl left too long in the kiln. Her eyes widened. The man retracted his fists again, thrust them toward the wall.

They impacted with an ear-splitting stroke of thunder twice as loud as the ones before.

And the veil shattered.

XX - Kuneprius - The Evenstar

*T*HE CIRCLE OF PRIESTS disbanded, the newest initiates leaving first, followed in succession by the more senior amongst them. When the time came for Kuneprius to go, Kristeus laid a hand on his shoulder, stopping him until the emigration finished and only those two and the golem—with Vesisdenperos trapped inside—remained.

Kuneprius shifted from foot to foot, glanced from the smooth dun eyes of the mud-beast to the corpse of the Small God.

He had a name. Thorn.

His body lay slack and drained of blood while a blissful smile lingered on his face, as though he found death a pleasant thing. The sculptor's keeper found it difficult to divert his gaze from his satisfied countenance. What had prompted it? Had life been a burden for this gray man, a thing thankful for the ending? Or did he know more about death and what came after than Kuneprius did? To be fair, he knew nothing of the end of life, other than now shouldering responsibility for the deaths of two—the woman-soldier who'd protected Vesisdenperos as a babe, and this Small God. Their demise at his hands brought an acidity to his mouth. He may have stared at the corpse, trying to solve the riddle of its expression for the rest of time, if Kristeus didn't lay his hand upon his shoulder again.

"Walk with us, keeper," the High Priest said, prompting him the same direction the others had taken to leave the sacrificial altar.

Hesitant, he twisted, guided by insistent pressure from the High Priest's touch. The space between them and the arched doorway leading out of the temple lay empty, the other Brothers having hastened out with the ritual complete. The bottoms of Kuneprius' sandals dragged on the colored stones as he allowed the High Priest to guide him. They'd already singled him out, forced him to be the one to sacrifice the Small God, Thorn—what more could they want from him? He inhaled a shuddering breath and turned his attention to his feet, struggling to lift them when his legs had little desire for the effort. Without meaning to, he began counting stones of matching color, starting with ones the shade of blood.

One. Two. Three. Is it blood?

The hand of Kristeus remained on his shoulder while the golem followed, each step marked by the quiet slap of the muddy soles of his feet on rock floor. They walked in silence until they reached the arched doorway leading out to the flat clearing surrounded by the wall of ocean. Kuneprius counted one hundred and thirty-two red stones by the time they stopped.

"Let the evenstar go first."

The sculptor's keeper acquiesced, stepping to the side to allow the golem a clear path through the portal. This near the opening, the noise of sea water rushing toward the sky roared more loudly than at the center of the temple. Kuneprius attempted to peer out the doorway but the living statue stepped in front of him, its gray-brown back blocking his view.

The mud man crouched to get through the arch. As soon as it passed through, a cheer rose, a roar loud enough to disguise the rush of water. Kristeus added his voice to the cacophony, the noise far too close to his ear for Kuneprius' liking.

How do so few Brothers make so much commotion?

The golem basked in the ovation before crossing the stone bridge and stepping aside upon reaching the other end. The High Priest increased the pressure on the keeper's shoulder, prompting him forward. Kuneprius resisted at first, fear gripping his spine. His mind raced through his previous life—raising Vesisdenperos, mentoring him as he grew and learned, the heartache when he gave himself to animate his creation, and then Thorn's death. His throat tightened and, if it weren't for the proximity of Kristeus and the other Brothers, he might have broken into tears. He clenched his teeth, determined to control them, and stepped through the archway onto the span.

The cheer continued and Kuneprius' mouth fell open. The couple dozen who had accompanied them to the temple and joined the circle when they forced him to kill the Small God had grown to a number greater than his ability to estimate. Hundreds? A thousand? Maybe more. Men, horses, and wagons as far as he could see. They stretched on and on across the flat land to the sea wall in the distance; more than he'd ever seen in one place.

The High Priest's palm pressed against his back, ushering him on when he wasn't aware his forward progress had stopped. He stepped with caution, the noise near deafening but cognizant of the water rushing under the bridge. He got to the end of the crossing and Kristeus guided him to stand beside the golem. The man made of mud raised one hand and the cheers ceased, cut off like a length of string severed by a sharp knife.

"Our time is nigh," the evenstar said through the statue's mouth, its rock-dragged-against-rock voice carrying across the expanse filled with men, wagons, and horses. "Go forth and prepare to meet my brothers."

The throng turned as though they had rehearsed the entire performance, then they began funneling out through a narrow opening at the far end of the area. There, the wall of water parted, but Kuneprius saw nothing more. The High Priest's hand remained on him, but he exerted no pressure. To his other side, the golem lowered his arm, watched the sea of men receding across the plain. When he spoke again, he didn't turn his head toward them.

"Go with the Brothers, High Priest."

Out of the corner of his eye, Kuneprius saw Kristeus nod.

"Shall I bring him?"

"No. Leave the sculptor's keeper with me."

The High Priest removed his hand from Kuneprius' back and stepped in front of them, bowed to the golem. The sculptor's keeper fought the urge to count the spots on the man's head, visible through the wisps of white hair lazily strewn across his scalp. He wondered if the High Priest had always appeared so old.

He turned on his heel and hurried after the others, his black robe flapping around his legs. When he reached the line of men, it swallowed him up amongst them, making him disappear from view. Kuneprius fought the urge to shiver despite the lack of chill in the air.

They stood beside each other, both of them regarding the army flowing off the plain, grains of sand squeezing through the neck of an hourglass. The hulking golem loomed over Kuneprius, his presence as much sensed as seen. The scent of the mud forming his vessel penetrated his nose through the aroma of briny sea water surrounding them. After a time, the brute turned to him, his muddy body slurping like a foot treading in a puddle. Kuneprius didn't face him.

"You were always a good subject, keeper."

Without realizing, he'd begun counting the men leaving, the number much more tolerable with so many of them having already gone. He stopped, directed his attention toward the living statue, and regarded the empty eyes, the emotionless and flat gray features. He looked away.

"You helped liberate the sculptor from the Goddess' caravan, then raised and mentored him as if your own. In this, no one could have asked more of you."

He paused, the grating voice echoing in Kuneprius' ears. The keeper inhaled, mud and salt filling his nostrils.

"But things have gone awry, haven't they? Since Vesisdenperos gave himself to the vessel of my return."

His breath caught, and he turned toward the hulking figure. "No, I—"

"I've been watching you. And that which I didn't see, the sculptor has told me."

His heart sped and the earlier threat of tears he'd fought against returned. This time he did not hide them. Why had Vesisdenperos betrayed him? He had dedicated every moment of his existence to the sculptor's well-being, given up any vestige of his own life to provide his comfort and success.

"I know you spilled your seed while thinking of the woman, and you wished to help the Small God. Knowing this, how can we trust you?"

The keeper's knees wobbled, and he faltered a step. The golem's face remained expressionless, exactly how Vesisdenperos had fashioned it, but the behemoth's chest moved and roiled. Kuneprius stared, tears smearing the sight into a gray blur. He blinked, rubbed his arm across his eye. The movement abated, leaving behind a shape—the ridge of a brow, two divots for eyes, the bump of a nose, the lines of a mouth. A likeness he'd spent his life caring for, nurturing, teaching.

The lips parted, formed a soundless word.

Run.

The keeper's instant of hesitation before he spun away to follow the command of his one-time companion was all the golem needed. It reached out a gray arm layered with muscles fashioned by Vesisdenperos and sausage-thick fingers grasped Kuneprius around the throat, cutting off his breath. He scratched at it, trying to break free, mud filling the spaces under his fingernails. The thing lifted him until his sandals scraped the ground, useless. His eyes bulged, his vision blurred, and air brushed his cheeks, drying the tears streaking his skin.

Icy water shocked him as the golem dunked him headfirst into the channel around the temple. Salt stung his eyes, scoured his tongue, but the beast's hand remained clutched on his throat, holding him under. He grasped at the thick fingers, yanked and pulled to release their grip. On his back facing up, he saw foggy streaks of light cross the sky through the sting and the blurred lens of sea water.

And then everything went black.

ell

Vesisdenperos watched in horror through the golem's eyes.

He'd done what he could to warn his friend when he realized what the living statue's new inhabitant intended, but it was too late. All he had left was watching the man who'd raised him battle against the behemoth's grip. A struggle destined to end quickly. Fluid entered his lungs, his resistance waned, and his arms dropped, splashing in the briny water of the moat surrounding the temple. In control of the golem, the evenstar held Kuneprius' limp body under a while longer, ensuring his life extinguished.

Even without a form of his own, something twisted inside Vesisdenperos. He ached to cry out in anguish, to wail and ask why, but he possessed no more ability to do so than he'd had to warn his friend. The feeling took his essence like a rope wrapped around him, binding him to keep him from experiencing his grief.

The golem released his friend's lifeless body, left it half in the moat, stood watching it. If it did so for some reason of its own, or to torture the sculptor, he couldn't have said for sure. Not until the mud statue extended one leg, pressed a toe against the corpse, and pushed firmly enough for it to over-balance and slide into the water. Kuneprius bobbed at the surface for a moment, his wide, unseeing eyes staring toward the sky before he sank, slipping into the moat's dark depths.

"This," a voice said. It didn't speak out loud, but filled the interior of the golem. "This is what happens to those who betray. Those who don't believe."

The twist that would have been inside him if he had insides tightened, accompanied by the uncomfortable and frustrating sensation of wanting to cry and not being able to.

"You believe, don't you, sculptor?"

He couldn't think how to answer. Instead of replying, he fought to control his thoughts, keep them from betraying his grief and sense of loss. Surely the evenstar must know everything he felt, all he thought. Were they not one inside the beast?

It didn't seem he expected a response. He turned the clay body from the moat, glancing toward the sky at the streaks of light crossing the firmament before striding across the plain. The other priests and brothers had exited the narrow opening, found their way out of the open space within the sea, the holy place known as Teva Stavoklis. As the animated statue, brought to life through Vesisdenperos' literal sweat and blood, caught up to the others, the sculptor diverted his attention away from what his creation saw. His world became the dull shade of gray of the mud he'd used to create this thing imprisoning him.

A thing he wished he'd never made.

XXI - Evalal – The Barren Mother

*S*HATTERED *MAY NOT* HAVE been the right word, Evalal would later decide. Exploded might suit better.

When the man's fists hit the last time, the green veil burst into uncountable pieces, like a shell on the beach ground beneath a heel. She shrieked and lifted her arm to protect her face, closing her eyes and waiting for fragments to rain on her, cutting her with sharp edges, perhaps ending her life.

None struck her as five rapid heartbeats sped by. She opened her lids and peered over top of her raised limb.

The shards and splinters of the magical barrier hung in the air, shimmering in the sunlight, dazzling as it reflected off edge after edge of the tiny surfaces. Broken, yet the pieces stayed in place, held by the thickness of the atmosphere. Evalal attempted to draw a breath and found it impossible.

Her gaze flickered between the man—his fists frozen against the wall, a concussive wave rippling outward along its surface from the contact—and the gray figures on the other side. The cracks and crannies and shards turning the barrier nearly opaque made them more difficult to see, but she realized they had lowered their arms and their chins, each one of them directing their scrutiny toward him.

Waiting.

Mesmerized, she watched the glimmer and glint until the pieces of the shattered veil fell. They tumbled together, a wave falling from the sky, but not even the tiniest bit of it hit the ground. The once mighty barrier rolled up and folded on itself until it disappeared. The hum and buzz stopped, the last roll of thunder dissipated; silence returned to the meadow.

Evalal stared, open-mouthed, seeing clearly for the first time the small people previously hidden by the green of the wall. Their skin was gray, as she'd suspected, their flesh smooth and free of blemish, like the surface of an egg boiled until hard. Taut muscle rippled beneath, revealing the sinewy strength of wild things while intelligence gleamed in their eyes.

Every one of them as well as the man who fell held their places, frozen in this unbelievable tableau. A Small God from the sky, the Small Gods of the Green. Evalal was seeing something no one had ever seen, a sight few would have believed. Her heart hammered against her ribs, breath burned in her chest.

A gray fellow twitched, the sudden tiny action acting as a signal, an impetus, because all of them moved. They dashed forward without sound from their lungs and mouths, small feet beating a cadence on the ground as they rushed the pale man who stood more than twice the height of the tallest of them.

He had time to raise his arms in protection before they swarmed him. The initial wave seized him by the legs; the next climbed on the first, using them as a stepping stool to encircle his torso. They flowed around him like sand dumped into a container with a rock, and it happened in silence save for the slap of bare hands and feet on bare flesh. The man uttered no sound; the little people said nothing. They moved as though controlled by a single consciousness. It took a matter of moments before he disappeared, his pale and slender frame consumed by a swirl of bodies paler and lither than his.

Gone from her sight, he finally made a noise. It started out as a dull moan, but grew, the tone and volume rising until it became a howl. Evalal clenched her teeth hard, making her jaw ache. Her gut knotted as she watched, unable to redirect her gaze. She imagined what was happening to the man who fell from the sky beneath the writhing heap of gray men. Was his blood being spilled? His bones broken? Limbs torn from his body?

Her stomach lurched at the thoughts, and she fought the urge to call out, beseech them to stop. Her entire life, they had raised her to respect all living things alongside her preparation for her role in saving the world from the return of the Small Gods. But here she stood, one of those creatures possibly being rent limb from limb, standing by in debate with herself over which was more important: the preservation of a single life or what might mean the safety of many.

Her gut churned, but she did nothing more than observe, her voice stilled even as her mind struggled. She couldn't have said whether he was truly a living thing. She'd seen him crash to the ground from the sky and survive; watched him gored on antlers, bitten by sharp teeth and walk away unscathed. He'd lived through things no human should endure—he couldn't be a man, so did not have life as she knew it.

The justification did not ease her discomfort.

The gray men at the top of the pile climbed off, then the next level, and the next. As the layers peeled off, Evalal tensed, waiting to see if she'd discover pools of blood, torn flesh, shattered bones, but she found none of those. In fact, she spied nothing but flattened grass. The space taken up by the man fallen from the sky lay empty.

What did they do to him?

She swallowed hard, saliva clicking in her throat, and one of the small gray men turned toward her as though it had been as loud as a clap of thunder. He raised his arm, extended a finger and made a sound. At another time, she may have recognized the word but, with fear crashing in around her, its meaning became as foreign as the call of a bird.

Not to the others. Almost as one, the gray men faced her, heads swiveling on necks, feet shifting, trampling grass. They stared at her for what felt longer than it was. The thought of fleeing occurred to her, but her body did nothing with the possibility her mind provided. But for the wild beating of her heart in her chest and the breeze stirring her hair, she didn't move as the closest took the first strides in her direction. A sour taste filled her mouth and a droplet of sweat ran into her eye.

Other gray men behind him mobilized, though they weren't in the same rush as when the green wall crashed to the ground. They walked toward her, steps measured, knowing she couldn't flee from them no matter how much she wanted to.

But they didn't swarm her. Instead, they created a circle around her, standing shoulder to shoulder and blocking her line of sight. Only distant views remained where she stretched to look over them; she spied two shapes unlike the men surrounding her. She saw only the tops of their heads—one sprinkled with sparse gray hair, the other fuller dark hair, but cut short. Evalal ignored the figures near her and concentrated on the others as they approached.

When they got close, the small men in front of them parted, creating an opening in the circle. A man entered first, his cheeks covered by nearly white whiskers, the skin on his forehead weathered as that of someone who'd spent much time in the sun. He moved at a slow pace, but she guessed from his expression it was because of exhaustion rather than purpose. A woman trailed behind him, holding his hand as he led her into the circle. Evalal recognized her immediately, dropped to one knee and bowed her head.

"Barren Mother," she whispered.

"Rise, child," the woman said, "and take me to the seed."

XXII - Ailyssa - Seed of Life

THE GIRL—EVALAL, THOUGH AILYSSA didn't understand how she knew her name—took her by the hand and led her away from the spot where, moments before, a magical barrier erected to protect the Small Gods from the outside world had fallen.

They picked a route through the beaten grass, parts of it tinged a rusty red. The former N'th Ailyssa Ra wondered about the coloring until she spied the twisted corpse of an elk lying to the right of their path, its black eyes staring toward the sky, unseeing, like her curse until so recently. The thought made her wish for time to relish her rediscovered sight, but urgency pushed against the inside of her chest, her heart beating against her ribs as though the organ led her rather than the girl. She pressed her lips together, inhaled slowly and released her breath, wished Horace's hand was in hers the way it had been so much lately. She resisted the urge to look back to find out if he followed them or not.

Dry grass crunched under her feet, louder to her ears than it should have been, but everything around her seemed to have heightened in intensity. The yellowed blades shimmered gold, the rusty red of dried blood shone an opalescent ruby. The grassy scent, the pungent odor of her own unwashed body, the aroma of damp soil enhanced her vision. Was this her mind's reaction to her sight returning after having it stolen from her for so long?

Over the girl's shoulder, she spied their destination. What appeared from her perspective a mound covered in flowers standing as tall as the grass lay ahead of them. As they got closer, the bouquet of the vast variety of plants and buds reached her, engulfing the other smells. Her nose singled out certain perfumes from others: honeysuckle and rose, lilac, wisteria, and sweet alyssum, which she'd imagined the Sisters had named her for.

Recognizing the aromas made her breath catch in her throat and threatened to bring her feet to a halt. These were the scents of the prayer garden at Olvana, a place where she'd spent so much of her life, and her last memory of being N'th Ailyssa Ra who belonged to the Goddess until she proved unable to produce a second daughter for her.

And yet I am here. Chosen.

The thought made her shiver, and Evalal glanced at her. Ailyssa nodded at the girl, confirming nothing was amiss and encouraging her to continue, all this communicated in a gesture though she lacked surety of any of it. Part of her wished she was still in Juddah's barn. There, she'd been scared, but safe in a strange way, the steady breathing of the nameless man to calm her and confirm they both still lived.

She forced the reminiscence from her mind. She realized death had awaited her in Juddah's barn, and only more unfortunate and awful events had prevented it. She shook her head to loosen the memory, but a sliver of it remained.

What happened to the man with no name?

After she fell through the veil—before first the beast, then Horace found her—the world on the other side disappeared, her vision ending with the lack of his touch. The sounds and textures of life had gone, too, leaving her more alone than she'd felt since those days waiting for her inevitable expulsion from Olvana. She thought of those chalk marks on the wall, unbroken by her blood, and the emptiness inside her, each fresh line drawn etching itself into her soul. Falling through the barrier had created similar feelings in her, but instead of small lines, it felt as though someone had tried to lop her spirit in two.

Ailyssa inhaled, expanding her tight chest as far as her ribs allowed. The sigh brought the odors again, and she fought to suppress the memory of the prayer garden. A season had turned since such thoughts might be pleasant and comforting. So much had happened, and her fear of what lay ahead added foreboding to the unpleasantness.

The tall grass on either side of them fell away, opening into a small, near-circular clearing around the flowering mound. She peered over the girl's shoulder again and corrected herself: this was no knoll covered by flowers, but a mound made of flowers. Evalal stopped before they reached the edge of it and Ailyssa halted beside her, still clasping her hand.

"What is this?"

The girl didn't respond immediately. While she awaited the answer, Ailyssa's eyes found their way across the tangle of flowers, stalks, leaves, runners, and vines. Jade foliage, blooms of crimson, chartreuse, goldenrod, lilac, and so many more. Vines twisted and interacted as though living creatures displaying their fondness for each other. She spied a plump strawberry amongst them, and the deep purple of a cluster of blueberries, and her stomach rumbled at the sight. How long since she last ate? Horace had done his best to forage for her, but shoots and berries provided sustenance for only so long.

And the smell. Ailyssa chose not to inhale through her nose to avoid those aromas prompting more memory. As she drew breath through her teeth, her tongue tasted them, identifying each scent as though she had been doing so in this manner for her entire life. She pressed her lips together tight, shook her head, and prepared to ask the girl the question again, as she must not have heard. Before she opened her mouth, Evalal spoke.

"Here lies Danya, princess of the Windward Kingdom. And with her, the Seed of Life."

Ailyssa's jaw fell open, and she stared at the thicket of flowers and leaves. She inhaled more than once, this time ignoring the smells, avoiding the memories. She understood Goddess had meant for her to be here, every step and challenge meant to prepare her for what she must do. But that knowledge and certainty did nothing to guide her, or indicate what she should do next.

She looked from the knotted garden to the girl beside her, but Evalal stared reverently at the spot where the princess lay dead beneath those blooms. Behind them, small feet shuffled in dry grass and she stopped herself from turning around to seek Horace and the comfort seeing him might offer.

What do I do?

Evalal's hand slipped from hers and the girl faded back a step. Ailyssa glanced at her, then returned her attention to the mound. No wind touched her face, but the blossoms and leaves shifted as though blown by a stiff breeze. A thick vine fell away from the rest of the tangle, thumping against the ground on a spot of rusty grass. It lay motionless for a moment as she stared at it before the tip curled up and its entire length rolled toward where it had come from, a finger beckoning her. She inhaled a surprised breath, not knowing if the plant's unusual action or its movement prompting her to take a stride forward had caused it.

A second step followed the first, then a third. Two more paces brought her to the edge of the muddled garden. She heard words spoken behind her, thought they carried Horace's tone and lilt, but her attention refused to be torn away to discern what he said, or if the words belonged to him at all. Maybe it was a memory—of him or someone else. Perhaps the ghost of one of her sons speaking to her from the other side.

The thick vine extended itself again, this time hovering above the ground, reaching up to curl itself around the fingers of her left hand. She looked down at it, half expecting it to twist its way up her arm, yank it from its socket, but its touch was benign. It tugged gently.

Ailyssa resisted at first, out of fear, but also because she recognized nowhere to rest without crushing one of the delicate blossoms or dainty leaves. The vine prompted her again, still tenderly, but with more firmness this time, enough to tug her off balance and force her into taking a step. She pressed her lips together at the thought of destroying the exquisite flowers with her clumsy step, but a broad leaf rose to meet her, cradled her foot with surprising strength. The vine pulled again, and another leaf accepted her next tread.

She needed no further encouragement.

The Barren Mother took three more steps to reach the apex of the mounded garden, each met by a leaf stronger than it should have been. When she reached the top, she turned. As her gaze swept over the grassland, she observed the creatures who had forfeited their lives to protect the seed which lay somewhere beneath her feet. A lancet of pain pricked her heart for each one of them and she silently blessed them for their sacrifice.

The Small Gods fanned out across the meadow, stretching to where the veil once stood. Not long past, Ailyssa would have said Goddess erected the barrier to keep them in, but she realized now they'd formed it to keep the rest of the world out, to protect themselves. By facilitating its fall, these creatures served themselves up to the possibility of death as surely as the elk and other animals lying dead around them. She sighed a sad breath, whispered a prayer for their protection.

Horace stood with them, Ivy's hand holding his—for comfort, to keep him from rushing to her. Ailyssa smiled at his knotted gray hair and his beard grown wild in the time since he'd fallen into the sea. He stared at her in return, appearing as the proverbial—nearly literal—fish out of water amongst the hairless creatures surrounding him. His lips moved but, whether he spoke aloud or meant to and failed, Ailyssa could not discern. She wished to go to him, touch his face, tell him everything would be all right; she wasn't sure she'd be telling him the truth.

The vine curled around her hand released itself, snaked its way around her waist as others twisted about her legs. The combination of vines and leaves supported her as they tilted her back, the old sailor slipping from her view. Before he did, she said a prayer for him, wishing him life and happiness and everything a hero deserved.

He disappeared from her sight, then the Small Gods, the grassland, the forest, until the endless blue stretching out above her filled her vision. Leaves and flowers caressed her back, supporting her. Love spilled out of their petals and into her, soothing the fear she'd made so much a part of her since her expulsion from Olvana. Loss, sadness, disappointment vanished as stems and leaves, pistil and stamen touched her arms and legs, flowed over her as though she'd lain on a beach and the ocean lapped up and over her.

A dim streak of light cut a path across the washed-out sky above her and the Barren Mother closed her eyes, waited for the garden to take her.

XXIII - Trenan - Goddess Warriors

*I*N *THE MORNING,* THE rain tapered to a mist, dampening soldiers and spirits as readily as did the fat raindrops that fell through the night.

Somewhere behind the bank of clouds, Trenan appreciated the sun shone, but as the men struck camp and returned to the road to Draekfarren, he wondered if it would ever shine again in his world.

Two riders struck out ahead of the rest, ranging far enough along the track Trenan no longer saw them from his place in the middle of the pack. Osis had offered for him to accompany the sergeant at the head of the small column, but the master swordsman insisted on riding nearer to the prince.

He was glad he had when the first of the dead reappeared at the side of the road.

The face stared at him from between two trees, hair stuck to his forehead by the fresh blood oozing from a gash in his scalp. Trenan's breath caught when he spied the fellow. He scanned the surrounding soldiers to find out if anyone else noticed the apparitions. It appeared no one did—except Teryk.

The prince gazed at the phantom, head turning as they rode past to keep his attention on him. Trenan gulped hard and closed his eyes. How did these abominations present themselves? The dead didn't rise, ghosts weren't real. It must be an effect of the black priests' magic, but why did Teryk catch sight of them at some times, then not others?

More appeared at the side of the track, glimpsed between trees and brush. They peered from behind trunks, sometimes watched him in the open where anyone might see them, if anyone else could. The master swordsman did his best to keep his eyes trained straight ahead, but it proved near impossible. The dead drew his gaze, as did Teryk. Irrational guilt welled up inside him and more than once he considered climbing from his mount, approaching whatever slain soldier stood in front of him to beg their forgiveness. He fought the urge, instead clamping his back teeth together, the muscles in his jaw knotting with the effort of remaining ahorse.

They hadn't been riding long before a shout from the head of the group drew his attention.

"Trenan!"

Osis' voice startled him, thankfully pulled his scrutiny from the most recent accusing spirit, this one with his lower jaw and his right eye missing. Trenan didn't remember whether he'd left the man in this state or if his injuries might have occurred after the master swordsman had killed him. Either way, it relieved him when the riders moved aside for him to urge his horse forward and away from him to catch up to Osis.

The sergeant slowed his mount for Trenan to approach, but did not resume his speed when the swordsman did. Instead, he pulled on the reins, halting his steed, then holding up a clenched fist indicating for the rest of the troop to do the same. Trenan stopped beside him, glanced at his friend.

"What's happening?"

Osis gestured with his head down the road ahead.

Before he looked, a shiver ran up Trenan's spine. He knew what he'd find if he turned his gaze along the track: a group of dead men he'd killed gathered in the lane, blocking their way. They'd revealed themselves to the others, ready to punish them for the death Trenan alone had brought to them.

He sucked a deep breath through his nose, held it as he gripped the reins tight in his hand and forced his head to redirect his gaze along the track.

Horsemen clogged the road ahead, distant enough they appeared as dark shapes in the mist. Spirits of the horses and riders he'd killed? They awaited too far away to discern wounds and blood, split heads or cloven arms. His stomach clenched, and he fought to keep from shivering.

"Who is this?" he asked, then worried a shake in his voice might have betrayed his fear.

If Osis heard any quiver, he made no sign. "We'll find out soon." He nodded down the road again.

The riders began moving toward them in an ordered formation, unrushed. Osis rested his fingers on the hilt of his sword and prompted his horse forward. Out of instinct, Trenan's hand fell to where his weapon should be, but found his scabbard empty. He gulped a lump of saliva down his throat and put his heels to his own steed.

The other soldiers followed, the slosh and slap of hooves in mud loud to Trenan's ears. He glanced to the side of the track, glimpsed a man with a gaping wound in his chest, heart and lungs exposed, then redirected his eyes along the road. At least he couldn't see any grisly wounds on the riders ahead—not yet.

The space between them closed, but with the grayness of the day and the mist of precipitation, anything more than their shape remained hidden. Trenan squinted, but doing so did nothing to aid him in identifying them. So far as he could tell, they hadn't drawn their weapons; they either meant no harm or harbored no worry over the troop of king's soldiers. Dead men had no reason to fear.

Soon they came close enough Trenan saw none of the riders bore wounds, their armor free of blood. But they wore no markings to identify them. Now they drew near, their leader halted, those following did the same without any signal to do so. Osis stopped, too.

"My name is Osis, sergeant-at-arms of the King's Army. My men and I are on urgent business of the kingdom. Clear the track so we may pass."

"Your scouts are safe and unharmed," the point rider responded, the voice of higher pitch than Trenan expected from a slain man, or any other man.

His heart jumped a beat.

Yoli! How is she alive?

He tensed in the saddle, the faces of dead men lining the side of the road forgotten. He opened his mouth to call out to her, to ask her how she yet lived, but he thought better of it and closed it without speaking. How would he explain knowing this woman to Osis?

The sergeant-at-arms prompted his horse forward a few paces and stopped again.

"I wasn't concerned for the fate of my scouts. Until now. What is the meaning of this?"

"You will not be returning to Draekfarren," Yoli said, her voice confident and unwavering. "You are coming with us."

Osis barked a laugh bereft of humor. "I think not, young lady. We both know you and your friends are no match for soldiers of the king. I might have you thrown in the dungeon for stopping us while on a mission for His

Majesty, but I am in friendly spirits today, so I will ask you once again to clear the way. Do so and no harm nor punishment will come to you or your group."

Her eyes flickered to Trenan, then to Osis again. His own gaze darted from Yoli to the others with her, counting them to make sure all the women had survived the encounter with the black priests. It surprised him to count thirty of them—half a dozen more than when they'd left Ikkundana with him.

"No harm will be done anyone," she said. "But you will not be leaving. We outnumber and surround you, so you will do as I say."

Both of the men turned in their saddles, looked past their own column of warriors to find another group of mounted soldiers behind them. Trenan squinted, attempting to determine the number, but distance and the narrowness of the track prevented him from getting an accurate estimate. At least as many as stood before them, to be sure.

How did they get there?

He'd seen no paths leading onto the road from either side, but the phantoms of those he'd killed watching from the fringe had consumed much of his attention.

Why is Yoli here doing this?

Osis turned toward Trenan, caught his eye. The sergeant's features went hard, his mouth pressed into a tight line, the muscles in his jaw and cheeks bunching. He held the master swordsman's gaze as though he awaited his friend to speak. Trenan didn't. Osis' lips peeled away from his clenched teeth and he faced the women in front of them. Without a word, he yanked his sword from its scabbard.

The female soldiers both ahead and behind did the same, the damp air filling with the hiss of steel rubbing against leather. The men in their troop clambered to free their own weapons, the move executed more noisily and with far less grace than the women had done it. A heartbeat later, Yoli, Teryk, and Trenan were the only ones without swords in their hands.

"Let us pass or endure the consequences," Osis grated.

Yoli prompted her horse closer, her expression reflecting nothing but resolve. She stopped, turned her mount sideways to further block the track; the move left her facing Trenan. He gazed at her face, a swell of pride he didn't deserve to feel growing in his chest. When she directed her attention to him, he felt as though he might burst.

"Tell them to put their weapons away, Trenan."

He swallowed, saliva clicking in his throat, and looked to Osis. The sergeant-at-arms' gaze jerked toward him, eyes wide.

"You know this woman?"

Trenan froze, unsure what to do.

"Everyone knows of the one-armed master swordsman," Yoli said, saving him. "And everyone knows he commands the King's Army. Now tell them to sheath their weapons before someone cuts themselves."

He made a show of surveying the group before them, then standing in his stirrups to peer at those behind them. She was right: the women outnumbered them, and he had firsthand knowledge of how well trained they were. Should it come to a fight, the men of the king's army would likely be bested. He didn't think she'd attack, but Osis didn't realize that. As he settled into his saddle, his gaze dragged across the shadowy dead watching from the edge of the trees, their pale, placid faces fixed on his. Trenan suppressed a shudder.

"Put them away," the master swordsman said over his shoulder, then directed his attention to the sergeant-at-arms. "Let's find out what the woman has to say."

A murmur ran through the group. Another time, he'd have chastised his charges for even such minor disagreement but, truthfully, there would have been no such dissent at other times. Whatever the priests had done to him must show to them, that was the only explanation. He glanced to the edge of the track, at the dead men with their bloodied faces, their horrific wounds he'd inflicted seasons in the past, and thought he saw them smiling.

XXIV - Ishla – Mother of Death

*H*E REALIZED SHE DIDN'T want him to follow, but he'd taken on keeping her safe, and doing a suitable job meant more opportunity, maybe cushier assignments. If such things existed. Plus, if she preferred him not to watch out for her, why did she drop those hints suggesting she'd be operating outside the king's approval? No matter what either of them might think, the queen needed him around, wanted him protecting her.

Strylor peeked round the corner, careful to stay out of the queen's sight. It turned out he needn't have worried; she moved along in the shadows halfway down the block, her form nearly invisible in the gray cloak she'd donned before sneaking out of Draekfarren.

When he'd first seen her leave her chamber, he acted as though he intended to heed her wishes and stay put, but the things she said about finding the truth herself and the folded garment under her arm gave him reason enough to ignore her command. He'd crept after her in the castle, keeping a reasonable distance between them so as not to alert her to his presence. At one point, he thought he'd lost her, because he wasn't aware of the tunnel. If she hadn't left the trapdoor in the wine room's floor ajar, he'd have missed it altogether.

Following her through the underground passage proved both easier and trickier. Locating her became easy—he followed the light of the torch bobbing along in front of him. While it showed her location, it did nothing to illuminate his path and, forced to take care with his footing, his steps slowed with strain and labor. He moved with stealth and quiet and avoided attracting her attention most of the time. Occasionally, an unseen stone skittered away from his foot or an invisible corner thumped against his knee or elbow. After each of these, he stopped, waiting for any change in the torch's pattern of movement. None came.

He realized the tunnel had come to its conclusion because the flame moved upward instead of forward, then disappeared. He paused then, giving her time to move away from the exit.

Once outside, he inhaled a deep breath his lungs appreciated. Despite the pungent and distinct odor of Fishtown, it felt and tasted better than the warm, moist air of the underground. It reminded him too much of the period he'd spent confined to a dungeon cell—a part of his life he wanted to forget and never wished to repeat.

The streets were near deserted but, where they weren't, the queen crept across the lane to avoid whatever drunk or denizen she might have encountered. She needn't have worried; Strylor kept his hand on his weapon, ready to lunge forward and protect her if the need arose. Once, it looked as though he'd have to. Ishla walked by what appeared a simple heap of discarded blankets or clothing but, after she'd passed, the pile rectified itself into the shape of a man. He shambled after her and Strylor increased his pace, a tangle of excitement and nerves igniting in his belly.

He hurried forward, caught the man by his elbow and spun him round, flashed his dagger in the man's face before he cried out or protested. The fellow's eyes went from narrow and angered to wide and frightful in less time than it took to blink them.

"Leave the woman," Strylor whispered through his teeth, the threat in them turning the words to a growl. "Make yourself scarce."

The man did as he'd commanded, cowering from him and then slipping away into shadows in the direction from which they'd come. Thankfully, he did so without further incident.

The queen's guard crept around the corner, continuing in pursuit of his charge. Where did she go at this time of night? Fishtown and beyond was the correct way if she desired any chance of finding her children, but not without a horse, supplies, and support. Last he knew, they'd headed toward Ikkundana. He supposed someone might walk right to the City of the Sick if they wanted, but it'd take an age. She'd need at least a donkey to carry the food and accoutrements to make it.

Maybe she's got herself a lover.

While the thought of the queen lying with a man other than the king brought him a measure of hope and excitement—if she chose to be with someone else, why not him?—he also realized how unlikely she'd have a consort in this part of the Horseshoe. Females weren't the same as men; they didn't sneak off to a whorehouse, satisfied with whatever cunny they might pay to get themselves into, especially not classy women such as Ishla.

Probably not a man, then.

But what else? They'd passed out of Fishtown now, the reek of the place replaced by the salty odor of the sea as they moved closer to the wharves. Did she intend to hire herself a boat? Quicker than walking, to be sure, but Ikkundana possessed no water access. Strylor shook his head and kept after her, wondering if the woman might merely be out for a moonlight walk and nothing more. Ahead of him, the queen's gray-clad figure rounded another corner and disappeared from his view. He increased his pace, left hand gripping his sword's scabbard to prevent it from banging against his leg or a wall, the sound betraying his presence if she halted around the bend. As before, his worry proved unfounded.

When he reached the intersection and peered beyond it, the queen had stopped not far ahead, facing away from him, staring at a blank wall. She threw the hood of her cloak back, the moonlight shining between the buildings surrounding her highlighting her hair with the sheen of a silver coin. Strylor leaned against the corner, waiting to see what she'd do next, and admiring how the lighting brought out her features. Seeing her this way made it easy to understand why the princess had grown to be so beautiful.

Ishla took a step toward the end of the alleyway, then another, like an unseen rope attached to her waist drew her on. Strylor squinted, stepped into the alley himself. The different positioning offered an alternate point of view; it showed the plain, unbroken wall built of brick with a small, black door in its middle.

How did I not see it before?

The queen continued moving toward it, her pace slow and deliberate. She moved in the manner of someone who knew what she'd find on the other side and experienced no fear over it. Her willingness to proceed gave Strylor bravery of his own. Truthfully, if she didn't show such courage, and he didn't need to look after her, he'd have turned and found the quickest return route to Draekfarren.

A noise behind him made him pause. He pivoted, hand gripping his sword's pommel hard enough he felt the blood leaving his fingers. He hesitated at pulling his weapon for fear the sound might alert the queen to his presence.

Though he'd tread but three paces from the corner, the entrance to the alley lay more distant than it should, beyond a narrow passage and high, foreboding walls. The queen's guard pressed his tongue against the roof of his mouth, swallowed a gulp of saliva.

"How?"

He spun away from this new and startling puzzle, facing toward the queen, and found another mystery. His breath stopped and his eyes widened.

His charge had disappeared.

~•~

Ishla breathed a sigh of relief as the door closed behind her. She wasn't fond of the oaf Strylor following her, but having protection at this time of night in this part of the city was a necessity. True, he may tell Erral or someone else where he saw her go, but she doubted it. He struck her as a man who'd do anything possible to avoid looking bad and—more so—being the subject of punishment. Surely he'd realize the wrath he might see from the king for losing the queen.

The corridor's dank air filled her nostrils, its odor a mix of herbs, lantern smoke, and an unidentifiable, underlying sweetness with as much chance of being an unpleasant stench as a pleasing bouquet. During her other few visits here, she'd wondered what it might be; today she ignored it in favor of finding her way through the labyrinthine halls. This was her first visit to the passages on her own. Every other time, a guide had led her through the corridors. As she walked, she pondered what might have become of the adolescent girl in the wooden mask and olive cloak she'd met not long before she'd lain with Trenan.

Trenan.

Her heart squeezed at the thought of his name. Sadness and grief brewed in her belly, threatening to overcome her if she let it. She breathed deep of the noisome air, swallowed hard and took a step along the passage. Her footsteps echoed down the stone corridor but, when she paused at an intersection to consider one way or the other, the sound of footfalls continued. They neither grew louder nor faded, always carrying on in a distinct and easy to follow direction. She realized the oddity meant for her to follow them.

After following the ghostly stride around three more corners, another noise joined the tap of leather soles on stone floor. At first she thought the mewling might belong to an animal in pain. She slowed her pace, taking care some beast with teeth or claws and an intent to injure her didn't catch her unaware. As she moved along the corridor, the sound grew in volume until it became recognizable.

The cry of a newborn babe.

The delicate wailing drew her to a wide wooden door mounted on gloomy iron hinges. Instead of a knob or handle, a length of thick rope hung from it, a fist-sized knot tied in its end. When she stopped in front of the portal, the echo of her steps halted along with her.

She raised her hand and set her palm upon the rough wood but hesitated before she lay her weight against it. The thickness of the wooden portal muffled any other sounds she might have detected, whispered words or the scrapes of foot on floor lost in the baby's desperate plea. Ishla drew a deep breath and leaned in, bringing her ear closer. The crying stopped, cut off suddenly, and her heart jumped into her throat. Motherly instincts aching for use since realizing her children's absence leapt into action. She pushed hard against the door, swinging it open on hesitant pins.

To her surprise, a cluster of people filled the room. Most of the ones smaller in stature wore the olive cloaks and wooden masks she'd seen before—the youngest initiates of the Goddess' order. Robes of a variety of shades of green clothed the others, each hue denoting a position, standing, experience, or age in the temple's hierarchy. Ishla had never learned what each symbolized, nor did it concern her then. The group of women directed their attention toward her, but she ignored them in favor of the wide chair placed in the center of the chamber.

It looked out of place in the sparse, undecorated room. Its rich purple velvet and overstuffed cushions stood out in stark contrast to the dull gray walls and bare floor. The robe worn by the woman seated on the plush seat approximated the color of the stone. Had she not rested upon the violet fabric, she might have blended into the surroundings.

A baby as small as any Ishla had ever seen suckled at the Mother of Death's teat. The babe's pale, wrinkled flesh made the girl—the Mother's milk honored only females—appear incredibly old rather than newly born. On the queen's other visits, she'd noted the woman revered by the temple's members ripe with child, and heard unseen babes crying from behind closed doors, but this marked the first time she'd seen a newborn. Did all of them look as ancient as their mother when she gave birth to them?

"Ah, Ishla, you have come," the old woman said. She supported the baby in one arm resting on a still-pregnant belly while stroking its hairless head with her other gnarled hand. "It is good to see you again. And you get to meet Goddess' newest warrior."

The queen didn't know what to say or how to act, so she lowered her chin in deference. "Mother."

"You are wondering why I have brought you here."

"But you didn't bring me. I attend you of my own accord. I need help to find…" Words caught in her throat. She swallowed. "…my children."

"Tut, tut, child. You came because Goddess needs you, so I called and you heard."

"But Teryk and Danya—"

"Have their parts to play, too. Separate from yours."

She wanted to protest further but knew the futility of such an effort. The Mother of Death paid heed to but a single entity. The queen's gaze slipped toward the old woman's belly. Did the babe she held belong to one of the other women? She couldn't have birthed so recently and be so ripe with child again. The two times Ishla had given birth, she didn't want Erral near her for months after, never mind producing more offspring. The thought caused another.

I've never seen a man here.

She glanced around the chamber at the female faces watching their interaction. Were these all her children?

"Some," the Mother of Death said. Ishla raised an eyebrow, not sure what she meant. "Many of them are mine by birth. The young ones. My offspring end up at Ikkundana, training to defend the Mother of Mothers. Others are brought to us by those who can't care for them, but all become my daughters."

Ishla's throat and tongue wanted to question how the woman read her thoughts, but her mind reeled, unable to instruct her speaking parts what to do. The Mother of Death offered her version of a smile, the wrinkles gathered on her cheeks suggesting it might as likely have been a grimace. The babe in her arm wiggled, her nipple popping out of its lips. Its tiny mouth opened as the little one's face screwed up in an expression illustrating unfathomable anger and disappointment. The noise it made sounded more akin to the bleating of a newborn pig than the cry of a child.

"My children," Ishla managed. "What do you need of me that's more important than my children?"

"Goddess doesn't tell me everything, only to summon you. She will guide you. Your friend hiding in the alley has a role, too."

"Not my friend."

The old woman nodded. "Which doesn't change the fact he has his part. We all do."

"But, Mother—"

"I'm sorry for what you think has happened, Ishla. Goddess doesn't give explanation, she does what needs to be done. But your time has come to take up the fight."

What I think has happened?

"Take up the fight? Mother, what—?"

The initiate closest to Ishla laid a hand on her arm, interrupting her. The Mother of Death's eyes slid shut, and a gentle snore escaped her lips within the space of two heartbeats. Behind the queen, someone opened the door and a breath of musty air entered from the corridor. She stepped back, then turned, ushered out of the room by the woman touching her forearm. She guided her along the hallway, which now led in a straight line from the chamber to the portal to the outside world instead of following a winding path.

Another robed sister awaited them by the door, pulling it open for them. Before stepping across the threshold, Ishla looked back the way they'd come, found herself baffled by the corner a few steps away where a moment before there'd been none. She blinked and shook her head but didn't mention it to the Goddess' followers. The one who'd guided her from the chamber nodded toward the alley, encouraging her to step out of the temple. She complied, and the portal closed after her.

As soon as she lay foot in the moonlit courtyard, the queen's guard appeared out of the shadows at the far end. His expression held equal parts fear and concern, but she assumed both those facets pertained to his own well-being, not hers.

"Queen Ishla," he called, rushing toward her. "I thought some ill befell you. I promise I won't let you out of my sight again."

She sighed and rolled her eyes, walked past him without knowing where she should go. Back to Draekfarren? It didn't seem what Goddess intended for her, judging by the Mother of Death's words. She halted in the center of the courtyard when she heard the nickering of a horse.

"Strylor?"

He stepped up beside her. "A woman in a green robe brought them."

Movement flickered at the far end of the open space, right where an alley leading to the boulevard began. Ishla moved three paces closer and stopped again.

Two horses waited in the shadows, one such dark chestnut as to be near invisible, the other so white, it was a wonder she hadn't seen it; the beast practically glowed.

"What did she say?"

"Nothing. Handed me the reins, then disappeared into the doorway. Surprised you didn't walk right into her on your way out."

She closed the distance to the animals, aware of the creak of Strylor's armor as he followed. The sheen of the white horse's coat drew her; she reached out, set her palm against its cheek and it nosed her shoulder.

"Why are they here, my queen?"

The steed nuzzled her again as she looked at the saddle on its back, the bags attached she knew already contained enough stock for a trip. She wondered what Goddess might have in store for her, but she let the thought slip away. Regardless of why she was here, this was her opportunity—the only one she would have.

She turned toward Strylor, wished for an instant to leave him behind, but the Mother of Death had said he had his part to play, too. Ishla clenched her teeth, inhaled through her nose to calm the rise of emotion trying to fight its way into her throat. When she'd quelled it, she looked into the queen's guard's eyes, set her brow.

"They are here so we can find the truth."

She inserted her toe in the stirrup and mounted the white horse, pulled the cowl of the gray robe up to cover her head. Without waiting for Strylor, she put her heels to the steed and guided it along the alley toward the boulevard beyond. Somewhere out there, the truth waited, beckoning her, and she would do everything in her power to find it.

XXV - Trenan – Camp

*T*RENAN SAT LEANING AGAINST a tree, the chunk of bread one of the female warriors gave him held loosely in his fingers. He possessed no appetite, despite not being able to remember the last time he'd eaten. The feeling left behind by whatever the priests had done to him and the accusing stares of the dead inspired no desire for sustenance. Teryk leaned against another trunk opposite him, arms propped on his knees, hands dangling, eyes staring at nothing.

Osis had said little since they gave themselves over to the group of female warriors, choosing to fall back to ride with the troop rather than beside Trenan. When they stopped for rest, the sergeant remained standing, surveying the men and women while keeping his eye on Trenan.

A benefit to stopping: the dead kept their distance, remaining outside the rough circle of resting soldiers. They hung at the periphery of his vision, but didn't approach close enough for him to make out faces or wounds. Water dripped from boughs high above, plopping on armor and skin, the forest floor, in an asymmetric rhythm. Trenan listened closely, attempting to lose himself in the sound, trying to forget the phantoms, the princess, Ishla.

"You should eat some."

In his forced distraction, he hadn't expected Yoli's approach. He held up the chunk of bread, shook his head, and let his hand drop again.

"Can't yet. I don't understand what they did to me."

She nodded, her stern expression showing a hint of compassion. "Their magic is potent now stars have fallen. But if you don't eat, your body will fail you."

"I will. I'm more worried about him." He gestured at Teryk.

Yoli glanced at the prince but did not respond. The master swordsman took this as her agreement.

"Osis will attempt to send a rider to Draekfarren."

"Yes."

Her lack of concern caused Trenan to stiffen, blood rushing into his cheeks. If a messenger made it to the Horseshoe, everyone would guess his failings. It would destroy Ishla and wrench from him everything left important in his life.

He glanced across at Teryk, any anger and misgivings he might have experienced toward the young man draining out of him. On the other side of the small clearing they'd chosen for rest—the king's men in the center, ringed by Yoli's warriors—Osis stood hands on hips talking to his two best soldiers. His eye caught Trenan's, and they held each other's gaze for a moment before the master swordsman looked away.

"What do you need of me?" he asked.

"Keep your eye on your sergeant. He is none too happy with being invited into our midst."

"He sees it as being captured."

"Yes, and may try to take action. With what is coming, it is a fight none of us needs."

He nodded and peered at Osis, who had returned to talking to his men in what Trenan now interpreted as a furtive manner. Beyond him, the Goddess' warriors stood at guard, then lay the forest. Even from this distance, he spied blood-soaked faces peeking between tree trunks and snatches of foliage. He suppressed a shiver.

"Most of all, I need you to heal as best you can." She reached out a hand and laid it on his forearm—the closest she'd come to showing emotion or concern in the time since he'd met her.

He stared at her fingers splayed against his armor and wondered if she knew about the phantoms haunting him. He opened his mouth to ask, but shut it again. If she didn't, he didn't want to tell her. He nodded, giving no more response until he swallowed and tilted his head toward Teryk.

"I'm more concerned about him."

Yoli lifted her hand from his arm and shifted to look over her shoulder at the prince. He noticed the touch taken from him as if someone tore the blankets off his bed during a peaceful sleep.

"He has experienced much trauma. I will do what I can to help him."

She moved away. Trenan set his bread down and reached for her, intending to grab her wrist and make her stay with him a while longer. With her near, the ghouls glowering from the forest seemed less fearsome. But he checked himself short of touching her, pulling his hand away before the tips of his fingers so much as brushed her. He let his arm drop and watched as she approached Teryk, then stopped and stood looking down at him, assessing. She stayed for a few heartbeats, then left, picking a route through men who did not try to move from her path. He realized this wasn't her normal way of being, but she chose not to cause trouble in the name of a greater good.

She disappeared behind a group and Trenan dragged his gaze away, looking beyond at the vague faces hidden in the forest, staring at him, accusing him, until his eyes encountered Osis. The sergeant's hard stare and pinched lips accused the swordmaster as surely as did the expressions worn by the ghouls. Trenan jerked his attention elsewhere, let his chin droop to his chest and shut his eyelids, feigning sleep to avoid confrontation.

But he found no relief behind closed lids. The faces of the dead swam through his mind's eye, their blind stares skewering him like daggers. But more than the memories of those he'd killed plagued him this time. He saw Danya's features, blanched white by the loss of blood. Teryk stabbing her replayed over and over while a crowd of rotting soldiers lurked in the background, witnesses to the treachery of the prince, and Trenan's failure to protect them both. Dansil skulked amongst the audience, though his countenance didn't appear decomposing like the others'. Instead of watching the princess' death, he stared at Trenan, a broad smile on his lips. Beside him, a man with no legs and one arm leaned against him, while a black-robed figure stood to the other side.

Trenan squeezed his lids closed tighter, trying to dispel the image. It didn't work; they followed him into his dreams.

—◆◆—

At first, he didn't know what woke him. The bloody faces of men long dead continued haunting his mind, carried out of sleep with him, but he soon recognized the harsh tones of confrontation. Trenan scrubbed his eyes with a knuckle and peered across the camp.

A group of four soldiers engaged with two stone-faced sentries. He couldn't hear their words, but their tone sounded threatening. Others around the encampment had noticed, too, and men and women alike rose from where they'd been sitting or slumbering, some moving toward the ruckus. The master swordsman levered himself up, pushing against the mossy tree trunk at his back. His spine creaked, ached, and he winced with the unfamiliar pain, but ignored it as he stepped away from his sleeping spot.

The men continued their verbal abuse of the woman warriors, one of them raising his arm and pointing into a sentry's face to emphasize a point. Trenan's gaze flickered to Teryk, who remained unmoved by the commotion. His eyes then flitted around the rest of the camp, noting who was up and moving and who wasn't, and scanning for the all-too-constant faces streaked with blood.

Osis leaned against a tree, arms crossed, regarding the proceedings but making no move to stop his men. When the volume rose further, he straightened but, instead of crossing the clearing as Trenan did, he glanced over his shoulder. Seeing him do so tempted Trenan to do the same, but he resisted. With no ghosts haunting his line of vision, he didn't want to redirect his attention and find the phantasms lurking somewhere else.

"Witches!"

The word made its way through the night air to his ears, pulling his awareness from the sergeant-at-arms. Two of the men moved forward, standing almost chest to chest with the sentries, one of them yelling in the face of a woman. She didn't react except to shift away from the spray of spittle carried on his words.

"Ye ain't nothin' but a bunch of witches. No chance you lot'd stand against the king's army."

"Really? I think you've forgotten who has captured whom."

Yoli spoke from the edge of the crowd formed around the shouting men and the stony sentries, arms crossed over her chest and a bemused expression on her face Trenan hadn't noticed before. She seemed unconcerned about the attitude of the soldiers, but his heart beat faster. He knew firsthand the fighting prowess of the women in an exercise yard, but two of the men confronting her warriors he recognized as the same pair he'd seen speaking with Osis earlier—both excellent, battle-tested fighters. The coincidence of their involvement concerned him.

"Mind your business," one of them said, pivoting to face Yoli. "If I want your opinion, I'll give it to you."

The other men chuckled. The female warrior unfolded her arms and took a step toward him.

Stop. This is what they want.

Surely she must see the trap being set, yet she still engaged them, willing to spring it.

"You'll get my opinion whenever I desire to offer it, useless oaf."

The man's upper lip curled into a snarl and he lurched at Yoli in one quick movement she had anticipated. She side-stepped, turned her body, grabbed him by the arm, and used his momentum against him. He pitched forward, and she rode him to the ground, landing with a knee in the middle of his back, driving air from his lungs with an audible whoof. Before the other men moved to help or enact revenge, five more women emerged from the group and wrestled them to submission with movements so conservative and precise, Trenan himself couldn't have said how they accomplished it. They drew no weapons. The sentries remained where they had stood, unmoving except when one raised her hand to wipe drying saliva from her cheek.

"Enough."

Trenan stopped as Osis strode past. He gave the master swordsman a sideward glance, but neither paused nor spoke to his superior. He went to where Yoli knelt on the man, pinning him, and crouched beside them.

"Don't you feel foolish now?"

The fellow grunted, wriggled under the female warrior's weight. She leaned forward, exerting more pressure and soliciting a groan from him. Osis looked at the others, similarly incapacitated, and shook his head.

"Soldiers of the king, indeed." He stood, directed his attention to Yoli. "My apologies on behalf of my men. They are not used to being prisoners."

"You are our guests." She gave her knee a firm push against the man, causing another pained expulsion of breath, before standing and freeing him. "But we expect guests to act politely."

"Guests. Of course."

"Let them up."

The other women stepped away from the three men they held in various states of submission. They all clambered to their feet, revenge burning in the scowls on their faces. King's soldiers and Goddess' warriors faced each other, the tension in their limbs bleeding into the air.

"Stand down," Osis said. "You've made fools enough of yourselves this night."

A grumble rolled through them, but they forfeited their fighting stances and slouched away from the group. If they'd been children, Trenan would have thought of them as sulking. The man Yoli had pinned climbed to his feet, brushed dirt and fir needles from his front, and stalked away without so much as a glare at the woman who'd bested him. The master swordsman peered at the leader of the Goddess' army, expecting to find a satisfied smile on her lips. To his surprise, her expression held nothing but the mild annoyance it always portrayed whenever she found herself in the presence of men.

The rest of the throng dispersed, leaving the sentries at their post and Osis and Yoli facing each other over the bit of ground where his soldier had lain. Trenan watched them from his place halfway across the camp as people settled into their places around him. Neither of the leaders of the opposing troops spoke, but something appeared to pass between them—a promise, a threat—he knew not which—or perhaps both. They stayed like that for more than a dozen heartbeats, each looking like they waited for the other to withdraw first. Finally, Osis acquiesced. He bowed so shallowly it could only be considered an insult, then took his leave.

When he passed by Trenan, he nodded almost imperceptibly.

The master swordsman remained for a moment regarding Yoli, thinking about her touch on his forearm. She paid him no attention, so he left, returning to his sleeping spot. He directed his gaze toward his feet to avoid stepping on those stretched out around him, but also to keep from spying any of the lifeless eyes possibly peeping at him.

He reached the tree, set his back against it, and slid to the ground, knees drawn up to his chest and face pressed against his arm, hoping he might sleep before the dead men found him again.

XXVI - Teryk – Temptation

THE CHIRRUP OF CRICKETS, the creak of wood, and the soft snores of sleeping warriors filled the night.

Teryk blinked to clear his bleary eyes, pushed himself up on his elbows, and wondered what had woken him. He was warm and dry enough, and he heard no sound out of the ordinary. In the distance, he thought he saw the stealthy movement of a sentry patrolling the camp's perimeter, but he couldn't be sure. Either way, she didn't make sufficient noise to have roused him from his sleep.

He inhaled the aroma of the damp forest filled with mosses and lichens, peat and dirt and wood. These and similar odors had made up too much of his life this past while, but it suited him better than the salty stink of the ocean. He shivered at the memories it coaxed—the sinking ship, the land across the sea, the strangeness that followed. Shadowy branches dangled over him as he lowered himself to the ground, wondering what had happened to Rilum.

He was in the Green.

The thought of the sailor surviving on his own seemed unlikely—one more death to weigh on his conscience. Rilum, Danya...how many more before this was through? Since he wasn't the firstborn, did killing his sister make him responsible for all the deaths to come?

Would the fall of mankind be his fault?

He closed his eyes, laid his forearm across his face. Crickets continued singing, uncaring for his dismay, warriors snored. Were they aware the end of their lives was close and getting closer every day, and he was to blame?

His chest tightened, and he longed to slip into the stupor that had protected him from this guilt over the last few risings and settings of the sun. This world wasn't a place he wanted to be, knowing fault for its impending end lay with him.

The scant breaths he drew did nothing to calm the storm brewing in his gut; at least the sound of his inhalations blocked the noise of forest and fighters both. It made him feel alone; maybe no one else could die because of him.

It took a while before he realized it wasn't the rasp of his breathing which relieved his ears of the crickets and the snores—they'd ceased. He stopped his own breath, listened.

No rustles or moans of sleeping soldiers, no buzz of song of insects, no whisper of wind in leaves. Nothing until the crack of a twig snapping under a foot. Teryk jerked up to a sitting position, scanned the surrounding area.

"Who's there?"

His eyes saw nothing but darkness at first until they became accustomed to the lack of light. Warriors lay scattered round him, Trenan somewhere amongst them, yet none of them made a sound.

Are they already dead?

He scuffled his way to his feet, the scrape on the ground of the boots supplied to him by the king's soldiers plain to his ears. A shiver ran up his spine and he wrapped his arms across his chest.

"Hello?"

Shapes at the far end of the camp where there'd been nothing a heartbeat ago caught his attention. They moved toward him, the shuffle and scrape of their movements as real as if he made the sounds himself. If so, why were the soldiers so completely soundless?

Teryk backed away two small steps before his ass found the trunk of the tree under which he'd been dozing. He glanced over his shoulder at it, noting its rough bark and the green moss. When he returned his attention to the shapes, they'd crossed half of the distance to him.

His mouth opened and closed and he stared without blinking as they picked their way through the sleeping soldiers carpeting the forest floor. They didn't take particular care in doing so—the taller, erect figure moved lithely, but the hunched, squat fellow showed no concern for making noise or stepping on the occasional prone form.

"What do you want?"

His voice trembled, and he pushed himself harder against the tree, wondered if he should attempt to bolt. He didn't try; if he did, his feet would tangle with one of the sleeping men and make him easier to catch.

Neither of the figures answered; they kept moving toward him in their steady advance, none of those they passed waking or noticing their presence. If the soldiers weren't dead, then these two must be ghosts.

Teryk shook his head. He'd seen the specters of those killed by Trenan. So many of them, with their split skulls, shorn limbs, and spilled innards. The memory of them visited, then disappeared, but it gave the prince hope.

"Trenan!"

His throat betrayed him and the word caught, got broken in two, so he cleared his airway and tried again.

"Trenan!"

"You think you find yourself in a time of need and you cry the name of the man who spent your entire life lying to you? Why do you call for your betrayer?"

Teryk swallowed hard and gaped at the figures, now two horse lengths distant from him. A sliver of moonlight made its way through the boughs and fell across them, showing him his stalkers for the first time.

The taller of them wore a black robe, its cowl drawn up to hide his features, though long and white fingers protruded from the sleeves. The other man wasn't short as he'd thought—he had no legs, and one arm; his tongue lolled from the side of his mouth like a dog's.

"I remember you," Teryk managed, his words carried on a breath not more than a whisper. "You're the healer."

"If you like." With the cowl covering his face, the voice floated in the forest air, unattached to anyone. "These days, I believe I've become more of a collector."

The term made him shudder. Juddah was a collector, the barn in which he'd imprisoned him and Ailyssa jammed with tools, implements, and barrels stuffed with things the prince didn't want to find out about. He blinked hard, shook his head to dispose of the memory.

"What do you want of me?"

"Have you considered our last conversation?"

His forehead creased. They had spoken, hadn't they? In a grim place, without the one-limbed man at his side. They'd talked of blame and betrayal, vengeance for his sister's death upon the men who'd manipulated him into it. He opened his mouth to reply, but no words came forth. What would he say? Did he want to cause more deaths, no matter the reason? If the world would perish because of his actions, why did he need to seek retribution first? He closed his lips, thoughts left unspoken.

"Ah, I see you are hesitant. Understandable. Despite his treachery, the one-armed man is your father. He raised you—be it amidst lies and deception—so you feel a connection. Perhaps greater than for your sister."

He shook his head. "No. I love—loved—Danya."

"You did. Right until you slid a knife into her neck. Which wasn't your fault."

Teryk looked away from the robed figure, gaze dropping to his feet. Mud covered the toes of his boots, splashed more than halfway up the sides. When was the last time he was clean? He raised his eyes. They were closer. White flashed beneath the cowl as he glimpsed the healer's pale face.

"But vengeance is not a concern for you. How noble. You've set aside selfish revenge in favor of worry for the greater good. Perhaps royal blood flows in your veins, after all. Not the type to make you the firstborn capable of saving the kingdom, however, an honor belonging to your sister—and now she's gone."

The man beside the robed figure—no legs, one arm missing—watched them, his gaze flitting between them as though he understood their words by watching their lips move. His tongue lolled out of the side of his mouth, a line of saliva glimmering on his chin, enforcing his dog-like appearance. Teryk stared at him, sensing something familiar about him, but he couldn't say what. It startled him when the healer spoke again.

"All is not lost."

"What do you mean?"

"I have particular talents. You of all people should know that."

Teryk shook his head, a knot in his stomach distracting him, adding to the confusion spinning his brain. Why did he recognize the legless man? Why weren't any of the soldiers aware of their presence? How did they get here? What interest did this collector have in him? He blinked, stared past the two of them to where Trenan lay sleeping. Betrayal and lies or not, he wished to have the master swordsman at his side right then. He closed his eyes, directed his gaze to the healer. Closer, and he'd pushed down the cowl so the dim glow of the moon gleamed on his smooth white features.

"You were near death when I healed you. I have crossed the great chasm before and returned with those who had slipped away."

The prince blinked, his mouth fell open. "Are you saying—?"

"I can get your sister, too. Return the firstborn to the world so she can save the kingdom."

The surface of Teryk's skin tingled, starting from his face and spreading down his neck to his chest, his torso, his limbs. Could the healer be telling the truth? What he spoke of seemed impossible—not only the return of his sister to the living, but diverting the bleak fate of mankind. His hairless head bobbed as though he heard the prince's thoughts and agreed.

"You might not be the firstborn of the prophecy, but you may be the one to save the kingdom."

The father's—no, the king's—face flashed to his mind. He didn't need to prove anything to the man—he was no longer heir to the throne—but after so many turns of the seasons being berated and belittled, maybe he could still validate his worth.

"You can bring Danya back from the dead."

He nodded. "I can, but it carries a cost."

Teryk raised an eyebrow, prepared his tongue to ask the obvious question, but again the healer responded as though partaking of his thoughts along with him. He canted his head toward the legless man, moonlight gleaming on his white pate. He vibrated at the attention being paid to him.

"My pet here can tell you of the cost. Mind you, he has not sacrificed to have a soul returned from the void. Such a feat requires the steepest of prices."

The prince swallowed hard, the saliva scraping along his throat like a sharp-edged rock. He'd have sworn it brought the tang of blood to his tongue.

"The...the steepest?"

"Reviving the dead is no insignificant thing. Legs and arms won't do. If you want a life snatched from the black lands, then one must be given in return."

The tingling sensation along the surface of Teryk's skin penetrated into him, raising goosebumps on his flesh and a shiver in his limbs and spine. He glanced away from the robed man to the other.

Stirk. His name is Stirk.

He'd been so different before, but he'd given so much. For what? To save Teryk? Stirk bounced up and down, shifting from one stump leg to the other, his hand pressed against the ground providing balance. Teryk looked down at his own hands, his legs. He didn't think he'd sacrifice them, but this was more important than anything. Bringing Danya back meant the return of his sister to the land of the living, but also the safety of the kingdom, the fulfilling of the prophecy. But to do so, he'd have to relinquish his life?

"Do you have a soul to offer?" the healer asked, then once more made Teryk suspect he had access to his thoughts. "It needn't be yours, just worthy of the trade."

The prince lifted his gaze, looked past the legless man, his eyes moving between the sleeping warriors until they found the prone form of the one-armed swordsman. Trenan, who'd raised him, trained him, his father, the man who'd lied to him, deceived him, betrayed him.

"How? How do I bring you a life?"

The healer smiled, his lips a sickening slash across his pale face. Teryk shuddered, the tremor shaking along his spine, refusing to stop. He raised his hands, covered his eyes, and wished for the two men to leave him be.

XXVII - Trenan - Messenger

A BATTLE RAGED, BUT no weapon filled Trenan's hand to defend himself. He dodged and ran, ducked behind any bush or tree suitable for providing cover. The army fighting against him pressed on, their faces painted with blood, some with limbs missing, intestines hanging out of abdomens, eyeballs dangling on stringy muscle. No matter where he fled or hid, they found him, but they carried no weapons, either. Instead, their jaws snapped open and closed, teeth clicking as they sought to ingest him, as though eating him might return them to their previous way of being.

The dream shuddered, breaking into glass-shard puzzle pieces before re-congealing. The attack continued, the scene shook again, shattered, and Trenan opened his eyes.

Sleep cast a fog over his sight so the face looming over him appeared a lighter smudge in the dark. Part of it gesticulated, produced a word which might have been his name. Startled, Trenan jumped, dug his heels into the loamy earth and pushed himself away. He expected the blurry visage to reconcile itself into a leering demon, saliva dripping from its pointed teeth, blood lining thin lips.

"Trenan, it's me. It's Osis."

His back against the nearest tree, Trenan stared at the sergeant-at-arms, heart hammering against his ribs. His breath heaved in and out in quick bursts, rushing blood and rapid airflow causing his head to swirl. The soldier moved closer, rested a calming hand on his friend's forearm.

"It's okay. Nothing but a dream."

Trenan swallowed, nodded, though the touch gave him no reassurance about the veracity of his words. He glanced past his friend at the forest behind him; sentries stirred in the distance, but he spied neither Stirk and the robed healer nor any of the phantasms plaguing him on his journey since the Green. Not yet, at least.

"What...what is it, Osis?"

The master swordsman tried to meet the sergeant's eyes, but couldn't prevent his gaze from flitting from one side to the other, convinced night and forest hid things waiting to haunt him.

Osis leaned closer, spoke in a tone barely more than the sound of an exhalation. "We got a rider away for Draekfarren."

Trenan stopped his surveillance, gaped at the sergeant.

"Really?"

"Yes. Erfin found his way out during the distraction. He is on the road and riding as fast as the wind by now."

"Is this the best idea?"

He shook his head. "Of course. We are captives of an enemy."

"Are we?"

He raised one brow at Trenan, but didn't respond to the query. "It will take Erfin five sunrises to reach Draekfarren, maybe less. Erral will send troops for us."

"Osis, you don't understand—"

"You've been through much, swordmaster." His tone hardened to a firm whisper. "Leave this to me."

The master swordsman opened his mouth, the temptation to snap at him threatening on his tongue. Osis stood, moved away a step, preventing him from doing so without raising his voice enough to disturb others. The sergeant-at-arms raised a finger to his lips, turned and crept toward the place where he'd made his bed for the night. Trenan stared after him. He'd avoided repercussions from the king, and the queen's devastation, when Yoli and her crew intercepted them. Not so.

I can't let it happen.

As soon as the soldier settled, Trenan pushed his spine against the tree behind him and worked his legs until he got in a position to stand. He did so with care, doing his best not to create sound and attract attention. If Osis had made his way here without notice, he should be able to find Yoli at the opposite end of the camp.

He started out, concentrating on where he placed his feet to keep from making noise and to avoid looking into the darkened forest. He didn't need to glimpse long-dead men returned to haunt him. With jaw clamped tight and hand pressed into a fist, he picked his way to where he'd find Yoli.

Ahead and to his right, he spied Teryk sleeping under an ancient fir, the ground beneath carpeted with brown needles. He moved in his sleep, disturbed, and Trenan halted, waited. A shiver ran along his limbs as he looked at his son, face sprinkled with uncharacteristic stubble, his hair long and stringy. He hardly resembled the prince who'd sneaked out of Draekfarren. In fact, he realized he appeared far different than he should, given the time passed, as though he'd aged faster than nature intended. He shifted again, discomfort tensing his sleeping features.

Dreaming.

Satisfied he hadn't disturbed his son, Trenan continued on, directing his attention to his footing, but a portion of his mind remained with Teryk. He'd been through so much, and the master swordsman realized he had but an inkling of what the prince had encountered. The haunted light in his eyes suggested much more.

We have all experienced so much.

He glided past his own troops, then those of the Goddess, recognizing many of them from his time training them at Ikkundana—far more women than when they struck out for the Green. He wondered where they had come from, and so quickly, but put it from his mind.

"What has you sneaking through my camp at this hour, swordmaster?"

Yoli's words startled him from his thoughts and he reached for the empty scabbard hanging at his waist. When he raised his head and found her gazing at him with an amused tilt upon her lips, he released his breath. She'd removed her outer layer of armor, the dark-colored underclothes blending into her surroundings. Her hair flowed over her shoulders and along her back, free of any constraint. Trenan couldn't recall ever seeing her in anything other than full armor.

He took a step closer. "Osis came to me."

"Did he? To tell you he sneaked a rider through our lax sentry, I'd guess."

Trenan opened his mouth, not sure if he meant to confirm her suspicion or ask how she guessed, but he closed it again without speaking. A movement over her right shoulder caught his attention. Worried it might be Osis spying on them, he diverted his gaze and found a blood-streaked face peering at him, gray brain matter showing through cracked skull. He looked back to Yoli.

"You know?"

"Of course." She laughed, the sound lacking in humor. "Do you think my sentries left time and space large enough to sneak man and horse through?"

"But why? Erral will send an army."

"I'm counting on it."

Trenan shuffled foot to foot and glanced at the bloody face behind her, noticed other dead men joining the first. He didn't bother examining them.

"What's wrong, swordmaster?"

She pivoted to what he'd looked at and he nearly leapt forward to stop her. Despite the faces looming behind her, she saw nothing.

"We can't let the rider get to Draekfarren."

"We have to. Goddess needs the king's soldiers."

He sucked the top edge of his bottom lip into his mouth, chewed it, eyes darting between Yoli and the dead men behind her. He noticed her brow crease at his demeanor, but he couldn't stop himself. With Osis and his troops here, no one would have brought the news of Danya's death to Draekfarren yet; Ishla wouldn't know he let her down. Only if the weapons merchants took it upon themselves to tell the king might the world at large find out, but what reason could they have for doing such a thing? No, the surest way for his love to find out about his failure was through the messenger.

"They won't be coming to your aid," he said, returning his focus to her. "They will come to put you to the sword."

"Yes, but by the time they arrive, they will have no choice but to fight beside us. The war is close."

He moved a half-step closer, leaning in; Yoli tensed with a man so near to her. "They don't know what has happened. The messenger will tell them. She'll find out the princess is dead."

She leaned back, and he sensed her eyes upon his face, but he couldn't bring himself to meet her gaze, instead peering toward his feet. Hesitant, she touched his forearm, and he made himself raise his chin.

"You must look past yourself, Trenan. Goddess has a larger plan at work, one we see but small trappings of, but everything has been for a reason. That includes what you think you saw."

His gaze flickered away; a veritable crowd of the dead had formed behind her. He shivered.

"Are you all right?"

He nodded. "It has been a troublesome time."

"And more difficulties will come. We must press on, and the addition of the king's army is necessary." She lowered her hand from his arm. "I promise nothing will happen to you, or any of my soldiers."

He opened his mouth, intending to protest. Who was she to think he needed her protection? He held the highest post in the army and had likely killed more people than she'd known in her life. The thought made him glance over her shoulder again at the cast of phantasms gathered behind her. His offense at her words melted, running out of his chest and threatening to turn his knees to water. He kept his balance, and she continued to look at him with concern. Instead of arguing, he nodded.

"Rest, Trenan. We have hard travel ahead."

He raised his eyes to hers, saw what might have been pity reflected in her expression, a look he was not used to seeing in others when they regarded him. He thought to question it, but the gathering of the dead watching over her shoulder prevented him from doing so. Instead, he nodded once more and turned, heel digging a divot in the forest floor, and walked away.

As he did on his way to see her, he kept his eyes to the ground, more to avoid seeing any ghoulish faces following him or tripping than to keep from making noise. Some soldiers sleeping around him shifted, disturbed by his passing. None of the women he'd trained at Ikkundana, including Yoli herself, seemed any different, despite their exposure to the black priests. How were they unaffected while dead men haunted him, and Teryk appeared all but lost?

Trenan glanced to the tree where the prince—his son—lay in the throes of restless sleep. He was more animated while unconscious than awake, a fact which gave the master swordsman more worry than he needed. What would it take to pull the young man out of his lethargy? And for Trenan to vanquish the ghosts haunting him?

He continued past, focusing on the spot where he'd made his bed, determined to find his way to the land of sleep, but unsure of finding the path to slumber. The ghosts still clung to his mind, even if he couldn't see them, as well as worry for Teryk, and now the surety about Ishla finding out what happened. The overwhelming wave of it crashed upon him, weighing down his last few steps to his sleeping tree. He sagged before reaching it, crumbling to the ground when he did.

He lay on his back, eyes closed and arm thrown over his face, hoping for sleep to claim him, but slumber proved reluctant. After a time, he pushed himself up to sitting, brushed dead needles from his palm on the front of his trousers. Hesitant, he raised his head and scanned the forest; apparently the phantasms hounding him since they left the Green had called it a night. Crickets chirped, wind stirred branches overhead.

His gaze fell upon Osis. The sergeant-at-arms leaned against a tree halfway between Trenan and the circle of female soldiers surrounding the king's men, his arms crossed as he stared at the master swordsman.

Did he see me speaking with Yoli? Does he think I've betrayed him?

A shiver crawled its way along his spine and he lay on the ground, turning away from his friend. He closed his eyes, praying for sleep to come and relieve him of the worries of the world.

XXVIII - Erral - Messenger

*S*OUNDS OF MEN SHOUTING to each other, the clank and bump of armor and equipment, and the shuffle of horses' hooves floated through the window, but Erral paid them little attention. He'd given the man, Dansil, his orders—nothing more for him to do than wait for them to return with the traitor in tow.

His explicit instructions: bring him back alive.

The king sat at his desk, the fingers of his right hand holding the flagon of wine in a death grip, while his left hand curled into a fist, tapped the desktop at irregular intervals. He stared straight ahead at the door in front of him, though he saw neither the grain nor the color of the wood. The scenes in his head distracted him.

Stolen glances. Subtle touches. Circumstances manipulated to bring them to the same place at the same time.

They played me for a fool.

An idiot could have seen what was going on, and likely many had. But no one considered telling the king they suspected his general and his queen of being...involved. For his own part, he'd noticed long ago, but chosen to do nothing. The master swordsman had, after all, sacrificed to save his king's life.

As any man should.

His fist struck the desk top harder, rattling the quills at rest in their jar. The muscles in his jaw flexed and relaxed, flexed again. The visions in his mind flashed to the day of the battle, of Trenan lunging between him and his would-be killer. He conjured the memory often, every time he caught them in one of those moments when they thought no one else watched. Each instance inserted a sliver of doubt, a dollop of anger. And now, as he sat with the clues pointing to a surety, he tried to recall him and Trenan before the swordsman's arm had come off.

Had they ever been friends? Had his lust for the queen always hidden in the background?

He'd given so much latitude because Trenan had sacrificed his limb, but what dutiful man wouldn't do the same for his king?

But he isn't a good man. He's a cad. A traitor.

No, they'd never been friends. He'd acted out of a sense of duty and debt, but a king should never do anything for those reasons. A king is a king and needs no reasons.

Fist met desk again, harder this time. A leaf of parchment sitting near the edge quivered, teetered, then fluttered to the floor. Erral ignored it the same as he did everything else around him. He had overlooked what went on in front of his face for all these turns of the seasons—he'd ignore them no more.

And the boy. The difference in how the swordmaster treated him during his training was obvious. Knights whispered of it, their gossip quiet, but everything eventually made its way to the ears of the king. Trenan didn't push him as hard or have the same expectations, took it easy on him when they sparred. Rarely did Teryk break a sweat in besting the master swordsman when no other in the kingdom stood a chance of doing so.

But more than that. The prince looked so much like his mother, but certain features, at particular angles...a hint of someone else in him, too? One who wasn't the king of the Windward Kingdom?

Both fists hammered on the desktop, and wine sloshed over the rim of the flagon onto Erral's hand. He turned his gaze toward it, glared at the red liquid slopped across his fingers and onto the desk, then hurled the vessel across the room. It thumped against the door, the vessel's edge bending in while leaving a dimple in the wood where it struck. Wine splattered against it and the cup hit the floor, bounced once, then rattled along as it rolled away. An instant later, a thump on the door sounded again, as though a delayed echo of the king's anger. A second followed, and then a third.

"What is it?" Erral snapped.

A voice on the other side responded; the thickness of the wood and his pulse beating in his ears kept the king from discerning the response.

"Enter," he said and stood, wiping wine from his hand onto his breeches before it dried and became sticky.

The portal swung open and Dansil—the former queen's guard and the soldier intended to lead the platoon to find Trenan—strode into the room. Erral wondered if, having been around the queen more than anyone else, this man knew of her transgressions with the master swordsman, and kept this knowledge from the king. If so, could he be trusted?

A second soldier followed him into the chamber, covered head to toe with road dust and looking exhausted. Erral was sure he'd never seen this fellow, though he wore the colors of the Windward Kingdom. They both crossed to the middle of the room, stopping a few paces from the desk, and bowed their heads in deference.

"What is the meaning of this? You are meant to be bringing the murderous traitor to me."

"Yes, my king, but as we readied to leave, a messenger arrived. You will want to hear what he has to say."

Erral looked from the former queen's guard to the other fellow, who awaited the king's command before speaking.

A man who knows his place.

"What is your name?"

"Erfin, your majesty. I was with Osis' detail and have ridden hard to bring you his message."

"Yes, I can see. Out with it, then."

"Their troop has been captured, my liege."

Erral focussed hard to keep from showing surprise in front of his men. He'd known of no movement from the Leeward Kingdom, though the relationship remained as volatile as usual. Unrest existed in parts of the kingdom—some were always unappreciative of paying their taxes, but none so much as to capture a squad.

"Who has done this?"

The man gulped as though forced to eat something unpleasant. "A troop of women."

The king stared at him, trying to decipher what he said. He felt sure he hadn't spoken a foreign language, but what he'd declared made no more sense than if he had.

"Women?"

"Yes, your majesty. Soldiers of the Goddess."

Erral barked a laugh. "There is no such thing."

"I assure you, there is. Dozens of them. They have Osis and the others held captive. Trenan and the prince, too."

The king's mirth died. His gaze snapped to Dansil. "What do you know of this?"

The former queen's guard shook his head. "Before Trenan killed the princess, he'd been traveling with other riders, but I didn't see them." He scratched his cheek with a three-fingered hand. "It's possible they might've been women. Definitely the prince and master swordsman were together."

"And what is the intent of these...women? What do they mean to do with my soldiers?"

The messenger shrugged, shoulders sagging far more than they rose under the weight of his exhaustion. "All I know is they're taking them to the City of the Sick."

"Ikkundana."

The man nodded.

"This makes your task easier," the king said, facing Dansil. "But it changes everything. What do the followers of the Goddess have to do with this?"

Neither of the soldiers replied; a good decision on their part, as Erral didn't expect them to nor did he want their input. He stepped out from behind the desk, right hand raised to his chin as he pondered this fresh development. The aroma of the wine spilled on his fingers floated to his nose.

Soldiers of the Goddess? How did I not know about this?

His intelligence and spies had failed him. Somehow, someone had built an enemy force within his kingdom without his knowledge. Incredible and unforgivable.

Trenan.

He wanted the queen for himself and probably had designs on the throne. It was the only possibility. Erral let his wine-scented hand drop to his side, fixed his gaze on the former queen's guard.

"Hold the men and call my armorer. Send riders to every corner of the Horseshoe. I want every swinging dick in the king's army ready by nightfall. In the morning, we ride for Ikkundana."

The two soldiers responded with shallow bows, then turned and hurried from the chamber, the messenger's boot contacting the empty flagon and sending it spinning and clattering away. The door swung shut behind them, leaving him alone again. He crossed to the window and stood looking out, waiting for the armorer's arrival. Men and horses milled about, each of them awaiting their orders, none of them suspecting what lay ahead for them.

"An army of the Goddess," the king mused aloud. "And Trenan with them."

Everything made sense now. He'd been their agent all along, perhaps recruited after he lost his arm. Erral realized he carried resentment over his sacrifice—the reason he'd seduced the queen and been manipulated into serving another power. Disgruntled men were always easier prey; wasn't that one of a woman's primary weapons?

Now he realized the truth, what needed doing became obvious.

Trenan must pay with his life.

XXIX - Trenan – Ghosts

*T*HEY FOLLOWED HIM EVERYWHERE.

When Yoli and her warriors first came, the phantoms disappeared for a while, then only showed themselves at night. Now, they stayed with him constantly. Every time he turned his head, glanced from one place to another, he found them leering at him, accusing him. They hid behind trees, lurked in bushes. They lined the sides of the road, an unbroken row of severed limbs and bloody faces, toothless mouths and exposed guts. Some pointed at him, others tried to say things, but their slack lips thankfully made no sound. Nobody else saw them, but would they hear them if they spoke? Would they recognize the voices of the dead calling out for vengeance?

Trenan kept his eyes on the horse's neck, using the ripple and roll of its muscles to distract him from his grisly accusers, but it proved difficult. After a while, he remembered them, the memories of their deaths returning to him unbidden. He saw a fellow he'd killed in a fight at a tavern for speaking against the king. He'd smashed his head so hard against the stone door frame, it split like an overripe melon; it surprised him he recognized his bloody features at all. Often he spied the soldier who'd attempted to kill Erral and took his arm instead. Sometimes this man wore his own face, other times he resembled the prince. Trenan always diverted his attention when he appeared, unwilling to find out which visage he'd be wearing.

The sun hung near the peak of its arc at midday when he sensed a rider pull up beside him, closer than necessary for traversing the dirt track. He looked up from surveying the horse's mane to discover Yoli looking at him from the saddle. Ghosts stalked the verge at the side of the road behind her, flickering at the edge of his vision, but he concentrated on her face to keep from their distraction.

"Are you all right, swordsman?"

"It has been a long trek full of sorrow, Yoli." He resisted the urge to glance over her shoulder at whatever disemboweled phantasm lurked at her back.

"It has," she agreed. "And yet something weighs on you beyond the loss of the princess."

He shrugged, directed his gaze to the horse's neck. His thoughts raced through everything he'd seen since leaving the glade outside the Green, how Teryk had acted, the array of ghosts and ghouls following him, and he considered telling her. But how could he? Seeing the phantasms of every person he'd killed sounded as though he'd gone crazy.

He raised his head, staring straight ahead. "What happened to you and the others?"

Yoli didn't respond for a moment, but he sensed her gaze on him like a finger pressed against his temple.

"What do you mean?"

"I saw the black priests." He faced her, closing his eyes as his view transitioned to her to minimize the number of dead men flashing across his vision. "On the hill with you when I was fighting Fellick."

"They were."

She said no more, and her unwillingness to give more brought a shiver down his back; he did his best to suppress it lest she inquire further about his own struggles. When she didn't appear she'd expand, he prompted her for more.

"And what happened? Did they—" He paused, swallowed. "Did they do anything to you?"

A question flashed across her eyes, but she left it unasked.

"They surrounded us, prevented us from aiding you."

"That's it?"

"Should there be more?"

Trenan shrugged; his gaze flickered away to a headless corpse stood at the side of the road, its arm raised, finger extended in accusation. He looked to the warrior.

"They're black priests. I thought they might have hurt you. Cursed you. Put a spell on you."

She shook her head. "They encircled us, used their power to keep us from leaving, but they could do no more. This is why my warriors train topless."

Trenan's brow crinkled.

"They hold little sway over women. We expose ourselves so they know they cannot conquer us."

"So they raised no sword to you?"

"Nothing more than a holding spell."

"And no..." His gaze flickered over her shoulder again. "No other effects?"

Yoli's eyebrow arched. "What is it, Trenan?"

He shook his head. "Concerned about you and the others."

She nodded once, though she remained dissatisfied with his response. Her eyes left him, surveyed the side of the road; he held his breath, hoping she'd discover one of the dead faces, make an exclamation of surprise, but none of this happened. Instead, her gaze found its way to the front where she peered past the riders in front of them at the track beyond.

"Two more sunrises and half a day—maybe a bit more—will bring us to the walls of Ikkundana. We will need you at your best, master swordsman."

The warrior didn't regard him when she said it, perhaps worried his response would be the wide-eyed, uncertain nod he produced. Staring ahead, she didn't notice it, so he cleared his throat and tried again.

"Of course."

It wasn't enough, but she nodded once and urged her steed forward, picking her way through the throng of riders toward the front of the column. Trenan watched her go, admiration for her filling him, but it tweaked another feeling inside him. He remembered not so long ago acting with the confidence she showed, a surety bred from season after season of training and proving oneself. But the dead men accusing from the side of the road left him a shadow of himself.

"We will need you at your best, master swordsman."

His chin sagged to his chest and the leader of the king's army let his eyelids slide shut, feigning sleep rather than watching the line of phantasms judging him from the roadside.

"Trenan?"

The word prompted him from the dream begun when he hadn't realized he'd fallen asleep—the same one every time he closed his eyes: an axe, the prince, his arm.

He snorted and shook his head, blinked twice and shifted to find Osis riding at his side in the same spot where Yoli had been.

"How long did I doze?" He raised his face skyward, but the sun appeared as naught but a smear of light through the haze of sleep veiling his vision.

"I don't know. Some time has passed since the warrior witch rode beside you. It is after midday."

Trenan frowned at the sergeant-at-arms' epithet directed at Yoli, but he let it go. No point arguing with him about someone he considered an enemy to the crown; his connection to the Goddess' warriors already strained their relationship enough. Instead of calling him out, he nodded.

"We should stop to eat soon."

"Your friend wants us to dine in the saddle today. It's her intent to make it to the City of the Sick as quickly as possible."

He glanced sideways at Osis, who stared straight ahead, a stern expression on his face. Trenan perceived he had a reason for riding beside him, but he didn't ask; he waited for the soldier to broach whatever was on his mind himself.

"What's happened to you?"

The question caught the master swordsman off-guard. Did he know about the ghosts? Did he see them? He glanced to the side of the track at the pale and bloodied faces staring at him. He gripped the reins in his hand tighter, resisted the inclination to ask the sergeant-at-arms if they appeared to him, too. If he did, he'd have phrased his inquiry another way; if they didn't appear to him, then Trenan would seem crazy.

Am I?

When he went without response, Osis rephrased his query to clarify.

"The Trenan I know is loyal to the king. He'd never consort with an enemy."

"These women are not our enemies."

"I have a troop of captured soldiers who might argue with you."

The sergeant—his friend through many battles and even more turns of the seasons—turned his head to fix the master swordsman with a penetrating gaze. He realized he should return the look, and wanted to, but found himself unable to do anything but glance, then peer away, careful not to let his vision stray to the sides of the road.

"I know how it appears, but they are doing what they think they must."

"But why?"

"To save the kingdom."

"Ha!" Osis scoffed, the sound much louder than his speaking voice had been. "There is no need to save the kingdom. And saved by a bunch of women? Ridiculous!"

"Do not underestimate Yoli and her soldiers. I have seen their skill; anyone who takes them lightly will regret it."

"Your words have the feel of a threat."

He shook his head, spied the blurred visages of ghosts glowering from the periphery of his vision and stopped. "Not a threat, Osis. A fact."

"It matters not. We sent a messenger through the ring of guards." He paused and Trenan sensed his gaze holding on him. "The rider got through, yes? I saw you speaking with the witch after I told you."

The master swordsman's cheeks grew hot. "He did. Yoli wanted him to take your message to the king, wants Erral to bring his army." He swallowed. "You should stop calling her that."

"She won't be too pleased about letting him through once they arrive. And they will come. You'll want to sort out your allegiances before they show up, Trenan. After everything, don't get yourself on the wrong side of your king, friend or not."

Rage bloomed in his chest and he snapped his head around to meet the sergeant's eyes, intending to tear a strip from him for questioning his loyalty. He'd lost an arm for Erral, given up the only woman he loved for him, and any semblance of a life. His failure to save the princess from her fate and the prince no more than a log sitting a horse didn't mean he hadn't done his best.

The last thoughts drained the anger from him before he opened his mouth. His gaze met Osis', but the vehemence with which he had turned left him; the tension in his jaw slackened, and he wondered what the sergeant might see when he looked at him. He thought concern and pity flickered in his friend's eyes. He wanted to look away, but diverting his attention meant looking upon the faces of the dead.

"What is it, Trenan? You don't seem yourself."

The swordmaster shook his head, gaze darting to his hand gripping the reins too tight. "You are the one who should be ready. There is a fight ahead."

"Humph. More threats. This is not what I'd have ever expected of you."

"Then it's not what you think. Maybe you should have some trust in me."

"I have trusted you as long as we've known each other but you are not the same man."

Osis clicked his tongue and put his heels to his steed, ushering the horse forward, relieving Trenan of any chance to respond. He opened his mouth to speak, unsure what he might say. Would he have told his friend the black priests had cursed him? About the faces of every man, woman, and child he'd killed in a life of killing haunting him? Maybe he'd admit Teryk was his son and his concern for the prince had stolen his edge? No, he'd have said none of that. All he may have done was to protest the sergeant's words, or implored him to trust him. Neither of which would have made a difference, so he remained silent.

It didn't take much time before Trenan's spine protested his position on the saddle with his head hung and back arched, leaving him no choice but to straighten and raise his eyes. Not so long ago, he'd have sat a horse through sunrise and sunset without a complaint from mind or body; not so now. His neck hurt, his spine ached, and his ass stung as though someone had beat it to a pulp with a switch. The sooner he climbed down off this beast, the better, but it sounded like Yoli planned to push on, likely until nightfall, if not longer.

Trenan stared straight ahead, trying to avoid the accusing looks of the dead, but found it impossible to escape them. Even without looking to the side, he spied them lining the track ahead of the column of horsemen like serfs forced to cheer a coronation parade. A few riders away, Teryk slouched in his saddle; he concentrated on watching him, wondering what went on in the lad's head. Did he still see the specters, as well? Was that why he kept to himself? Other than the one time, he hadn't acknowledged their presence again, but neither had he acknowledged the living.

Trenan thought about urging his mount forward between the mix of female soldiers and captured men of the king's army separating him from his son, but he resisted. Speaking with Yoli had been difficult; dealing with Osis even more so. Did he want to stare into Teryk's blank eyes? Gazing into the young man's features—reminiscent of his sister's—would do nothing to ease the master swordsman's heart or mind.

I'll check on him tonight.

Instead, he returned his gaze to his horse's neck, steeling himself for the pain awaiting him but preferring it to the mental anguish inflicted by the ghosts of the dead. His thoughts strayed, but he did his best to keep it controlled, diverting it from thoughts of the princess' face, pale with blood loss, or the prince's empty stare. But keeping it from both these sent it to the one other place he didn't want it to go.

Ishla.

What would she do when she found out what happened to her children?

Trenan closed his eyes, hoping to doze again and escape his thoughts but knowing if he did, his dreams would betray him, too.

XXX - Teryk – Watching

THOUGH NO ONE SPOKE to him directly, Teryk watched and listened to everything going on around him—this was the last night before their arrival at Ikkundana.

He knew nothing of the place, but the way Osis and the other men reacted told him all he needed to know. None of them wanted to visit this place. 'City of the Sick', he'd heard it called. From what he gathered, no one who visited ever returned. Had he control of his body like he did his sight and hearing, the once-prince of the Windward Kingdom would have taken his horse and ridden the opposite direction, but his arms and legs only intermittently allowed him their use so the thought went skittering from his mind.

Men snored around him as he leaned against the tree where they set him at day's end. He'd slept for a bit, but his dozing ended a while ago, leaving him wide awake, his eyes moving from subject to subject. He gazed upon sleeping soldiers, women patrolling the perimeter, their leader, Yoli, who never appeared to sleep herself. None of them held his attention for more than a dozen beats of his heart.

None until his gaze came to rest on Trenan.

The master swordsman lay propped against another tree and, though he looked to be asleep, his body twitched and moved at irregular intervals. Teryk watched as he raised his arm in front of his face, as though fending something off, then let it drop. His legs kicked out, first one, and then the other. His head jerked side to side. The bastard's dream must have been unpleasant.

Teryk's lips curled as he watched. Whatever he went through in his sleep, he deserved worse. How could he have lied to him for all these turns of the seasons, letting him believe himself something he wasn't? How could he have betrayed his father? No, not his father—the king. He was Danya's sire, not his. And there lay the swordmaster's biggest sin—allowing Teryk to kill his sister when he was not of his right mind.

He clenched his teeth hard enough to make his jaw ache. His gaze remained on Trenan, but his thoughts wandered to the black-robed healer and his companion, Stirk, with one arm and no legs. He'd said he possessed the ability to return the dead to life and Teryk had barely stopped thinking about it since he spoke the words. But had he truly been more than a dream proclaiming such a thing? Was he the feverish imagining of his sick brain manufacturing the conversation?

Someone to his right turned over in their sleep, rustling leaves, but he didn't look away. Trenan waved his hand in front of him, like shooing a fly. His every movement added to the anger and resentment brewing inside Teryk, stacking up in his chest like the game of tower sticks he and Danya played in their youth. The memory poked a firm finger into his heart.

He closed his eyes, allowed his jaw to slacken and his chin to droop. His sister didn't deserve what had happened to her; she went to the Green out of concern for him. She'd given up comfort and happiness at Draekfarren to search for him, to return him to safety. Though Trenan hadn't stopped him from plunging the knife into her throat, Teryk still shouldered the responsibility for her presence and his opportunity. If he hadn't chosen to strike out on his own, she would be alive and safe.

Guilt rested with him.

"It is not true."

The speaker of the words did not whisper them, in no way attempted to conceal his presence from anyone else.

Teryk opened his eyes and shifted his head—all the movement paralysis allowed his body. The black-robed healer stood before him, the cowl thrown off to reveal his face. Light from torches burning around the encampment shone on his shaven pate and threw shadows across his features. His left hand rested on the scalp of the one-limbed fellow beside him.

"Had you not believed yourself the firstborn of the rightful king, none of this would have happened. But you did, because they deceived you."

The former prince glanced away from the men standing in front of him, surveying those around them to see who else might be close enough to listen to the conversation. Nobody awake paid them any attention; they didn't even realize the healer's presence. When he brought his gaze back to them, it fell on Stirk. The mutilated man's eyes darted from one thing to the next, never resting on anything for more than a heartbeat, as though the only way to expend his energy.

"Look at me."

He did.

"Everything has its roots with the man who begat you. He kept the truth from you, even when he knew what the prophecy foretold. Should he not have known you adequately well to realize what you would do? Was it not he who taught you your values?"

Teryk sucked his bottom lip into his mouth, bit it hard enough to feel the pain but stopping short of drawing blood, and nodded. The healer nodded along with him.

"Then the question is simple: who deserves to live? He whose deceptions caused all that has happened, or your sister, the victim of his lies?"

Anger bubbled into Teryk's chest. He looked past the healer to the tree where Trenan—his father, the cause of the grief in his life—rested. Had someone handed him a knife now the way the tall, skinny man once did, he'd have rushed through the tangle of sleeping men and sunk it into the master swordsman's heart while he dozed. But not only did he not have a weapon, he couldn't move.

"I can help with one of your problems."

Feet hidden by the hem of his robe, the healer appeared to glide across the ground to reach him. Stirk didn't move with such grace. The man without legs shuffle-hopped beside the hairless fellow, the healer's fingers still on his head as though supporting him. They stopped an arm's length from Teryk.

He wanted to cower away from them, but his useless body denied him. Instead, he watched the healer reach out with his right hand. He laid it on Teryk's shoulder and removed his other from Stirk. This one he held out, palm up.

"Give me you hand, pet."

Stirk's attention snapped to his master, and he raised his arm. Teryk's gaze flickered to the man's hand as the healer grasped it and saw Stirk had a thumb and three fingers, and was missing part of his palm.

The robed man closed his eyes and his companion stiffened. Teryk glanced between them before a tingling sensation distracted him. It intensified, spreading through his shoulder and into his chest. He inhaled a hard breath, half-filling his lungs as the vibration emanating from the healer exerted pressure on his insides. It built until air no longer entered or exited his body.

Out of reflex, Teryk raised his arm and grabbed the healer's wrist, yanked his touch away. As he did, the strain inside he thought might end with his death relented. The black-robed man opened his eyes, stared at him with an intensity making him want to cower.

"I have released you." He pulled away from Teryk and let go of Stirk's hand at the same time. When the three-quarters-limbless man drew back, Teryk saw he now lacked yet another finger. "Do what you must do to get your sister back."

Teryk lowered his gaze, raised both hands and patted his chest, relishing in his own touch. How long since his limbs and digits last worked as intended? How odd one sometimes does not appreciate such things until they are unavailable.

When he lifted his head again to thank the healer for what he had done, though the sentiment sat uneasily with him, the black-robed man and his companion were gone. Instead of seeing them, he looked across the cluttered clearing at Trenan, the man responsible for his sister's death; the man whose life might be the key to her resurrection. Teryk leaned hard against the tree, using it for leverage as he climbed to his feet.

——ele——

The closest of the dead men lunged toward Trenan, the rusted tip of his polearm extended at his face. The master swordsman threw his arm up in defense, kept from crying out. But the wicked point didn't penetrate his flesh, the same as the others before it. He lowered his defences, eyelids as close to closed as possible while remaining able to see the throng of phantasms gathered around him.

The one who most recently poked at him leered at him with a broken-jawed smile, then stepped aside to let another take his place. This fellow was missing half an arm, the cut which had taken it continuing into his side where a loop of intestines sought to find its way out. He gripped no sword, the blow which had lopped off his limb having relieved him of whatever weapon he might have held with it, leaving it lying on a battlefield along with the severed arm. What field of battle, Trenan didn't remember and didn't care to. If he figured it out, he'd face a different dead man waiting to replace this one, then another.

With no sword or axe, this ghoul grabbed for the leader of the king's army with fingers caked with dried blood. Trenan waved his own hand, seeking to bat it away, but it met no resistance, passed through the other's arm as though it didn't exist.

Because it doesn't.

The realization should have encouraged him, but it didn't, for another man waited, and another, and another. Each desired revenge for the death Trenan had dealt them, and no prayer he said afterward begging for mercy on them had relieved them of a sliver of their suffering. No matter what god, nor how desperate, they remained dead, and none of their souls had moved on.

They've spent their deaths awaiting this moment, waiting for their opportunity for vengeance.

He wanted to cringe away from them, close his eyes, seek refuge in sleep, but his body and mind refused to give him relief. Instead, he feigned slumber so none around him knew what he experienced.

An axe crashed down by his head. A spear shot forth, directed at his chest. A sword looped through the air, aimed for his neck. Trenan fought not to react but jerked and moved in response.

Until the girl stood before him.

She wasn't like the others—no severed limbs defined her, no cloven skull or leaking gashes. A hole in the side of her neck, nothing more. Fresh blood covered half of her face and soaked her clothes. At first, he didn't recognize her, both because of the red masking her features, but also because he didn't try to. It took but one more step closer.

"Danya."

His lips moved to speak her name, but no sound emerged. Her gaze didn't waver, her eyes boring into his.

Why are you here? I didn't kill you.

She made no move toward him, no killing lunge or vengeful strike. She didn't need to. Her stare penetrated him, found its way through him, into his heart. He fought against his paralysis and forced his eyes shut, breaking contact; the pain in his chest remained. The forest pressed close around him, like a crowd standing too near, exhaling their squalid air on him, attempting to suffocate him. He held his breath, forced his lids closed tight, until a noise startled him—a branch snapping.

He pried his lids open, and it took a few heartbeats for his vision to readjust. When it did, he saw the dead faces gathered around him, but it was no longer Danya standing before him. Instead, her brother loomed over him. Trenan opened his mouth to tell him he'd seen his sister as Teryk raised his dagger toward the night sky.

XXXI - Vesisdenperos – Battle

*T*HE SCULPTOR HID.

He was aware of the rhythmic bounce of the golem's gait, heard words spoken nearby, sensed the change from day to night and day again. The clank of armor and weapons, the sounds of horses, the whisper of wind in trees. Though he possessed this awareness, he ignored it. He feared that, should he concentrate on any one thing and attract the evenstar's attention, then he'd know his thoughts, see fear and grief and anger tangling up inside him.

And he fought against those as hard as he did everything else, picturing himself curled into a ball, tucked in a distant corner inside the clay golem. Whenever his recollections strayed to his mentor's dead eyes staring at the sky, he snatched them back. When memories of learning his craft and fashioning the body which now imprisoned him bubbled up, he sent them skittering away like a pebble kicked along a flagstone path. He tried to keep his mind blank and empty, but Kuneprius returned to him repeatedly.

The work you do is important, he had said to Vesisdenperos so many times. *You, my son, will change the world.*

Had he known changing the world included the death of the man he'd considered his father, he'd have chosen a different life.

You didn't choose this life. They chose you for it.

More of his mentor's words, and no relief in them. The ball he imagined himself in tightened; he thought of pulling his knees to his chest, pressing his face against them. He wished he could cry, or scream and yell, something to relieve the pressure of his emotions building and building.

Your time will come, and you will be the most important, the most admired of the evenstar's men.

He'd have traded everything for Kuneprius to live again, to watch his lips move as he counted his steps climbing the path to visit the sculpting cave where he honed his skills. He'd start over again for one more of his bland meals, a last droll joke, a final positive platitude. But it was too late; time did not roll backward, it carried on, leaving death, despair, and ruined lives in its wake.

The golem moved inexorably forward. Its sculpted muscles never grew tired, its solid clay stomach never growled, nor did the sculptor's. With the husk of his body left lying in the sculpting cave, only his essence lived on. Until the evenstar's arrival, he had powered the muddy beast, lending his energy to its limbs, his guidance to its mind. Now the priest Ine'vesi guided it, his will imparting far more power through the mud than the sculptor could have imagined. He sensed it flowing through the living statue, energizing it, giving it strength, and leaving Vesisdenperos to wonder why the evenstar hadn't ended his existence.

The way he killed Kuneprius.

For a long while, he drifted away, focusing on nothing, emptying his mind of painful thoughts and memories. A crash pulled him from the depths in which he'd lost himself, waking him like a man from a deep slumber.

"Come, see what you helped create," the voice around him said.

Then he noticed the sensation of movement—not the machinations of the vessel carrying him, but a rising of his own self. An instant later, he peered through the eyes of the golem.

They stood at the border between forest and grassland, a vast field of tall, yellowed grass stretching before them to the stark, gray wall of an immense fortress. No windows dotted its surface, no doors. Nobody perched atop, overlooking a parapet. It appeared one great slab of stone.

Halfway across the plain, armies clashed. Sun glinted on steel as a mass of bodies heaved and pitched in a nonsensical, violent dance. Vesisdenperos stared; had he a mouth, it would have fallen open at the sight. Where had these warriors come from? If Kuneprius was with him he'd have attempted counting them, as he liked to do—a task to fill an entire day, perhaps longer.

A rumbling chuckle boiled up inside the golem, starting somewhere below the sculptor, shaking him.

"That is not all, sculptor."

The golem's head canted, raising Vesisdenperos' field of vision to follow a light streaking across the sky, smoky trail stretched out behind. It hit the ground with a sound like the one which had brought him out of his hiding. The falling object cut a trench in the earth, throwing up chunks of grass and soil, bowling over soldiers, indiscriminate of whom they fought for. When it came to a halt, a moment passed while wisps of smoke wriggled their way skyward, and then a man climbed out of the hole it left. Naked, he spread his arms. A mounted warrior rode toward him, weapon swinging at his skull. The man dodged, caught the rider's horse by a hind leg, and sent both of them toppling.

More chuckling shook the sculptor again as another fireball struck the ground, then another.

"See, Vesisdenperos? See what your skill and prowess have wrought?"

The evenstar's words hit him like a punch to the gut, knocking unreal wind from imaginary lungs. He tried to pull himself away from the golem's vision, return to the hole he'd dug for himself on the journey to this place; the fallen Small God wouldn't let him. Fireballs fell, battle raged, and he watched with eyes incapable of blinking as though someone had pinned his lids open to torture him. The chuckle again, shaking him, rattling his soul.

"This is because of you, sculptor."

The golem's legs moved, carrying them toward the fray. Again, Vesisdenperos tried to scurry away from the scene, but Ine'vesi held him.

"You are going nowhere, my friend," the fallen god said, using the sculpture's mouth this time and speaking aloud. "I need you, for a while, at least. You bind me to this creature. Soon I will have another place; then I can let you go."

Had he knees to shake or teeth to chatter, they'd have done so, but he didn't. He felt pressure against him, forcing his essence into the extremities of the clay beast, spreading him throughout like a layer of butter on a thick slice of bread. The golem's limbs became his, though he didn't control them. He filled its groin, its head, its chest, sharing it with the evenstar come to earth to crush them. They crowded the space together, the two of them as one. Except for one spot, a single place where Vesisdenperos found himself alone.

I am the heart of the beast. That's why he needs me.

The golem raised an arm skyward, increased its pace to a loping run.

"To battle," the rock-grating-on-rock voice yelled. "The kingdom will be ours."

XXXII - Teryk – Breakdown

TERYK PICKED HIS WAY between the sleeping soldiers, careful with each step not to disturb any of them with his passing. Halfway to his goal, he stopped. What was he going to do when he reached Trenan? Throttle him? Surely he'd make sufficient noise to rouse the others, and he counted many friends amongst the men. He'd never squeeze his life from him before somebody intervened. Similarly, he'd not have the time to beat him to death with his fists without someone stepping in. And that supposed his target, a trained soldier, didn't overpower him to begin with. They'd sparred enough times for him to know the master swordsman's strength and skill far surpassed his in any and every sort of combat.

The young man surveyed the warriors sleeping around him. The women had disarmed the king's men, their weapons stored in a centralized location, packed along in a wagon pulled by two horses and surrounded by a complement of female soldiers. No way to get to them and liberate a sword. To succeed with this task, he needed to kill his father without attracting attention.

Kill my father.

Despite all the man was responsible for, the thought rang a hollow bell inside him. Patricide. End the life of the man responsible for him having one. Kill the man who loved his mother.

No. Kill the man who lied to you. End the life of the one responsible for stealing yours. Kill the man who betrayed you, and his king, and whose actions resulted in your sister's death.

In a different frame of mind, he might have recognized the voice in his head didn't belong to him but sounded more like the healer's.

He drew a slow, deep breath and continued. His gaze swept the ground ahead of him, both to be careful of where he stepped, but also hoping to find a method of ending Trenan's life. To his surprise, he found what he searched for within three paces.

The dagger's pommel stuck out from under the small of the woman's back. When he first spied it, he thought he might have been mistaken as the rest of the women who slept amongst the men appeared as disarmed as them. A rock or a bit of stick fooling him. He leaned closer, reached his hand down, stroked the grip with the tip of his finger.

Not a rock or a stick.

Moving with care, Teryk crouched, aware of each part of his body and ensuring none impinged on anyone else's space. He wrapped his fingers around the handle, dragged it toward him, holding his breath. The woman lying on it sighed in her sleep and he stopped, wondered what might happen to him if she caught him stealing her weapon. When she neither moved nor opened her eyes, he pulled again. The dagger came out easily once he freed the guard from beneath her.

He held it up in front of his face, examining it. The knife appeared bigger than the slim blade he'd used to kill Danya, still by no means imposing. Its edges looked sharp, its point deadly and, as his sister's death proved, one needed little more.

Standing, he took a moment to scan his surroundings—everyone around him remained sleeping. None of the sentries turned toward him, and Trenan's dream-fueled thrashing had settled, so he continued.

Men snored, bats fluttered through the high forest boughs. His own footsteps, cushioned by layers of moss, sounded loud to his ears. Ten paces before he'd reach his objective.

The end of the master swordsman's life.

He moved more quickly with his goal tantalizingly close, careful but pushing to get to him as fast as possible. In his hurry, his toe caught the leg of a burly soldier as he went to step over the man. He landed more heavily than he intended and paused, expecting the fellow to awaken. An emphatic snort sounded, and he rolled over—the extent of his disruption. Teryk released his held breath and carried on.

Three more steps passed under his feet; four more remained until he reached the master swordsman. His pulse beat in his ears, blocking out the other sounds of the forest. Trenan turned his head away in his restless sleep. The remaining space disappeared hastily until Teryk loomed over his father, the man who raised him, and trained, and lied to him his entire life.

He stole everything from me.

He stared down at him in his disturbed slumber. The cords in his neck stood out as though he strained against something, and Teryk wondered what he dreamed of. Did he see the murder of his sister? A precognition of his own death?

The former prince swallowed hard, pressed his lips together, and peered at the dagger in his hand, wan moonlight shining through the forest canopy reflecting on its blade. What would his mother think when she found out he killed his father? Would she care when she knew the responsibility for ending Danya's life rested with him? Time alone could answer these questions.

He gripped the weapon tighter, knuckles aching with the effort and the muscles in his forearm tensing. He raised it slowly, eyes fixed on Trenan's throat where he'd bury the blade, like before. When he'd stabbed Danya, she didn't make a sound, hadn't been able to with the steel in her neck. The master swordsman wouldn't be capable of calling for help, either, leaving Teryk time to watch his life drain from him. Whatever happened after didn't matter.

As the weapon reached its apex, the swordmaster's head pivoted and his eyes opened, found Teryk's. The young man hesitated.

"Teryk?"

Trenan's voice came out a croak, the name nearly unrecognizable, but enough to stop him from bringing the dagger down.

"I saw her," Trenan said, leaning forward and reaching out to grab the front of his son's tunic. "She stood right where you are standing."

Teryk stared at him, at the unfamiliar expression twisting the man's features. He struggled to understand what it meant.

"She didn't say anything. Did nothing. She just looked at me."

The young man shook his head. "Who?"

Trenan's eyes darted first over one of his son's shoulders, then the other. When he glanced back, he understood what caused his facial contortions: fear.

"Danya. It was Danya. But she did nothing; not like the others. They're here to get revenge. I killed them and they want to torture me for it."

Teryk blinked, resisted the urge to look around. He knew no one lurked behind him, nobody stood over his shoulder, living or dead.

"Don't let them take me, son." His voice strained with effort, his eyes glistened. "I said a prayer for them, begged for mercy for them, but it didn't work."

Without thinking about it or meaning to, Teryk lowered the dagger.

"I had no choice. I'm a soldier of the king. My job is to protect the kingdom. Tell them. Tell them it's not my fault."

This time he couldn't help but glance over his shoulder. He didn't expect men risen from the dead to haunt the master swordsman. He thought he'd find soldiers roused from sleep, or sentries investigating the disturbance. He saw neither...not yet.

"Don't let them take me, son. I didn't mean to hurt them. I didn't mean to hurt you."

The swordmaster of the kingdom, the leader of the king's army, collapsed forward against him, pressing his face against Teryk's chest as tears broke free, flowing from his eyes to dampen his son's tunic.

The anger inside him unwound, and the dagger slipped from his grip. He put his arms around his father and embraced him while he sobbed.

XXXIII - Fellick and Ive – Black Priests

*T*HE *CLINK AND* CLATTER of swords and axes settling with the movement of the wain set Fellick's teeth on edge. Each sound meant a blade requiring a fresh whetting, a piece of leather-bound grip in need of replacement or—Goddess forbid—chipped steel needing repair on a grinder. In his heart, he realized it didn't matter but, after so long dedicating his waking hours to the manufacture, care, and sale of the kingdom's best weapons, he found it hard to let go.

But tools of violence is not what my life has been for.

Ive sat in his customary spot in the driver's seat, reins loose in his fingers. Left up to Fellick, they'd have stopped to secure their cargo now they didn't have the added payload of two young women for whom to make space. Of course, the lanky weapons merchant had been insistent such trivialities must wait. Any other time, they'd have been at odds over it but, this time, his partner was right. And so the stocky fighter moved his bottom jaw forward and back, over and over, grinding his teeth in an effort to stop the way the nerves in them tingled with every clank of steel on steel.

"We will be upon them soon, my friend."

Ive's eyes peered straight ahead as he spoke the words, staring at the road, or the asses of the two horses pulling the wagon. Fellick glanced toward him but didn't speak, the fingers of his right hand gripping the hilt of the sword lying sheathed on his lap his only response. His partner required no more from him; such was the way of their communication. Often it involved the tall fellow speaking and not much more.

On this journey, he'd done far less speechifying than normal. As time passed, the gravity of their tasks ahead, the enormity of it, kept them both in reflection and quiet. Many times, Fellick wished their trips had been thus instead of filled with the vocal meanderings of his partner as he mused on every subject entering his mind. For once, he'd rather have put up with the inane chatter, he decided.

"Ive," he said, voice perching somewhere between grunt and fully formed word. He didn't move his gaze from staring down the road, but noticed out of the corner of his eye when the other weapons merchant glanced toward him. He chose not to respond, and Fellick rubbed the tip of his tongue on his bottom teeth, wondering what to say. It felt as though he should say something.

The wagon's left wheel hit a rut, jarring their wares with a clatter and bouncing the men in their seats.

"Are you all right? Not used to you being so quiet."

Ive drew a deep and noisy sigh, shoulders rising and falling with it. He returned his gaze to the road, both of them staring at what the world offered in front of them, neither of them enamored with what it presented.

"You know what lies in wait for us."

"Yes. But we've always known. We have prepared."

Fellick glanced toward his partner, watched him wet his lips, head moving ever so slightly in agreement.

"What is it, then?" the stocky man prompted.

"The girl."

"Mmm."

"I hate what happened to her and my part in it. Because of me, her life ended, and the prince is broken." Now he shook his head side to side, lips pursed. "I know you will tell me it was what must be, but the result doesn't change. So much potential lay ahead for them both. Remember what that was like, Mr. Fellick?"

"Aye," he said, though he wasn't sure he did. It felt as though it had been so long since the Mother of Death had laid out their roles. Had their lives ever been anything but this? He took his left hand from where it sat atop the sheath of his sword and set it on his companion's forearm. "For the greater good."

"Yes. Hurts my heart nonetheless."

Fellick nodded, lifted his soothing touch, and said no more. The wain rattled on, boards creaking, wheels clattering on hard ground, weapons settling. A bird flitted across their path, then three right behind it, then nine more. The sudden movement startled the horses, but Ive's practiced grip on the reins calmed them with little more than a faint whinny and a shake of their manes. It occurred to him they'd never named the beasts laboring to drag them and their wares from place to place, forever referring to them simply as 'the nags.'

They deserve better. We all deserve better.

He lowered his gaze, eyes falling to his dirty trousers, then finding his hands. He turned them palm up, looked at the way the dirt clogged the loops and whirls etched on his fingertips. Ive had once informed him the patterns on no two people's fingers were the same, and he wondered at its veracity, or how he might know such a thing. Truthfully, he couldn't, but such was his partner's the nature: speak with confidence and inspire belief. The man could have made a living in a pulpit, if he so desired, and Fellick had told him as much; he'd responded that he liked neither wine nor little boys enough for it. The stocky weapons merchant turned his hands over, examined the web of scars on the other side, certain no one else's in the land bore the same pattern.

A light wind shook the leaves on either edge of the road, a faint scent carried upon it as though someone had set alight the rind of an orange. Fellick raised his head and sent his thoughts skittering from his mind. He squared his jaw and squinted at the forest to his right.

"They're near."

Ive cleared his throat, sat straighter on the wooden plank serving as their seat. "Indeed."

They glanced at each other, gazes catching and holding. A corner of the lanky weapon's merchant's mouth crept up in a lopsided facsimile of a smile.

"Thank you, Mr. Fellick, for everything over all the seasons. You have been an ideal partner and companion. I couldn't have asked for more."

The warrior heart in the stocky man's chest shrank one size, rose to clog his throat. He didn't fear dying himself; he'd trained from his youth, expecting death at the point of a sword to be his destiny, no matter what path he took. But Ive's confident bluster and bullshit bravado masked a caring and beautiful soul deserving of better than what lay ahead.

He wanted to tell his friend this, let him know how much he meant to him, and opened his mouth to do so, but stopped. He inhaled a breath, tightened his grip on the sword hilt, and nodded once, then looked to the road, satisfied Ive understood.

—ele—

Birk moved toward the edge of the track, leaving the group of priests sitting in the fringe of grass before the trees began. Most of them chewed bread in danger of growing stale and gnawed pieces of cheese after having picked away the spots of mold. He'd heard the clatter of the approaching wagon, the sound drawing him from his own meal to stare along the road at the modest cloud of dust kicked up by two horses and a pair of wheels. He considered calling over one of the others for safety, but decided not to. Even brigands would have to be out of their heads to consider approaching Birk and the black priests.

He squinted toward the approaching wain, raised a hand to his forehead to block the sun. Soon, it drew close enough for him to make out the shapes of the driver and passenger—one tall and slight, the other a barrel of a man.

"Fellick and Ive?" he said to no one in particular. "What are they doing here?"

He stepped out into the road, boots scuffing on the dry ground, and raised a hand. A few heartbeats later, Ive returned the gesture from his spot in the driver's seat. Birk lowered his arm, put his hands on his hips, and awaited their arrival.

"What are the two of you doing here?"

The lanky merchant reined the horses to a stop, the weapons in their wagon clanking as they settled forward. A few paces remained between them, but he didn't close the distance; they could damn well climb off their perches and give him an explanation.

"This wasn't the plan. Explain yourselves."

"The thing about plans is they have a habit of changing," the lanky weapons merchant said as he dropped the reins and climbed out of his seat.

The wain bobbed and rattled as he and Fellick dismounted. Ive patted the ass of the horse on his side as he went by, approaching Birk with long, slow strides.

"What do you mean plans change? You were supposed to head to Woodsel to arm our men there."

"Yes, but this isn't Woodsel, is it? See what I mean about the nature of plans?"

Birk's brow furrowed. He'd never been sure if he liked either of the weapons merchants; in that moment, he decided he definitely did not fancy Ive.

"You need to turn yourself around and get those nags moving double time. The evenstar will arrive soon and we must be ready."

"Yes, yes." Ive waved dismissively, the breeze it created stoking Birk's newfound dislike. "But my companion hungers, don't you, Mr. Fellick?"

The stocky man emerged from behind the horses and grunted his assent, stalked past Birk without as much as a glance, a sheathed sword gripped in his left hand. Dislike wasn't the word he'd have used to describe how he felt about this half of the weapons merchants—fearful fit as a better descriptor.

"Do your friends have anything he might eat? Our stocks have run low. We'll resupply when we raze Krin's tavern, but until then," he shrugged, "the beast must be fed."

He reached Birk and clapped him on the shoulder with a long-fingered hand, his forward momentum turning the man and carrying him along as he stalked toward the robed men. Fellick strode a few steps ahead of them, his shorter gait quicker, devouring ground faster than the lethargic pace of his companion. He looked past him at the priests; with their cowls thrown off while they ate, they didn't appear so different from any other group of fellows who'd stopped at the roadside to eat lunch.

Ive's hand slid to a spot between his shoulders, thumb resting on one side of his neck, fingers on the other, a slight pressure from his palm ushering Birk toward the others. From anyone else, the position and firmness of the touch might have brought some apprehension, but his newly discovered dislike of the man transformed concern to annoyance. Why hadn't they done as he'd told them? He shrugged to get him to remove his touch from his back, but it remained.

"I don't understand why you are here. It would have been quicker to go to Woodsel as we planned and feed your brute at Krin's than to find us."

"Tut, tut. Don't let Mr. Fellick's appearance deceive you. His gruff exterior hides much more than you realize. More than you know and more than you'd ever hope to be."

He raised an eyebrow at the weapons merchant's words, unsure if he meant them as an insult. Five paces remained between them and the priests seated in the grass taking sustenance as even servants of the evenstar must; Fellick reached the semicircle in which they'd arranged themselves. Birk opened his mouth to question Ive's intended meaning, but the hiss of steel jerked from scabbard stopped him. The stocky man's blade sliced through the air, opening the throat of the priest nearest to him.

Ive's grip on his neck increased to the point of causing pain; he halted them both and stepped in front of Birk. Confusion and panic exploded in his chest and he opened his mouth, snapped at the weapons merchant.

"What is—"

He never saw the dagger piercing below his ribs and angled up toward his heart. The shock and surprise of it sent the air from his lungs as the lanky merchant leaned close enough for his breath to touch Birk's cheek when he spoke.

"Give my regards to Goddess, if she deigns to allow you audience."

He took a half step closer, jamming the blade farther into him, before stepping back again, wrenching the dagger free. Ive left him teetering, the weapons merchant spinning on his heel and rushing the last few paces to aid his friend where Fellick had already dispatched one priest. The remaining leapt to their feet, two of them brandishing blades and advancing to engage their attackers, the others raising their hands, collecting power from their banished gods.

Birk's knees failed him and he toppled, the impact jarring him and sending a gout of blood into his throat. He coughed it into his mouth, tried to spit the coppery taste out but lacked the energy to do so. It drooled from the corner of his lips onto the grass. He stared straight ahead, saw two more of the priests cut down by men he'd thought his allies, if not his friends. A circle of light too bright for his eyes grew around them, blades flashing, and he let his lids slip closed. The sound of metal on metal, steel cutting flesh, faded away.

He inhaled one last time, the stench of burnt oranges and singed bread hiding the stink of his own blood.

XXXIV - Horace – Waitin'

*H*ORACE PACED FIRST ONE way, then the other. He'd been doin' exactly the same thing for far too long with no effect on the situation. The sun rose and set a few since Ailyssa disappeared into the garden, but he couldn't make himself stop. Ivy sat cross-legged, watchin' him as she'd been for most o' the time he'd done it. She only stooped when she left for a while and returned with food and water to give him the energy to continue pacin'.

He stopped and stared hard at the hilly garden at the middle o' the beaten-down patch o' grass. The colors'd mostly drained from the blooms, leavin' flowers wilted and turned a shade o' brownish gray what reminded him o' the clay beast what'd stolen his friend Thorn. Vines'd shriveled and leaves'd drooped, the entire mound o' plants shrinking to half its original size, but no sign o' Ailyssa. He worried the thing'd swallowed her up and ate her the way he sometimes wished the God o' the Deep'd done to him instead o' lettin' him go through ev'rythin' since.

"Where is she, Ivy?"

But the Small God didn't respond, same as the last time he asked the question. Same as the time before, and the time before that one, and ev'ry time before those. He weren't sure if she refused to tell him, or if she didn't want to admit she didn't know. Part o' him wanted to leap forward and dig into the heap o' decayin' plants, find the woman and pull her out, but he thought Ivy and the others might not let him.

He took a half-step toward the shrunken garden, doin' his best at furtively glancin' toward her to see if she noticed. She sat in the same place she always did, watchin' him, not movin'. He slid his foot a little farther, a little farther, his boot sole scrapin' on ground dried out by the days passin' since Ailyssa disappeared.

When he'd moved the equivalent o' three paces, she got up, but did nothin' else before another o' the other gray fellas approached her. He stood taller'n Ivy, and broader. Both his stature and the way he carried himself suggested to Horace he might be a leader amongst their people—maybe the one he'd seen when he visited them before, but he found tellin' them apart difficult. He laid his hand on Ivy's arm.

"It's time," he said.

She nodded and lowered herself into crisscross applesauce, her head uncomfortably near the fella's thing danglin' between his legs, but she appeared not to notice. He strode away at any rate, gesturin' with his arms and speakin' the language o' them gray people what Horace didn't understand. The others strewn around the meadow began headin' toward him, and the ol' sailor returned his attention to Ivy sittin' in the grass.

She bent her head at him.

Not knowin' for sure what else to do, he nodded in return, then pivoted on his heel and closed the distance between himself and the wizened garden.

Standin' at its edge, he noticed the colors wasn't the only things gone from the tangle o' flowers, but also their bouquet. Weren't nothin' but a stink now—decayin' leaves, ol' soil, faded blossoms. Somewhere beneath it all, he thought he might've caught the scent o' one last rose, but it might as easily have been the sweet odor o' some dead thing. The possibility gave him a shudder.

He dropped to his knees at the edge of the decrepit plot, his joints poppin' and makin' him wince when they did. With his palms restin' on his thighs—aware o' dirt smeared on the front o' his pants, turnin' the fabric hard—he stared into the garden, attemptin' to discern any shapes between the tangle o' dyin' vines and droopin' leaves. Weren't nothin' to see but the death o' beauty.

And the death o' Ailyssa.

He inhaled a fearful, shudderin' breath and glanced o'er his shoulder toward Ivy, who sat in the same spot and appeared to be payin' him no mind. Her own hands rested on her knees, palms facin' skyward, face lifted up in the manner o' a child enjoyin' the sun on her cheeks. Horace watched her for a few heartbeats, but she remained unmovin'. But for a smidge o' size and the lack o' bits between her legs, it might've been Thorn sittin' there. It reminded the ol' sailor o' when the Small God turned up havin' stolen a pair o' breeches, the funny way he'd walked until he got used to rough fabric rubbin' against his gray skin. He chuckled, shook his head in a wistful nature, and returned his attention to the garden, chest cinchin' in around his heart and givin' it a squeeze.

He didn't want to lose another friend. If Ailyssa were in there, he needed to get her out.

Horace reached out with both hands and grabbed bits o' plants, intendin' to yank them out without realizin' he'd encounter thorns in doin' so. He jerked away with a whistle o' sharp breath between his teeth and turned his palms toward his face. Each now contained a couple o' pricks for his effort, one point havin' lodged itself in his flesh. He frowned, took its end between the thumb and finger o' his other hand, and gently pulled it out. A string o' somethin' sticky stretched out between the tip o' the thorn and his palm, makin' him frown. When the line o' stuff broke, a fat red drop squeezed outta the hole left behind. The ol' sailor first thought about puttin' his lips on it to suck the blood out, but he stopped, the filth on his skin deterin' him from puttin' his mouth on it. Instead, he wiped it on the thigh o' his breeches, smearin' blood along the dirt-darkened fabric.

This time when he reached into the garden, he did so with more care and attention. He chose his spot, wrapped his fingers around the desiccated fronds more carefully. When he felt no pain from it, he gave it a tug.

The handfuls o' plant matter came away easily, crunchin' between his digits and fallin' to dust. Encouraged, he leaned forward, eyed things up searchin' for planty defenses before reachin' in to grab more. Again, the delicate runners and vines broke with little resistance. Horace tossed the detritus o'er his shoulder, peeked at the tangled mess and realized that, at this rate, it'd take him a good long time to get ev'rythin' cleared and find out what lay beneath. He rocked onto his haunches, decidin' to use a different method.

With another grimace at the discomfort it caused, he uncurled his legs and struggled his way to his feet. He inhaled a deep breath, readyin' himself and tryin' to ignore the stink o' dead plants, then swung one foot toward the garden in a loopin' kick.

The withered flowers practically disintegrated from the force o' his attack, puffs o' once-red petals flyin' up into the air. With no resistance from them, Horace spun around with his own momentum and teetered at the edge o' fallin' on his ass. Seemed a miracle he kept his feet, but he did, and went right back to kickin' the shit outta the garden, this time doin' better at controllin' his enthusiasm.

This made quicker work o' the decayed foliage, but it proved more effort for the ol' sailor. A sweaty sheen soon built up on his forehead, and he stopped to wipe it on his shirt sleeve with a quarter o' the garden layin' in ruins. He bent forward, hands on knees, and examined it closer but saw nothin' hidden away inside. He took the time to draw one deep replenishing breath and got right at it again.

Chunks o' browned vine flew, landin' somewhere lost in the yellow grass. Once-beautiful blossoms exploded in muted hues o' their former splendor—rust and indigo and mustard rather'n the stunning reds and blues and golds they'd been. After spendin' most o' his time aboard one ship and another, Horace Seaman didn't know much about gardenin', couldn't imagine what might've sucked the life outta it in such a brief span. Nothin' natural, at least.

His foot exploded through a jigsaw o' leaves tangled together, sendin' chunks flyin'. At the edge o' his awareness, he heard insects buzzin'—flies gathered around animal carcasses scattered about the area like he'd stumbled into a slaughterhouse rather'n a meadow. He ignored them and ev'rythin' else to concentrate on demolishin' the twisted thicket.

Three more kicks and he stopped again to wipe more sweat away and labor a breath into his lungs. He realized he heard other sounds, too—the voices o' Small Gods chatterin' to one another, occasionally callin' out—but he heard somethin' else, too. Underlyin' the buzzin' flies and the talkative gray people were a sound more akin to a moan.

Horace's forehead developed a crinkle in it. He glanced toward Ivy, thinkin' she might be makin' the noise, but she hadn't moved since he'd last checked on her. Maybe one o' the other Small Gods hid in the tall grass, keepin' an eye on him as he demolished the wicked plants? His gaze swept the surroundin' area, but he saw nothin'. The crease over his eyebrows deepened, and he leaned forward.

The sound came from the garden.

The ol' sailor licked his lips, tasted dirt and flower dust upon them, turned his head and spat. Part o' him thought it might be somethin'—or someone—under the vines and leaves makin' the noise. A much larger part suspected the low, near imperceptible moan emanated from the plants themselves.

Are they cryin'?

As he raised his foot again, he hesitated. He'd seen so many strange things since the dummy Dunal'd knocked him o'er the side o' the cursed boat, flowers what cried wouldn't be no real stretch o' his imagination. He might've stopped, set his boot on the ground, walked away, but Ailyssa's face floated into his mind. If she were buried beneath the dried-up leaves, he needed to rescue her, whether they bawled at him or not.

His stomp turned what'd once been a broad, pink bloom to a cloud of dust. He switched legs, swingin' his left foot and sendin' a tangle o' vines dehydrated to twigs flyin' into the grass. Sweat ran from his forehead into his eyes, dripped from the tip o' his nose, but he didn't bother stoppin' to wipe it away. The low and constant moan drove him on, remindin' him ev'ry passin' heartbeat may be a precious one to Ailyssa.

He'd kicked it down to half the size it were when he started—about a tenth o' what it were before Ailyssa laid atop it—when he saw the ragged edge o' what he thought might be a scrap o' fabric. He ceased the destruction and dropped to his knees, ignorin' his poppin' joints this time. Wary from his first try, Horace pulled his sleeves down to cover his hands and began scoopin' away around the flash o' cloth.

Nearer to the ground, the low moan sounded louder. Hearin' it more clearly, he knew for certain it didn't come from no person he'd ever known. The sound sent a shiver up his spine; he did his best to suppress it, concentratin' on clearin' the debris.

The clothin' scrap grew bigger as he worked. The dirt and dust coverin' it made it impossible to know its color, or whether or not it might belong to Ailyssa. With ev'ry attempt to clear it away, more fell to replace it, so he stopped tryin'. He scooped a double handful o' dead plants and more crumbled in. After the same thing happened time and again, he realized the garden were loath to give up what it held. He rested on his haunches, shoulders saggin'; at this pace, he'd never get her out.

Horace thought about askin' Ivy for help but figured that, was she willin' or able to offer assistance, she'd have done so. Same with the other Small Gods. But didn't they have some kind o' magic? What were the point o' bein' a God if you neglected to use your power?

He sighed again and decided he had but one way to proceed. He reached forward, extendin' his hands out from inside his sleeves, and grasped the fabric in his fist and pulled. It shifted, encouragin' him, so he climbed to his feet, bent at the waist, and took hold again.

Rough and gritty cloth rubbed against his fingers, dirt and the dust o' the dried plants coverin' it the way a briny layer covered ev'rythin' after a ship got home from a stormy trip. He licked his lips without meaning to, expectin' to taste salt, instead found them tastin' o' rotted flowers. He spat before puttin' more effort into tuggin', wiped his mouth on his sleeve before realizin' doin' so'd add to the problem.

The ol' sailor gritted his teeth and leaned away, his spine lodgin' a protest which he ignored. His fingers dug into the rough cloth, threatenin' to peel back his too-long nails, and he began to pullin' again. The material coverin' part o' what he suspected a person shifted more'n he expected it to. His grip slipped with the movement and he toppled backward, landin' on his ass with a thump what clicked his molars together and sent his breath whooshin' outta his lungs.

He sat for a few heartbeats, half expectin' Ivy or some o' the others to point at him and laugh, but none did.

Of course they didn't. What they're up to is far too important to care if an ol' fella landed on his behind.

He collected himself and his air and got to his feet, brushin' dirt from his backside knowin' it'd do him no good; these breeches stood no chance o' bein' clean again. One step brought him to the withered garden's edge. He bent at the waist, grabbed hold o' the dirty piece o' cloth, this time prepared for it to move or not.

When he yanked, it moved, and it only took a bit o' effort for him to pull an arm out from under the tangled mess o' shriveled vines. With it exposed, he stopped, starin' at it, but nothin' about it told him if it belonged to Ailyssa or not.

Who else might it belong to, dummy?

He shook his head and curled his hand under the armpit half-covered by brown leaves and pulled hard. The unhelpful body budged, so he tugged again and again.

"Sorry if I'm hurtin' you," he wheezed between heaves.

She shifted a little more with each effort, and he soon recognized a head shape under a funeral mask o' dried up foliage. He thought to stop and brush it away, but the worry he'd find his companion lifeless beneath stayed his hand. Waitin' wouldn't change what he'd discover, but it'd at least let him keep his hope for a short while longer.

He leaned back, usin' his tired legs to do the work while his hands gripped under the arm. His feet skidded and scuffed in loose soil and dried grass. The shape hidden in the garden slowly made its way into the daylight—a shoulder, the top o' a chest. The mask o' leaves remained stubborn about coverin' the face, but ev'rythin' else appeared intact. Dirt and flower dust covered ev'ry bit, but he didn't think he spied blood anywhere; no bones looked to be pokin' out in ways they wasn't meant to. He kept workin' at it until most o' her body came free, then he stopped, sank to his knees beside her.

The broad leaves hid her face; Horace reached out a shakin' hand, paused before his fingers came into contact with them. When he did, the desiccated foliage fell to powder. He resisted the urge to brush it off her cheeks and forehead, worried about rubbin' it into her eyes or clog her nostrils with it. He leaned forward and exhaled gently, in the manner one might do when tryin' to light a fire.

The remnants o' dead leaves blew away easily, though he'd imagined it'd turn out more difficult, the way ev'rythin' else had after he got thrown overboard. Features came into view: a nose not the right shape, eyes a smidge too close together, thinner lips than he recalled, and a full head o' hair Ailyssa couldn't't've grown in the time since the garden had claimed her.

Horace stopped blowin' and tilted back, ass sittin' atop his own feet. For a minute, it felt like his heart fell outta his chest and into his gut. He'd watched her climb onto the mound, stared in disbelief as the vines and runners, leaves and flowers engulfed her, coverin' her until she disappeared from his sight. He'd spent sunsets and sunrises watchin' the pile o' plants as it withered and shrank, and not once did anyone leave it. If someone were buried inside, who else might it be if not Ailyssa?

His chin sank to his chest, and he inhaled a shudderin' breath what stank o' rotted flowers, wished he hadn't done so. The grit hangin' in the air tickled his nostrils; he sneezed and the person lyin' on the ground in front o' him coughed as if in response. The ol' sailor's head jerked up.

Her eyes opened, and she blinked a few times, clearin' the dustiness o' the dead garden from her orbs. Horace couldn't think what to do but stare. After a dozen heartbeats, the woman who weren't Ailyssa sat up and turned toward the man o' the sea. They stared at each other for a while, the corner o' her mouth tiltin' up in what might've been a smile.

"Who are you? Where's Ailyssa?"

The young woman—he saw she'd known the seasons turn fully maybe twenty times despite the dirt smeared on her cheeks—tilted her head and waited a few heartbeats before resopndin'.

"I am Ailyssa. And I am Danya, princess of the Windward Kingdom, firstborn child of the rightful king. And I am Rak'bana. I thank you, Horace Seaman, for waking me and for delivering the Barren Mother free of harm."

Horace's lip quivered; he closed his mouth tight to make it stop. She diverted her gaze from him, peerin' o'er his shoulder at the Small Gods beyond, and didn't return her attention to him. Instead, she stood, brushed dust off the front of her smock, the action makin' negligible difference to the number o' dead flowers clingin' to her. She took a step and the ol' sailor reached out and touched her hand. Danya stopped, looked down at him.

"What about Ailys—the B...Barren Mother? What happened to her?"

The princess smiled in a manner remindin' Horace o' how a parent might look at a child what said somethin' amusin'.

"The Barren Mother—your Ailyssa—has completed her task."

She turned and started walkin' as though she'd provided a genuine answer. His hand fell from hers into his lap and he allowed his head to droop again, looked at his hands lyin' there—dirty, wrinkled, callused, sprayed with gray hairs. Hands belongin' to an old man who'd given his life away to the sea and lost so much in the doin'. He closed his eyes and gave in to the knot formin' in his chest. His shoulders slumped forward, exhaustion permeatin' ev'ry bit o' him, and tears ran down, catchin' in his beard.

Horace might've been kneelin' for a short while, or it may be damn near forever; he didn't know which. What he knew were that Ivy scared the shite outta him when she snuck up behind him and touched him on the elbow.

"Are you all right, Horace Seaman?"

He blinked, took note o' how his heart hammered in his chest, and drew his arm over his face, wipin' tears away and likely smearin' snot across his cheek to boot. His mouth opened with the intent o' lyin' to her about ev'rythin' bein' fine, but the words refused to be spoke. He snapped his jaw shut and started o'er again.

"First my son, Rilum," he said, surprised at what he found himself sayin' but unable to stop. "Weren't never a good pa to him; I left him for the sea. Then what I did to Dunal."

He looked at his hands wringin' each other in his lap and expected Ivy to ask what he meant—she didn't.

"Fella were an idiot, but he didn't deserve it. Thought I'd make up for it by helpin' out Thorn, but I couldn't keep him safe." His gaze flickered to her; she watched him but made no move like she meant to interrupt. "Now Ailyssa. Ain't good for nothin', me."

"Not true." The Small God put her hand under his arm and prompted him to stand, her touch firm, stronger than one might've expected from a bein' o' her size. "We could not save the world without you."

Horace got to his feet, wiped his face on his shirt sleeve again despite knowin' the action'd spread more dirt than it'd clean. "What're you talkin' about?"

She gestured toward where once rose a shimmery green barrier. "Come."

The ol' sailor let her lead him, takin' one final gander at what now looked as though it had never heard the word garden. Ev'ry last bit had disintegrated, leavin' what resembled a burnt-out fire pit, its ash leanin' more rust than gray, without a hint o' Ailyssa anywhere within its remnants. When he stopped gawkin' and faced the direction they headed, surprise caught him good enough he nearly ceased walkin'.

Weren't just the Small Gods millin' about in the grassy space leadin' to the forest, but also a wide array o' forest creatures, too—near as many animals as little gray people.

"What's happenin'?"

"They are here to help."

Horace raised an eyebrow, but didn't bother askin' questions. He'd seen far too many unusual things for a gatherin' o' hairy beasts to warrant too much o' his attention. Still, as they walked, he eyed them up, noticin' a handful o' unique kinds he'd've called deer, and a bunch more what must've been related, but larger. Some possessed horns—no, they was antlers, he thought—some didn't. He spied other creatures, too: enormous pigs with curved tusks, cats with tawny fur and long tails, and a few creatures what resembled the one what'd accompanied Ailyssa when he found her, but none so big. To his surprise, none o' the animals so much as looked at one another, though he thought some o' them normally wanted to eat the others.

They passed by the spot where Ivy's friends'd attacked the naked fella, nothin' left behind but a pile o' bones what looked like they'd laid about so long, the sun'd bleached them white. He shuddered. Not far from that, a few o' the little folk gathered around the girl what'd been tendin' the garden. Her eyes was closed and discomfort pulled her young features taught as they administered aid to the arm she held gingerly against her chest.

The gray people they walked by bowed their heads slightly as they passed, and Horace wondered why—a brief distraction from grievin' for Ailyssa.

"Where are you takin' me?"

"Someone you should see."

"Someone?"

The ol' sailor's heart sped in his chest. Had Ailyssa survived and been magically transported to another spot? Maybe he'd find her hangin' in a tree or growin' outta the ground like she were a flower herself? He took to stretchin' his neck, attemptin' to peek past Ivy—easy to do, given her stature—and the cluster o' forest beasts; much more challengin'.

Though the shimmery barrier'd fallen and disappeared, it weren't no trouble figurin' out where it'd been; the end o' the meadow and the beginnin' o' the forest created a distinct line. As Ivy led him, the last group o' gods and animals parted, lettin' them by, and Horace got a glimpse o' who—what—she meant for him to see.

His veins froze and his feet stopped movin'.

Just outside the start o' the Green, the pale thing lay on the ground, though weren't much o' it still white. Smears and streaks o' fresh red blood and flaky patches o' rusty dried blood covered most o' its skin, the little what were left. Slices and gashes marred its flesh, revealin' somethin' else beneath—not muscle and guts. It looked from where he stood to be more skin.

"Why is that here?"

A sheen o' sweat found its way between his palm and Ivy's, and he felt pretty sure the Small God didn't perspire. It went right along with the sickly knot what appeared in his gut, pushin' itself uncomfortably against his insides.

"They tried to eat us. Killed Ailyssa's beast, they did."

"No, this one saved you."

Horace stopped breathin', gawked from Ivy to the creature. It took a distressed feelin' in his chest before he remembered to draw air again.

"What are you takin' about?"

She pulled on his hand, promptin' him to move past her. He resisted, so she yanked again, firmer, givin' him no choice but to stumble forward a few paces. He stopped, stared at her, and Ivy raised an arm, pointed for him to go on.

The ol' sailor swallowed hard and faced the injured creature lyin' on the ground not so far away from him. It appeared in no shape to be threatin' him, but he approached with caution, anyway. The memory o' this thing and its companions tearin' Ailyssa's ferocious beast to bits, rubbin' its dismembered parts against their faces where mouths should've been, struck him as though it'd happened moments ago. He crept toward it, body turned sidewise, ready to bolt if he needed to.

As he approached, he noticed the skin on its face'd been split and remembered seein' that before, and how he'd thought he spied another hidden beneath. Horace scrunched up his forehead, squintin' to see what the white cowl concealed, but a thick mask o' blood hid it. If he meant to discover the answer, he'd have to get closer. He sighed, the scent o' decayin' garden gone, replaced by the rusty odor o' blood.

Half o' the creature's face were peeled away, as if someone'd taken a knife to a piece o' sail cloth stretched tight o'er a barrel's openin'. He saw a nose, some lips, a scruff o' beard, and one eye. It were open and lookin' at him but, if whoever it were wrapped up inside still lived, he couldn't be sure. His feet shuffled in the beaten-down grass, carryin' him close enough to stretch a finger out and lay it on him if he'd wanted to—he didn't. The open eye flickered toward him, startlin' him, though not so much as the words what squeezed outta the half-covered mouth.

"Fuck me dead."

Weren't more'n a wheeze, them words, but weren't a doubt in his mind what'd been said, nor who'd said them.

"Rilum?"

Horace took an unsteady step forward, knees threatin' to buckle beneath him, so he let himself sink to the ground before they gave out on him. The eye followed him, and he'd have sworn the one exposed side o' mouth crinkled up in a half-smile.

"How?"

The man-inside-the-fiend shook his head once with obvious effort. "Long story. Doesn't even make sense to me."

The ol' sailor shuffled forward on his knees, took his son's hand, careful o' the talons pokin' out from the two fingers lookin' like they belonged to the creature what'd wanted to eat them. Tears fell from his eyes, unnoticed.

"What happened to you, Rilum?"

"Don't matter, pa." He coughed bloody spittle onto his lips, fresh and bright compared to most of what covered his half-face. "You're alive is what matters."

Horace leaned closer. "I...I don't understand."

He put an effort to shakin' his head, gave up. "Ain't no way to understand. Not this."

"What can I do?"

"Nothin'. Not for me, at least. I became an animal, and it's right I die like one. I'm jes' glad I got to see you one more time."

Saliva clicked in the ol' sailor's throat. He opened his mouth to speak, jaw quiverin', but shut it again before he made a fool o' himself by stutterin' somethin' indecipherable. Instead, he clutched his son's hand, swallowed again before givin' it another try.

"I'm sorry." A whisper. An apology. An admission.

"Don't need...to be." It looked to be gettin' more difficult for Rilum to speak. "Did your...best."

Horace blinked hard, squeezed tears out to roll into his beard. One fell and splattered against his son's shoulder.

"Wasn't there for you, boy. Was never a father."

Rilum's fingers flexed in his. An attempt to comfort him? A spasm o' muscles he no longer controlled?

"Gave me what...I needed. To make...right choices."

A gray tongue wiped across cracked lips, provided no moisture. Horace scanned the ground near them, hopin' to find somethin' to wet his mouth, but found nothin'; the sun'd done an expert job've dryin' things up since the last time it rained, and weren't no dew in the morns. Rilum's fingers flexed again, barely noticeable, and he returned his attention to his son.

"Pa."

"It's okay, boy. Son."

"Thank you."

His digits tightened once more, and the eye slid closed.

"Rilum? Rilum?"

The ol' sailor stopped himself from grabbin' his son's shoulder and givin' it a shake like he might wake him from a nap. His lips pressed tight; so much he wanted to say to the lad, so much to ask and tell, so much to teach, but the time were past. A last breath rattled outta his lungs. Rilum's lungs? Did they belong to somethin' else? Didn't matter. The final exhale meant it didn't matter whom they belonged to.

He's gone.

Horace sagged, chin droopin' to his chest. He wanted to put his palm against his son's cheek, but the thought o' the monster he'd become stopped him. He hated himself for his fearfulness, and for so many other things—for not bein' the father he should've and lettin' this happen to his child; for what he did to Dunal; for Thorn; for Ailyssa.

He squeezed his eyes tight, clamped his jaw to fight off the sobs threatenin' in his chest. It seemed like he'd be successful until a scrawny arm slipped around his shoulders, pulled him in toward a bony shoulder. He shifted his head to it and released the pain building inside him.

He cried and Ivy held him until his tears ran out.

When he stopped, he raised his face, the water caught in his eyelashes smearin' her features into a parody of themselves. The Small God lifted her hand and laid her palm on the ol' sailor's cheek the way he'd wanted to do to comfort his son. Warmth radiated from her touch; he remembered feeling it before, when she'd touched him, when Thorn'd done the same.

"You are a good man, Horace Seaman."

She stood, pulled him to his feet, and guided him away from his dead boy, the fallen veil, the mythical Green. As they passed through the gatherin' o' gray people and forest beasts—each steppin' aside and seemin' to nod with an understandin' o' what'd happened—a shadow fell across the meadow.

At first, Horace thought a cloud'd crossed o'er the sun, but it disappeared quick, then returned a moment later. The ol' sailor raised his eyes from peerin' at his feet to see the enormous bird come to light on the ground near what remained o' the garden. It looked one direction then the other in the jerky way birds move, then ignored ev'rythin' to preen the black feathers on its wing.

Ivy glanced o'er her shoulder at the sailor, a smile cantin' her mouth. "Say hello to Father Raven."

<<<<>>>>

The End of Book 5

Find out how the saga ends in the final the final installment of the Books of the Small Gods, *And Kingdoms End*, available at your favorite book retailer

Afterword

Dear reader,

In the world of writers and writing, we have two terms that come up quite frequently: plotters and pantsers. For those of you who have not heard the terminology, a plotter is someone who takes the time to outline their work (often in great detail) before they begin writing, while a pantser gets an idea and runs with it (writing by the seat of their pants, as it were). I fall somewhere in the middle. I definitely plan, and I know where I'm going, but there is a certain joy in discovering bits and pieces of the story as you go. That being said, trying to get somewhere without a road map can also take a little longer than you expected (apparently you can ask George R.R. Martin about that). We're finally here, though, with the Books of the Small Gods ending in the next volume, **And Kingdoms End**. I hope you'll join me to see what happens.

Visit Bruce online at www.bruceblake.net for
FREE SHORT STORIES, signed copies,
and to stay updated on new releases

Also By Bruce Blake

Curse of the Unnamed epic fantasy:

The Book of Shadow
Shadow Scarred
A Shadow Upon the Land
In the Shadow of the Dragon - coming July, 2023

Khirro's Journey epic fantasy:

Blood of the King
Spirit of the King
Heart of the King

The Books of the Small Gods epic fantasy:

When Shadows Fall
The Darkness Comes
And Night Descends
When Ravens Call
The Twilight Fades
And Kingdoms End

The **Icarus Fell** urban fantasy series:

On Unfaithful Wings
All Who Wander Are Lost

Secrets of the Hanged Man

Blood of the King (Khirro's Journey Book 1)

A kingdom torn by war. A curse whispered by dying lips. A hero born
against his will.
With a vial of the king's blood in one hand, and a sword of legend in the
other, one soldier sets out on an odyssey that will change his life... or end
it.

Forced into the army, Khirro never wanted to fight. And with the monarch
dead, any hope for the kingdom's survival hangs by a slender thread.
But when the king's shaman charges Khirro with a curse, he's compelled
to undertake a journey to the haunted land in search of the outlaw
necromancer. And if he fails... the very walls of the fortress itself will fall
to the blood-crazed undead.

Can Khirro complete his quest in time to save his realm from a brutal end?

*"Blood of the King is a masterpiece. It is as close to perfection as I would
consider a book to be."*- Ella Medler, author of *Blood is Heavier*
"Blake has a knack for bringing you into the story"
*"Mr. Blake's writing is masterful and clear, he draws you into his story and
when it's finished you feel like you're leaving an old friend."*

The Book of Shadow (Curse of the Unnamed Book1)

Llyris Fildarae is an outcast tainted by a sliver of magic in a world terrified
of the supernatural. Loathed and distrusted, she uses her ability to control
a magical Unnamed to survive.

Caedric Carpera is desperate to save his son from a deadly illness. He enlists
Llyris to locate a lost tome containing secrets capable of healing him, but
its location is a mystery that's already claimed lives. Thrust into a hostile
world, Llyris and her companions risk everything to find the relic and
return before the child's sickness prevails.

But who is the enigmatic old man who appeared out of nowhere to set them on this dangerous expedition? And what does he really want?

Only a perilous mission to an untamed land can save the boy and reveal the truth.
Except some truths are too shocking to be exposed.

"Bruce Blake has written a hell of a book and I am eagerly awaiting the sequel!"
"I'm usually a chapter per night type, but I couldn't put this book down."

On Unfaithful Wings (Icarus Fell #1)

To some, death is the end; to others, a beginning. To Icarus Fell, it should have been a relief from a life gone seriously awry.
But death had other plans.
Icarus doesn't believe that the man awaiting him when he wakes up in a cheap motel room is really the archangel Michael, or that God's right hand wants him to help souls on their way to Heaven. Icarus doesn't believe there's a Heaven, so why should they want his help?
But the man claiming to be the archangel tempts him with an offer he can't ignore--harvest enough souls and get back the life he wished he'd had.
It seems Icarus has nothing to lose, until he botches a harvest and the soul that went to Hell instead of Heaven comes back to make him pay by threatening to take away the life he hoped to win back.
To save the wife and son he already lost once, Icarus will have to become the man he never was. Somehow, he will have to learn to believe.

"The next book in this series cannot come out soon enough for this reader. Not just my favorite Kindle book of the year, but one of my favorite books ever."
"I loved this book."
"Bruce Blake's On Unfaithful Wings is a great urban fantasy novel. I love good character development in a story's protagonist and Blake nails it with Icarus Fell. I found myself rooting for him from the get-go and laughing out loud at some of his observations."

"On Unfaithful Wings was an impressive first novel. All of the characters were interesting and engaging, but in particular the main character and his struggle to reconcile with his new identity/job. This is one of those stories that stays with me long after I read it and I'll be on the lookout for more from this author."

"This is just, simply, amazing. Icarus is one of the best characters I've ever "met", chock full of virtues and faults and doubts and worries and a simple HUMANNESS that comes through so clearly, I almost expect to run into him around the next corner."

"Icarus Fell is a flawed man but a wonderful character. From the moment I started reading On Unfaithful Wings I was pulled along by this interesting character and wanting to know what would happen next."

About the Author

Bruce Blake lives on Vancouver Island in British Columbia, Canada. When pressing issues like shovelling snow and building igloos don't take up his spare time, Bruce can be found taking the dog sled to the nearest coffee shop to work on his short stories and novels.

Actually, Victoria, B.C. is only a couple hours north of Seattle, Wash., where more rain is seen than snow. Since snow isn't really a pressing issue, Bruce spends more time trying to remember to leave the "u" out of words like "colour" and "neighbour" than he does shovelling.

Bruce has been writing since grade school but it wasn't until the mid-2000's he set his sights on becoming a full-time writer. Since then, his first short story, "Another Man's Shoes" was published in the Winter 2008 edition of *Cemetery Moon*, another short, "Yardwork",was made into a podcast in Oct., 2011 by *Pseudopod*. Since then, he has concentrated on writing novels, publishing the **Khirro's Journey** trilogy (*Blood of the King*, *Spirit of the King*, and *Heart of the King*), three books in the ongoing **Icarus Fell** urban fantasy series (*On Unfaithful Wings*, *All Who Wander are Lost*, and *Secrets of the Hanged Man*), and the **Books of the Small Gods** series (*When Shadows Fall*, *The Darkness Comes*, *And Night Descends*, *When Ravens Call*, *The Twilight Fades*, and *And Kingdoms End*). *The Book of Shadow* is the first book in the **Curse of the Unnamed** series, to be followed by *Shadow Scarred*, *A Shadow Upon the Land*, and *In the Shadow of the Dragon*.

Bruce has many more projects simmering on the back burner, so stay tuned.

Visit Bruce online at **www.bruceblake.net** for
FREE SHORT STORIES, signed copies,
and to keep up to date with new releases